WINGS OF FIRE

WINGS OF FIRE

THE DANGEROUS GIFT

by
TUI T. SUTHERLAND

SCHOLASTIC INC.

Text copyright © 2021 by Tui T. Sutherland
Map and border design © 2018 by Mike Schley
Dragon illustrations © 2021 by Joy Ang

This book was originally published in hardcover by Scholastic Press in 2021.

ISBN 978-1-338-21455-0

10 9 8 7 6 5 4 3 2   22 23 24 25 26

Printed in the U.S.A. 40
This edition first printing 2022

Book design by Phil Falco

For Benjamin — welcome to the family!

And for the Pyrrhia-Pantala AU, with hugs
and awe for all your amazing dragons.

Tsetse Hive

Beetle Lake

Vinegaroon Hive

Hornet Hive

Cicada Hive

Mantis Hive

PANTALA

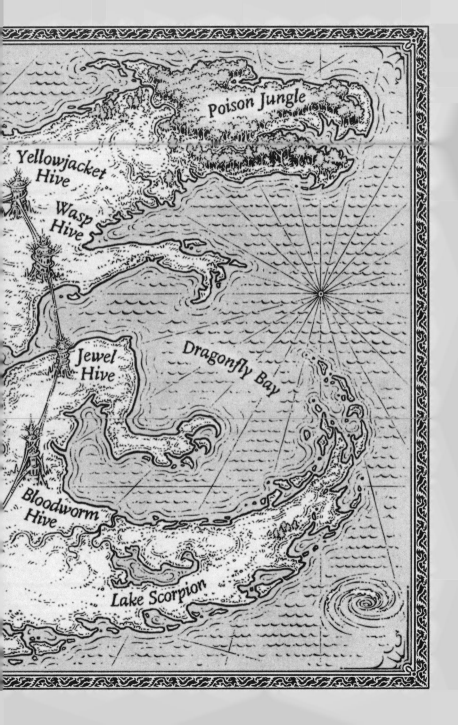

Tsetse Hive

Beet

A GUIDE TO THE
DRAGONS

Cicada Hive

Mantis
Hive

Yellowjacket
Hive

Wasp
Hive

OF PANTALA

Bloodworm
Hive

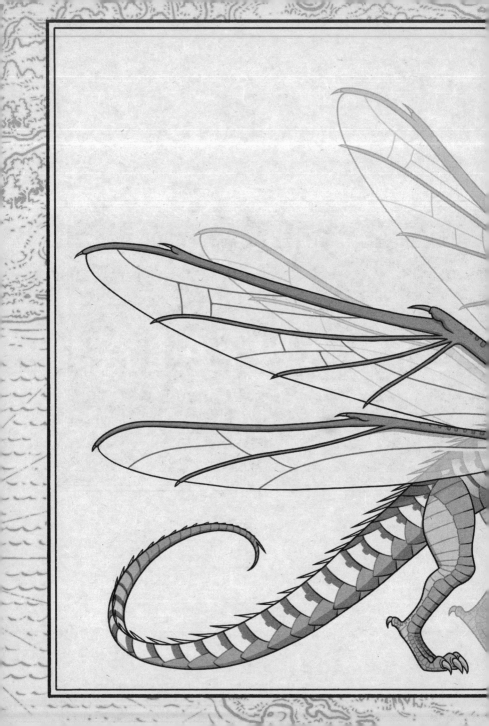

HIVEWINGS

Description: red, yellow, and/or orange, but always mixed with some black scales; four wings

Abilities: vary from dragon to dragon; examples include deadly stingers that can extend from their wrists to stab their enemies; venom in their teeth or claws; or a paralyzing toxin that can immobilize their prey; others can spray boiling acid from a stinger on their tails

Queen: Queen Wasp

SILKWINGS

Description: SilkWing dragonets are born wingless, but go through a metamorphosis at age six, when they develop four huge wings and silk-spinning abilities; as beautiful and gentle as butterflies, with scales in any color under the sun, except black

Abilities: can spin silk from glands on their wrists to create webs or other woven articles; can detect vibrations with their antennae to assess threats

Queen: Queen Wasp (the last SilkWing queen, before the Tree Wars, was Queen Monarch)

LEAFWINGS

Description: wiped out during the Tree Wars with the HiveWings, but while they lived, this tribe had green and brown scales and wings shaped like leaves

Abilities: could absorb energy from sunlight and were accomplished gardeners; some were rumored to have unusual control over plants

Queen: last known queen of the LeafWings was Queen Sequoia, about fifty years ago, at the time of the Tree Wars

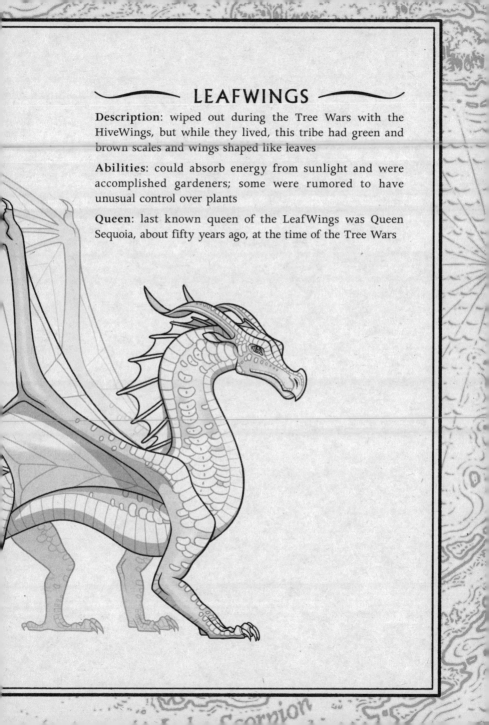

THE LOST CONTINENT PROPHECY

Turn your eyes, your wings, your fire
To the land across the sea
Where dragons are poisoned and dragons are dying
And no one can ever be free.

A secret lurks inside their eggs.
A secret hides within their book.
A secret buried far below
May save those brave enough to look.

Open your hearts, your minds, your wings
To the dragons who flee from the Hive.
Face a great evil with talons united
Or none of the tribes will survive.

— PROLOGUE —

Swordtail blinked awake in a haze of smoke. Smoke clung to the air and filled his nose; even the savanna grass seemed to still have wisps of smoke clinging to its blades. There were dragons all around him — hundreds, maybe thousands of dragons — but he didn't know any of them.

They were all lying in the tall grass, and on the other side of the smoky sky, he could see the blurred outline of the sun.

The last thing he remembered was falling asleep at night, in the jungle, next to Blue and Cricket and Sundew. Before that, he could remember lying there, listening to the carnivorous plants rustle and slither nearby, thinking about the battle to come. He remembered watching Blue rub his wrists nervously at the spots where his flamesilk glowed in the dark.

Flamesilk. Fire. Blue was going to set the bonfire of heart of salvation aflame, and the smoke would be the antidote to the breath of evil. His fire was going to set all the HiveWings free from Wasp's mind control. If it worked, maybe there wouldn't be a battle at all.

The smoke in the air suggested that there had definitely been a fire — a much bigger fire than one pile of roots could have produced, in fact.

But what had happened?

How did I get here?

He pushed himself up to standing and winced.

Everything hurt. His muscles ached as though he'd been flying for days. Even his claws felt bruised and sore.

From the sounds of the moaning and grumbling around him, many of these strange dragons felt the same way.

He suddenly realized that most of them were HiveWings. His enemies.

Why am I lying in the savanna, surrounded by HiveWings?

Did they capture me?

If so, they were doing a pathetic job of keeping him prisoner. No one was even looking at him. He wasn't tied up. He could fly away right now.

Which way, though?

Which way was Blue?

Or Luna. If I could fly to Luna, I would. So what if there was an entire ocean between them? He would find his way there, to her.

Juuuuuuuuuuuuuuuust as soon as he figured out where in Pantala he was.

He squinted around, looking for a landmark. Even if there was nothing but savanna around him, that would be a clue.

But there was something: two Hives, visible in the distance, with glimmering webs stretching between them. Which meant the Poison Jungle should be in the other . . .

A cloud of black smoke covered the horizon behind him, reaching from ground to sky.

Is that the jungle?

And suddenly he had a memory — a memory of standing beside Blue as flamesilk spiraled out of Blue's wrists onto the pile of roots. Swordtail remembered his own claws clutching a spear with sharp thorns twisting from one end. He remembered staring at the rows of HiveWings, all of them eerily still and white-eyed. They hadn't moved as he and Blue approached the pyre. They hadn't swarmed forward to try to stop them. They hadn't even looked at him.

He remembered now how that had worried him.

But he'd put his faith in the antidote. He'd watched the green-tinged smoke rise and fill the air, drifting over the front ranks of the HiveWing army. Slinking around his own head, and Blue's.

And then he'd felt his claws twitch and sink into the ground. His wings opened, but he hadn't moved them. His head turned toward Blue, and his mouth moved, and something that wasn't him spoke through him.

"Two little SilkWings, all for me. Just what I always wanted. And one of them a flamesilk! So nice when a plan sprouts exactly the way it's supposed to."

Blue had stared back at him, his talons also firmly planted. The LeafWings flying down from the trees would not have been able to tell that there was anything wrong. Only Swordtail could see the panic in Blue's eyes. Only the two of them knew that they were paralyzed inside their bodies, controlled by someone — or some*thing* else.

It felt like the toxin the HiveWings used on Misbehaver's Way prisoners, but worse.

The rest of his memories came flooding back. The smoke spreading over the LeafWings. Sequoia and Belladonna and Nettle caught by the breath of evil, just as Swordtail was. Blue's talons turning toward the jungle. His fire burning it all down.

Swordtail crouched into the savanna grass, trying to breathe. It was morning now. They must have spent the whole previous day scorching the Poison Jungle. He remembered being in the squadron that was sent to gather all the breath of evil from its hidden lair, before the fire reached that area.

He also remembered searching for the rest of the LeafWings. The thing inside him had driven him relentlessly through the crackling, smoking trees, looking for Sundew and Cricket and the young LeafWing princess. That was probably why he was so sore and singed and scratched-up. It was a miracle he hadn't been eaten by a frantic dying plant along the way.

But he didn't remember finding any LeafWings.

Swordtail jumped to his feet, ignoring the pain in his talons. He spun, searching the savanna around him.

Hundreds of HiveWings, a few LeafWings — but nobody he recognized. No Sundew. How had she escaped the smoke by the battlefield? Oh, wait . . . she hadn't been there when Blue went to burn the roots. He didn't know where she'd gone, but maybe that meant her mind hadn't been taken over.

And if they'd searched all day for her with no luck, maybe she'd really escaped, along with Cricket and the rest of the LeafWings who hadn't been near the smoke.

Where could they be?

He lifted one talon gingerly, then the other. He was controlling himself right now. His head felt curiously light, as if it had been caught in the grip of someone's talons all night and they'd just released him. Cautiously he started walking through the grass, toward a flicker of bright blue wings near one of the shrubs.

Blue? If he could find Blue, they could fly away together. Maybe the mind control had been temporary. Or maybe it didn't work over long distances; maybe they could fly out over the ocean, as far as they could possibly get, and escape its clutches that way.

It was Blue. Swordtail could see soot smudged along Blue's face and limbs and wings, but it was unmistakably him, asleep, with his brow furrowed in worry.

Swordtail was a few steps away from his friend when his legs suddenly froze. He felt a chill sweep through him, all his scales shivering away from believing that they'd been taken over again.

"Nice try," his own voice whispered. His wings folded in and he dropped to the ground, stuck in place. Trapped. So close to Blue, but so far from himself.

She has me in her claws, he thought. *But she can't read my mind; she can't stop me from thinking. Or hoping.*

Blue and I may be stuck here, but I believe Sundew and Cricket escaped. Maybe they went to find Luna.

And if they did, I know they'll come back for us. They'll find a way to set us free.

We just have to survive until they do.

PART ONE

BLIZZARDS & BURIED MAGIC

⟊ CHAPTER 1 ⟋

The youngest queen in the history of the Ice Kingdom was going to be the *very best* queen of the IceWings ever. Ever ever. THE BEST.

She was going to keep all her dragons safe. They were all going to be healthy and prosperous and safe and no one was going to die of any more evil magic plagues, like the one that killed the previous queen.

NO ONE.

NOT ON HER WATCH.

Queen Snowfall had a plan, or at least, she had a firm death grip on an idea that was kind of like a plan.

That plan was: STAY AWAY FROM OTHER DRAGONS.

No more getting involved in other tribes' stupid wars. No more summits with queens who talked down to her or eyed her as if *she* might be the one to start the next war. No more interactions with NightWings, *ever*.

None of this intertribal peace talk empathy-building drum circle nonsense!

IceWings were a GREAT tribe. They didn't NEED any other tribes. Those subjects of hers who wanted to go explore, to meet other dragons and study in their perilous, flammable schools? They needed to be STUFFED INTO IGLOOS until they came to their senses.

(Her council had talked her into letting a few IceWings go to Jade Mountain Academy, for now, instead of using her excellent igloo plan. There had been so much alarming enthusiasm for the idea of "connecting with the other tribes." WHY, was her question. How could anyone even *want* to be around strange dragons after what had happened to their tribe? She was hoping the students they'd sent would come back with stories about how terrible the academy was, and that by then all the other curious IceWings would have forgotten about ever wanting to leave.)

No, in Snowfall's vision of her reign, all IceWings would stay IN the kingdom, where she could keep an eye on them. Other dragons would stay OUT of the kingdom and there would be NO MORE dealing with tribes that weren't them.

It was a good plan, a straightforward plan, a nice, safe, brilliant plan.

Except for the problems.

Problems like queens who kept sending her messages about alliances and trade and building more schools like Jade Mountain Academy. (Shut UP, Queen Ruby; go AWAY, Queen Glory; deal with your OWN STUPID DRAGONS, Queen Thorn!)

Problems like the IceWings on her own council who wanted to meet with the NightWings and try to "build a bridge" over "centuries of violence and hatred" after the blast of magic empathy that had ended their last battle.

Problems like not knowing exactly where everyone was, and having to wonder whether the missing dragons in question had left the Ice Kingdom or were still lurking around somewhere, maybe plotting some cold-blooded murder.

Most urgent, though, was the problem that *hundreds* of strange dragons were apparently flying toward her shores at that very moment.

"You're *sure* they aren't NightWings?" she demanded again.

Her scout managed not to sigh, but she could tell that he *wanted* to, which was VERY DISRESPECTFUL and maybe she should have him punished. Wasn't that what a fierce, powerful very-best-queen-ever would do? Punish dragons for disobeying her, or thinking about disobeying her, or making faces as if they were trying not to make faces?

"I could see flashes of different colors from their scales," he repeated. "I promise you, my queen. Mostly green, but many, many other colors as well. No black dragons. They're not NightWings."

Snowfall paced from one corner of the balcony to the other. They were high on one of the tallest spires of the palace, with the wind whisking pellets of ice all around them. The sun was low in the sky off to the west, painting the clouds gold and orange as it sank into the sea. She knew they were out there, but no matter how fiercely Snowfall glared at it, she couldn't see any dragons flying out of the sunset.

She wondered if NightWings had found a way to disguise their scales. Maybe Darkstalker wasn't really gone, even though all those not-IceWings at the Jade Mountain Academy promised he was. Maybe he was still out there, and he'd come up with a way to turn NightWings into multicolored rainbow dragons, and then he'd sent them far out into the ocean to fly in an enormous arc so they could come at the Ice Kingdom from the west and avoid the Great Ice Cliff and soon they would be here to kill her and her entire tribe.

This was not far-fetched freaking out! This was completely reasonable, justified freaking out!

Her scout was looking at her as if he thought she might be losing her mind, though. She had to put her queen face back on and act as if an invasion of alarming rainbow dragons was the sort of thing excellent queens such as herself could easily handle, no problem.

"Well, if they're *not* NightWings, what *are* they?" she asked. He hesitated, and she answered her own question. "RainWings? I mean, RainWings. Of course. That's the only tribe with many colors, so . . . perhaps with SeaWings; those can be green. It's probably a group of RainWings and SeaWings." *Why would RainWings and SeaWings form an alliance to invade my kingdom from the west?* her brain screamed. *Coral and Glory have betrayed me! They decided*

I'm too young to be queen and they're coming for my throne! Which is very unfair because Glory is the same age as I am and she's queen of TWO tribes!

All right, Queen Glory probably wasn't coming to depose Snowfall because of her age. See, her brain could figure that out, and so it was, ipso facto, working perfectly reasonably, and that meant all these other worries were entirely legitimate.

Also, the RainWing tribe hadn't invaded another kingdom in literally hundreds of years. They hadn't even participated in the War of SandWing Succession. All they wanted to do was snooze around the rainforest eating papayas. They would be an utterly useless invasion force. If Glory did want to invade another kingdom, she'd have to do it with her NightWings, who liked attacking and killing and stabbing and violence and lying and destroying things.

So maybe Glory found a way to turn NightWings into rainbow dragons and sent them this way and so they ARE NightWings after all!

Snowfall rubbed her head, which was throbbing as though someone had shoved icicles through her temples.

"I don't . . . *think* . . . the RainWings and SeaWings would attack us," the scout said cautiously.

"Is your job thinking?" Snowfall shouted, making him jump. "ARE YOU AN EXPERT THINKER? Did we accidentally assign you to scouting because we missed your GIANT AMAZING BRAIN and all the AMAZING THINKS it could have shared with us?! DOES IT SEEM LIKELY THAT YOUR *THINKING* WOULD INTEREST ME?"

"N-n-no, Your Majesty," he stammered.

"No," she agreed. "You are a scout. Go scout again and come back with real, actual information."

He flew away immediately, and then she spent seven minutes worrying about whether she'd been too harsh with him and whether an excellent queen would have said any of that, and whether a certain sister of hers would have been more serene and therefore more excellent, and then another twelve minutes growling at herself about how excellent queens didn't second-guess themselves and how she needed to be more decisive, and then she realized that she was accidentally thinking about murdery black dragons trying to murder her again, and she had to lie down and cover her face for a moment.

When she finally sat up, her aunt Tundra was standing in the doorway of the balcony, watching her with impassive raised eyebrows.

"Hello," Snowfall said haughtily. *I was definitely* not *panicking. I was resting my eyes in a very normal queenly fashion. I do not need to explain myself. I am the queen and therefore whatever I do is queenly, no matter what her eyebrows think!*

"Good evening," said her aunt. "It is time for the wall."

"Of course it is," Snowfall said. "How MARVELOUS. My FAVORITE PART OF THE DAY."

Tundra had a face that repelled sarcasm. No matter what Snowfall said, no matter her tone of voice, it all slid right off that frozen expression. Tundra inclined her head slightly and held out the jeweled box that contained the IceWing crown.

As a little dragonet princess, Snowfall had looked forward to wearing the crown her entire life. Diamonds! Sparkles! Power! Everything she'd always wanted!

Until the moment it officially became hers, when it became clear what Queen Snowfall had had to lose to get it.

And now it was her least favorite thing in the world.

Well . . . maybe Tundra's face was her least favorite thing in the world. But they usually came together, so she could hate them both simultaneously.

Snowfall opened the box with an irritated sigh and lifted out the glittering, diamond-encrusted monstrosity. Spiraling spikes like icicles jutted up into the air, around a cluster of crystalline jewels and twisted silver arches. It weighed as much as a small polar bear and made her neck hurt the moment she put it on.

But she couldn't let Tundra see that. She tipped her chin up and flared her wings to usher her aunt ahead of her.

Everyone says the war is over. Everyone says Darkstalker is gone. Everyone says the NightWings won't attack us again.

But everyone could be wrong. THE NIGHTWINGS CAN'T BE TRUSTED. They want me dead. They want all of us dead. If I could find a way to wipe them all out first, I should.

Tundra's necklace of SkyWing teeth clicked noisily as they strode through the palace. Snowfall pressed her talons to her eyes for a moment, trying to drive the headache away.

Being the queen, it turned out, was like living inside a snowstorm that never ended. She tried so hard to start each day all new, with a list and a plan and energy. She'd get so much done! Each new problem was a mere snowflake. She could tackle them one by one. Little sparkly quick-melting problems.

Except the snowflakes piled up faster than she could fly, sparkles on sparkles on fluff on ice on cold on heavy wet layers of slush and freezing clumps, and by night she was buried far below them.

And then, every night, just when it was all too much, her aunt Tundra would appear with her cold marble face, and that meant it was time for the wall.

According to the ancient tradition of the tribe, every night the queen of the IceWings had to consider the wall that listed every important dragon in the tribe, and then she had to adjust the rankings of all the dragons in the aristocracy.

Every. Night.

Whose idea WAS this?

Snowfall had always considered the wall, known as the gift of order, to be one of the best magic things in the kingdom. She used to wake up before the sun and soar down to the courtyard to see where her name was each morning. She loved watching the word *Snowfall* climb higher and higher as she worked and trained and studied, until she was at the very top of the dragonets' side of the rankings. And there it stayed, moon after moon — apart from that unfortunate blip when her cousins messed everything up for a few days.

But then Winter was gone, and Hailstorm moved over to the adult wall, and Snowfall was in her proper place at the top again, and it was excellent to look at. BEST DRAGONET IN THE WHOLE KINGDOM, the wall reassured her, morning after morning. YOU'RE DOING GREAT. EVEN YOUR MOTHER THINKS SO. SHE PUT YOU RIGHT HERE AT THE TOP BECAUSE SHE SEES HOW UNDENIABLY GREAT YOU ARE.

Sometimes it felt like a secret message from Queen Glacier. Like, *don't worry, I remember you, even though we haven't been in the same room in a while. I am quite pleased to have a daughter like you. I appreciate that you are not embarrassing me.*

It wasn't like that now.

The wall did not tell Snowfall she was undeniably great anymore. It said WELL? and MAKE SOME DECISIONS and STOP DITHERING and A GOOD QUEEN WOULD HAVE NO TROUBLE WITH THIS and WHAT HAPPENED TO BEING THE BEST QUEEN EVER? WHY ARE YOU SUCH A DISASTER?

There were no more messages, unspoken or otherwise, from her mother.

Now the word SNOWFALL was set apart, in its own little queen corner, off by itself. Now the task of reordering the rankings every night was *her* job, and Snowfall had begun to suspect that the gift of order was less a gift and more an act of twisted revenge. Some queen must have angered her animus somehow, and he or she had responded by crafting this torture device, perfectly designed to drive IceWing queens insane for the rest of time.

Once upon a time, Snowfall had thought she would love this part of being queen. The fate of all her dragons in her own talons! The power to lift up those most loyal and knock down her enemies!

But it didn't feel like power. It felt like work, pinning her down like the weight of the crown.

Icy rain drizzled down as Snowfall stared up at the wall of rankings. The light globe floating over her shoulder lit up the names in front of her. Behind her, the three moons illuminated the snowy courtyard. Silver, empty, cold, and wet, speckled with weird shadows from the light tree.

Empty.

Only twenty IceWings had died of the plague (*only*), plus thirteen more in the battle with the NightWings, but since Snowfall became queen, the palace had felt as empty as if the entire tribe had vanished into thin air the day Queen Glacier died.

The entire tribe, that is, in addition to the one sister who had actually vanished.

Maybe the rest of the IceWings deliberately made themselves scarce whenever they saw her coming. Maybe that was always what it was like for a queen.

"Well?" Tundra asked smoothly. "Who are you going to move?"

YEAH, agreed the wall. YOUR MOTHER NEVER TOOK THIS LONG.

Snowfall's head hurt. Her *teeth* hurt. Why did her *teeth* hurt? *Every night* she had to do this.

Even when she had much more urgent crises to deal with than the hierarchy of palace dragons. Such as the dragons that were coming across the ocean right at this moment, preparing to tramp their dangerous talons all over her snowy kingdom.

She wished she had a list of *their* names, and an entire history of their tribes, and an explanation for their behavior and an outline of what they were planning to do when they got here, plus a battle strategy for getting rid of them.

Tundra cleared her throat.

Right. The wall.

Snowfall adjusted the heavy crown on her aching head. She couldn't remember even seeing half these dragons today. How was she supposed to know whether they deserved to move up or down?

When everyone avoided her, or spoke to her in polite monosyllables, where was she supposed to hear about the squabbles, mistakes, outrages, or triumphs in their freezing little aristocratic world?

How did Mother always know everything?

Snowfall glanced sideways at her aunt. Tundra had lost her husband, Narwhal, in the IceWing-NightWing battle.

One of her children lived in exile and another was in prison awaiting trial, while the third was recovering from a very bizarre magic spell. Snowfall didn't know quite what to think of Hailstorm these days. He seemed rigidly perfect on the outside and all melted together on the inside.

Tundra looked exactly the same, though. Snowfall never saw a hint of sadness or rage or resentment in her face. Even though they both knew perfectly well that Tundra had always hoped her daughter, Icicle, would take the throne from Glacier before Snowfall could.

Never going to happen now, Snowfall thought. *After all those years of competing, suddenly I'm the queen and Icicle's locked in the dungeon for being a traitor, and none of it was up to me in the end.*

She lifted her chin. *Act like a queen. All the time. No matter how much your teeth hurt.*

Hailstorm could go up a notch. He hadn't annoyed her at all today, and it would please Tundra, so perhaps she'd let Snowfall cut this short without too many more changes.

Snowfall stabbed her claws into Hailstorm's name and dragged him up a spot. She left Tundra's name where it was — safely in the First Circle, ever since Narwhal sacrificed himself to save the new queen.

She also left Crystal up among the top ten names, even though she could feel Tundra glaring at it intently every night. Wherever Crystal was, she was still a princess. She hadn't done anything terrible that Snowfall knew of. She wasn't *definitely* out there trying to raise an army to steal Snowfall's throne, and she wasn't *certainly* hiding in the palace trying to poison Snowfall's food. She was only *maybe* doing those things. Snowfall couldn't knock her down the list for maybe crimes, even if the maybeness of them was terrifying enough.

If she left Crystal's name in place, she hoped it would look as though she wasn't afraid of her sister at all.

She reordered a few other names, trying to keep her eyebrows arched in a bored, haughty way. *So easy, this boring task*, her eyebrows yawned. *Easiest task in the world, definitely not frying all my brain cells.*

"Really?" Tundra said once, as Snowfall slid her uncle Permafrost down a notch (for pointing out, again, how easy it would be for SeaWings to invade from the northern ocean side of the Ice Kingdom, a reminder that Snowfall really DID NOT NEED right now, thanks very much). Tundra snapped her jaw shut as Snowfall glared at her.

Finally Snowfall stepped back, shaking her talons. Her claws felt as if they might shiver into a million pieces in a moment. The wall always made them feel that way, and they were always fine after a while, but it was unpleasant.

"That's your . . . final decision?" Tundra said with *just* a hint of skepticism in her voice, easily denied if Snowfall had snapped at her.

"Yes." Snowfall couldn't take another moment of this. She had to figure out what to do about the approaching dragons. The only other IceWing who knew was the scout who'd reported it to her. That animus SandWing, Jerboa, knew, too. Snowfall had gone to her for a spell to protect them, but it hadn't been any help because animus magic was BROKEN, or Jerboa was lying to her, and either way she was useless.

So Snowfall needed to deal with the invasion by herself, somehow, although so far her strategy of pacing around her throne room all night hadn't been particularly effective.

Even so. Alone. That was what she wanted to be. Or, specifically, somewhere far away from Tundra.

She wrestled the giant crown off her head and shoved it into her aunt's talons. Her headache eased a little.

"Go away," she snapped. "Now."

Tundra bowed and swept off, leaving only a faint vibration of disapproval in the air behind her. She never said anything obvious to remind Snowfall that, only a few months ago, Tundra and Narwhal had been practically second-in-command to Queen Glacier. She never even hinted at memories of their former relationship. Back then, Snowfall had been so careful about every word she said, afraid of offending her aunt and falling down the ranks as a result.

Snowfall knew Tundra must hate the fact that she had to bow to her niece now. And *probably* Snowfall wasn't helping the situation by barking at her and ordering her around. She couldn't help it, though; she was too overwhelmed by everything else to add "be more polite to Aunt Tundra" to her list.

If there was *one* upside to being queen, surely it was

that she could finally snap at dragons who deserved it. Couldn't she?

Maybe she couldn't. Maybe that was *worst* queen behavior, not best queen. Maybe she was messing this all up every time she opened her mouth.

She glanced up at the wall again.

The wall didn't say anything (of course it didn't; it was a wall). But it was clearly thinking about how civil Queen Glacier always was, and it was definitely judging her.

This is sane. It is normal to feel judged by magic walls. I am a perfectly sane queen with a well-functioning brain and everything is fine.

Something snapped in the courtyard behind her.

Snowfall whirled around and stared through the icy raindrops. It all looked the same: pale, icy, wet, weird shadows.

But it wasn't empty.

Someone was there. Someone was watching her.

— CHAPTER 2 —

It's Darkstalker! He's here to finish the job of killing us all. Or another NightWing. Or Crystal. Definitely a murdery dragon about to kill me!

"Show yourself!" Snowfall shouted. "I know you're there!" She inhaled a gust of frostbreath, ready to unleash freezing death on her assassin, and charged toward the tree of light. A figure moved among the branches, wings spreading, and Snowfall bared her teeth.

"Ack!" the figure shouted. "Stop! Snowfall! It's me!" The dragon tumbled out of the tree and landed awkwardly among its roots, trying to stand and bow and duck behind the trunk at the same time.

Snowfall skidded to a stop. The dragon's scales were white, freckled with dark blue, not black. Not a NightWing. The dark blue meant it wasn't Crystal either. She swallowed her frostbreath back down and lowered her head to squint at the spy.

"Lynx?"

"Hi," said the dragonet. "Hello. Thank you for not freezing me. Hi, Snowfall."

"*Queen* Snowfall," Snowfall snapped automatically. Lynx had been her biggest competition all through school and training, at least after Hailstorm was captured by SkyWings. She was only the daughter of a minor noble, but she was hardworking and clever and good at making teachers like her, and Snowfall had wanted to strangle her more than a thousand times.

"Right," Lynx said, glancing over her shoulder as though she was already regretting this conversation. "Queen Snowfall. Sorry."

She didn't *sound* sorry. She sounded like she always had, challenging Snowfall to races around the palace or arguing over points of IceWing law in class.

Snowfall narrowed her eyes. Lynx was still a year away from moving to the adult wall, and without Snowfall or any of the cousins left on there, Lynx had been sitting easily at the top of the dragonet list. But Snowfall could move her down. Snowfall could flick her all the way into the Seventh Circle if she wanted to. Snowfall was the QUEEN now. Deciding that Lynx was a disrespectful nobody who deserved to be squashed back into her place was absolutely Snowfall's job.

"What are you doing here?" Snowfall demanded. "Are you spying on me?"

A normal dragon, with a healthy fear of punishment,

would have denied it immediately. But Lynx made a rueful face, spread her wings, and said, "I am, actually."

"Wh — you *are*?" Snowfall scowled at her. "WHY?" *Is she working with the NightWings? Or the invading dragons? Or Crystal? Or all of the above? Or writing to my cousin Winter about what a terrible job I'm doing? They were always too friendly, those two. Maybe she's convinced him to round up a bunch of SeaWings to attack us! I don't know why, but it's possible!*

"Because I'm worried about you," Lynx said frankly. "Snowfall, are you all right?"

Snowfall's ENTIRE BRAIN stopped working. It just rolled over and lay there, suddenly full of nothing to say after months of nonstop yelling about everything. Her mouth was all, *hello? any thoughts?* and the response was apparently, *nope, just flap around like a bewildered walrus for a while.*

"Snowfall?" Lynx said after a moment. "Are you — did I break you?" She reached out and tapped lightly on Snowfall's forehead.

NOBODY TAPPED ON THE QUEEN'S FOREHEAD! Snowfall jumped back and stared at her. Nobody asked if the queen was "all right" either. She had *never* been asked that question, and certainly not since she became RULER OF THE WHOLE ICE KINGDOM.

"Of *course* I'm all right," she snapped. "I am the *queen*."

"Those . . . two things don't necessarily go together," Lynx observed. "I'd think maybe the opposite, actually."

"Why don't *you* think I'm all right?" Snowfall demanded. "What are you trying to say? Do you think you'd be better at this than me?"

"Oh my goodness." Lynx edged away a step and looked even more concerned. "Not even remotely! I'd never want to be queen!"

"The CORRECT ANSWER," Snowfall said in an icy voice, "is NO, SNOWFALL, YOU'RE DOING AMAZING."

"You *are* doing amazing!" Lynx cried.

"See, now I don't believe you." Snowfall wrenched a globe off the tree and batted it up at one of the windows that overlooked the courtyard. Some aristocrat was going to wake up in the morning and be very confused about why he had a second light globe bobbing gently around his room.

Lynx watched it sail over their heads, then returned her gaze to Snowfall. "I'm just worried about the fact that the only dragons you ever get to talk to anymore are old and bossy and kind of mean."

Snowfall let out a snort. That certainly described the council of powerful IceWings who'd nominated themselves to guide the new young queen.

"Some would say I'm bossy and kind of mean, too," she said to Lynx haughtily.

"Oh, you are," Lynx said (which was NOT the correct answer EITHER), "but that means you need to order some kind, agreeable dragons to hang out with you. Ones that won't make your brain hurt all the time."

"Like you, I suppose?" Snowfall asked. *How does she know that my brain hurts all the time?*

"No, no," Lynx said. "I'm not agreeable at *all*. You'd be like, 'fetch me a narwhal!' and I'd be all, 'urrrgggh, whyyyyy, narwhals are heaaaaavy and I'm reeeeeeeading,' and you'd say, 'but I want one! right now!' and I'd say, 'then go GET one, bossytail,' and you'd bellow, 'I AM YOUR QUEEN!' and I'd be like, 'yes, but this book is at a really exciting part though,' and theeeeen you'd probably have me executed. I'd be so irritating! You already know this about me."

"How do you know that my brain hurts all the time?" Snowfall blurted. "I mean. That is. What makes you THINK that my brain hurts all the time?"

"Well," Lynx said carefully, flicking her tail. "You haven't stopped frowning since the beginning of the plague. That would give anyone a headache, I'd think. And *my* brain is always tired, when all I have to do is study and train and stay at the top of the dragonet rankings. *You* have to do alllllll the queen stuff. And, you know. Also the . . . the sad bit."

"No, no." Snowfall stamped right over Lynx's last words. "No time for that. I can handle all the queen stuff. I'm not a lowly noble like you. I can do everything just fine. This is what I've been preparing for my whole life."

"Sure, but — there was supposed to be more of a whole life first," Lynx pointed out. "Like, a couple more decades at least, I imagine."

"*You* don't know that," Snowfall said. "Maybe I was planning to challenge Mother for the throne, like, next week anyway. Because I'm so already ready to be queen."

The light from the tree was too bright and she could feel her eyes watering. She turned to pace back to the wall, rubbing her face with one talon. A couple more decades with Mother as their queen. Maybe longer. That was what they should have had; that was what Darkstalker stole.

She hadn't really had a plan for challenging her mother anytime soon. She'd thought there would be plenty of time ahead of them before she had to worry about that. Or that certain sisters would get there first.

"I guess I don't know," Lynx said, catching up to her. And walking BESIDE her instead of a few steps behind! How had this dragon done so well on her exams? Did she not know any royal etiquette at all?

"I guess," Lynx went on, "maybe it had to be sooner because you needed to challenge her before Icicle did, right? Or someone else? Maybe it's better this way, with her giving you the throne instead of you having to take it."

"I could have taken it," Snowfall assured her. "Anytime I wanted to."

She remembered Queen Glacier lying on her deathbed, gripping one of Snowfall's talons and staring intently up at her.

She remembered her sisters watching from the queen's

other side, Crystal's eyes glittering in the blue twilight, Mink sobbing.

"I will not have our tribe suffer the fate of the Kingdom of Sand," Glacier breathed between spasms of coughing. "*There will be no War of IceWing Succession.* Do you three understand me?"

Mink nodded frantically, although, at age two, she knew almost nothing about the war and probably couldn't even name the sisters — Blister, Blaze, and Burn — that she and Crystal and Snowfall might become.

"We promise, Mother," Crystal said in her frail, slippery-sweet voice. They were all sick at that point, although they didn't know yet that the plague came from Darkstalker's magic. But Crystal had draped herself in diaphanous scarf-veils that managed to make even the plague look glamorous. "Nobody wants another war."

Even though Crystal had actually fought in the War of SandWing Succession, she hadn't come back noticeably tougher or more aggressive. She actually seemed a bit less *there*. She kept staring out of windows and losing track of conversations, probably thinking about all the deaths she'd witnessed, Snowfall guessed. She could easily believe that Crystal didn't want the tribe, or especially herself, to face any more battles.

"We'll just fight each other," Snowfall said. "We won't drag anyone else into it. A normal duel, over in a day." *Could I beat Crystal in a fight? Maybe right now, while she's sicker with the plague than I am.* Crystal was three years older, slightly taller, a little lazy, and a bit of an overthinker. Snowfall could probably use those last two to her advantage.

Do I really have to kill her, though? Snowfall didn't know if she could handle one more dead IceWing. She didn't know if her claws could add to the death toll.

Mink sniffled, and Snowfall felt a small lurch in her chest. Mink wouldn't want to be queen, would she? Surely she wouldn't try to be in the duel . . .

"No," Glacier snarled. She crushed Snowfall's wrist in her talons with painful ferocity. "You *will not* fight each other. *I* am going to choose the next IceWing queen."

Crystal rubbed the edges of her wings together, a nervous habit that made a jittering sound, which drove Snowfall mad. "But," Crystal started. "But that — that's never —"

"You must swear on the spirits beneath the ice," Glacier said fiercely. "Whoever I choose to be queen, the other two will support her. You'll help her save the tribe and keep the peace. *No duels.* No fighting. No war. Do you understand?"

Snowfall glanced across at her sisters. Of course Mother would choose Crystal — the oldest, the calmest, the one other dragons liked. Crystal had never clawed her way to the top of the rankings like Snowfall, but she didn't seem to care even half as much. Did swearing this oath mean Snowfall would have to give up on the throne forever?

"For how long?" she asked. "I mean . . . tradition says no one should challenge a new queen for the first month of her reign — is that what you mean? Or for longer?"

"Longer," Glacier rasped. "The tribe will need stability after this plague." *If any of us survive it*, was the unspoken murmur under her words.

"So . . ." Snowfall studied Crystal's bowed head for a moment. "A year?"

Glacier sighed, a sad whisper of wind across a frozen lake. "I don't want you three to fight," she said, closing her eyes. "Ever."

"I won't," Mink cried. She climbed up onto the bed with their mother and crept under Glacier's wing. "I won't ever hurt them, Mommy, I p-promise. I love them and I love you and we'll all be r-really good."

Crystal lifted her gaze and met Snowfall's eyes. Hers were clear blue as the sky, and Snowfall couldn't read them at all. Was she angry that their mother was asking them to break centuries of IceWing tradition with a promise like this? Or was that a look of triumph, knowing that if she agreed, Snowfall would never be able to take her throne?

"I'll swear, too," Crystal said. "No fighting. Whatever you want, Mother."

"Snowfall?" Glacier said.

Snowfall felt as though sharp talons were raking the words out of her throat. "I swear," she choked out. "I'll support the new queen. I won't challenge her."

For now, her brain couldn't help adding. *For . . . a while, at least*. She tried to shut it off, but it kept whispering. *Maybe one day . . .*

"Good." Glacier opened her eyes again and tucked Mink in

closer with her wing. She reached for the glittering diamond crown on the side table. "The next queen of the IceWings is Snowfall. That is final."

A shocked numbness seized Snowfall's scales, spreading out to her wingtips and tail. She felt the heavy weight of the crown settling down around her temples. Crystal's face was unreadable, a blur over Mother's shoulder.

Me. She chose me. I'm the next queen of the IceWings. Not Crystal.

She thinks I'd be the best queen.

Is she right? What if she's wrong?

Now I'm the one who has to protect us from the NightWings.

And I'm the one who has to find a cure for this plague before any more dragons die.

Queen Snowfall.

Crystal bowed to Snowfall with a swoop of her wings, murmured something like "congratulations," and excused herself to check on something in the kitchens. She was beside the bed again, veiled and coughing, when Queen Glacier died later that night — shortly after the queen told Snowfall, far too late, about the animus who might be able to save them.

But the next morning, Crystal was gone, and Snowfall hadn't seen her since.

So. One could see why she might find that worrying.

She cut a suspicious glance at Lynx. "Do you actually think it's better? That I'm queen? You don't wish it was . . . someone else instead?"

"You mean Crystal?" Lynx asked, saying the quiet part loud again, like an absolute beluga. "I don't know her very well. She had just left for the war front when I came to the palace. Whenever I did see her, I got the impression she was hiding something."

"Isn't everybody?" Snowfall said with a snort.

Lynx scrunched up her snout and thought for a second. "I'm not."

"You were spying on me," Snowfall pointed out.

"Sure, but not very well," Lynx argued.

Snowfall was tired of being rained on. She turned away from the wall and went through the nearest archway, shaking her wet wings over the icy floor. It was marginally warmer inside the walls of the palace, but it would still take a while to feel dry.

Lynx followed her into the ballroom, where a pair of servants was changing the faded light globes in the chandeliers. They took one look at the queen, or maybe at the queen's thunderous expression, and fled through one of the upper balconies, their task only half-finished. Snowfall frowned after them.

"Well, I don't know Crystal," Lynx went on, "but I knew Queen Glacier and she was brilliant. She chose you. That's good enough for me."

"That's it?" Snowfall rounded on her with a hiss. "So you don't think *I'm* actually good enough to be queen? If it were up to you, it wouldn't be me! You're only supporting me because my mother thought it was a good idea?!"

"Three MOONS, Snowfall!" Lynx took a step back. "I'm sure you'll be a good queen! Except maybe if you have a meltdown because all the dragons around you are awful and you yell at anyone who tries to be nice to you!"

"Oh, is THAT what this is?" Snowfall said. "You're being NICE to me? Thank you SO MUCH, that's JUST what I needed."

"See, you're being sarcastic," Lynx said, "but it *is* what you need, walrus-breath."

"You can't call the queen a walrus-breath!" Snowfall shouted. "It's not allowed AND it's not nice! Where are my executioners when I need them?"

"You don't have those," Lynx said, with a distinct lack of concern in her voice. "Hey, I know what would help. Want to go for a swim?"

"NO, I OBVIOUSLY DON'T WANT TO GO FOR A SWIM!" Snowfall yelled, even though swimming had once been one of her favorite things. She wondered if Lynx had actually remembered that. "I don't have TIME for that kind of non-sense! I am RULING A KINGDOM RIGHT NOW, not that you've apparently noticed!"

"But don't you need a break?" Lynx asked. "I think it would make you feel better."

Snowfall dug her claws into the ice below her. "I don't

have time to feel better," she said through gritted teeth. "My sister has gone into hiding, probably so she can kill me; animus magic is *broken* so I can't use it to fix ANYTHING; and there are *hundreds* of evil mystery dragons flying DIRECTLY AT OUR BORDER RIGHT THE HECK NOW. They will probably BE HERE BY TOMORROW. To do SOMETHING NEFARIOUS, I don't know what, but PROBABLY INVOLVING MURDER! WHEN AM I SUPPOSED TO FIT A LEISURELY SWIM INTO ALL OF THAT, LYNX?"

Lynx stared at her, blinking fast for a long moment. "Well," she said finally, "no one said it had to be a *leisurely* swim —"

"EXECUTIONERS!" Snowfall bellowed.

"Great Ice Spirits, Snowfall, take a breath!" Lynx grabbed one of Snowfall's gesticulating talons and gripped it between hers. "Tell me about the hundreds of evil mystery dragons."

"That is top secret information," Snowfall said haughtily. "Not for insignificant dragonets to know."

"But you clearly need to talk about it," Lynx pointed out. "Just tell me and I promise I'll keep it a secret if you want me to."

Words started spilling out of Snowfall against her will. "Hundreds," she said. "*Hundreds* of strange dragons. On their way here. Right now."

"I got that part," Lynx said. "That's all the information I already have. But do you mean real dragons? Not paranoid-made-up-hypothetical dragons?"

Snowfall began to swell with indignation and Lynx jumped in before she could start yelling again.

"All right! Sorry, just checking! I believe you. Hundreds of mystery dragons. Um . . . from where?"

"I don't know!" Snowfall cried. "That's the problem! One of the problems! Maybe Crystal went to get an army to destroy me. Maybe the NightWings want to finish what they started with the plague. Maybe Coral and Glory have formed an alliance and decided to take me down!"

"But . . . why would they do that?" Lynx asked.

"BECAUSE EVERYONE IS EVIL!" Snowfall shouted. She yanked her talon out of Lynx's grasp.

"Snowfall! Everyone just got *out* of a war! None of the queens in Pyrrhia want to get back into another one! Listen, listen. How do you know about the hundreds of dragons?"

"One of my scouts," Snowfall said. "He was out scouting the western ocean and saw them coming from a distance. They landed on an island out there, but he said they were regrouping to fly again soon."

Lynx scrunched up her face in a thinking-hard expression that Snowfall knew very well from years of sitting next to her in class.

"From a distance? Across the western ocean?" Her eyes went suddenly wide. "Three moons. Snowfall! What if they're from the lost continent?"

"How have you ever beaten me on a test?" Snowfall

demanded. "Does your brain even work at all? The lost continent isn't real! It's a myth!"

"Unless it *is* real, and we're about to get hundreds of visitors to prove it!" Lynx was nearly dancing on her claws now. Snowfall wanted to drop a mountain on her.

"That is not better!" Snowfall shouted. "Dragons from a whole other continent?! Invading MY KINGDOM? They must be coming to steal our land! And treasure! What if they have extra-murdery superpowers we've never even thought of? Or WEIRD DISEASES, Lynx, what if they have WEIRD DISEASES THAT WILL KILL US?"

"We can't worry about all of that until it actually happens," Lynx said with an "I'm so practical" expression that made Snowfall feel like screaming.

"Yes, we can!" Snowfall cried. "I'm worrying about all of it right now!"

"OK," Lynx said. "Sure. But *maybe* they come in peace."

Snowfall's scales wanted to leap off her and go running up the walls, shrieking or exploding or whapping into everything. She couldn't even hold all the things inside of her that might go horribly and dramatically wrong.

"Snowfall," Lynx said. She folded her wings forward around Snowfall's head, like a dome of white curtains, and looked into Snowfall's eyes.

It was impertinent, but it cast an irresistible stillness around them.

"*Queen* Snowfall," Snowfall reminded her. It was kind

of peaceful not to be able to see the palace. This was what she wanted for the whole tribe: a wall of solid scales around them, blocking everything else out.

"Queen Snowfall," Lynx echoed. "You said they'll be here tomorrow? So let's fly to the western coast and meet them. Let's find out who they are and what they want before we panic. I mean, bit late for that, clearly, but we can save the more epic panicking for when we actually know something."

"We?" Snowfall said. "Meaning me and my whole army?"

"Meaning you and me," Lynx said. "And one guard, if you must."

"Terrible plan," Snowfall said. "The worst. I hate it."

"Great." Lynx grinned at her. "See you at the front gate at dawn."

She trotted away, like a dragon with no worries in the whole world, and Snowfall was left staring into the walls of the palace. Pale shimmering blue drizzled down through the translucent ice, reflecting the weather outside with phosphorescent magic. The gift of elegance, crafted by a long-ago animus with no sense at all.

Why couldn't it be a "gift of invincibility," or a "gift of unlimited-every-queen-gets-magic-now" or a "gift of crush-your-enemies-with-one-thought"? It was so unfair (and deeply suspicious) that animus magic stopped working EXACTLY when Snowfall found out about Jerboa. She should have had at least one animus gift — she had so many great ideas!

Didn't animus dragons know about the danger from other

tribes two thousand years ago? Was the one who made the Great Ice Cliff the only smart one?

Suddenly a thought hit her, a thought so brilliant it made her gasp.

There were other animus dragons before we lost Prince Arctic. Other gifts.

She knew where she needed to go.

The Forbidden Treasury.

~ CHAPTER 3 ~

Most of the IceWing treasure, including Snowfall's awful crown, was kept in the regular treasury — a guarded vault close to the center of the palace.

But there was another treasury, one known only to a few and spoken of in whispers. It was buried in an ice cave deep below the palace, and the only way to get there was through a secret passage from the queen's own rooms. No one but queens and princesses had been down there in hundreds of years, or perhaps ever. Only the queens and princesses were even sure it was real.

Had it been conjured by an animus sometime long ago? A gift of secrets? Or did a queen in their ancient past once order workers to carve out the cave and the passage with their own claws?

Snowfall didn't know. She didn't think her mother had known either, although now she wished she had asked more questions.

At the door of her royal chambers, a tiny dragonet was

sitting between the guards. Her eyes were large and dark blue, and her scales were white with feathery patterns of gray along her wings, like whiskers or tufts of fur. The guards had clearly been chatting with her, but they snapped to attention as Snowfall approached, and the little dragon scrambled to her feet as well.

"Hi, Snowfall," Mink blurted. "Um, um, um, I m-made you something." She reached into a small pouch slung across her back and brought out a tiny block of ice, carved with great care into, as far as Snowfall could tell, a blob.

Mink gently placed it into Snowfall's talons with an expression of bashful pride.

"Oh . . . uh, thank you." Snowfall turned it around a few times, wondering which end was up. "It's . . . great."

"It's a mink!" her little sister said. "Like me! But, um, an actual mink, not a dragon mink. See the whiskers? And the ears?"

"Sure," Snowfall said doubtfully.

"It's just to say I love you," Mink said shyly.

This would have been sweet, if it weren't for the fact that Mink loved literally everyone. Snowfall was pretty sure every dragon in the whole palace had at least one of Mink's "I love you" gifts. The queen's room was still cluttered with them: miniature unidentifiable ice sculptures on every surface.

Snowfall hadn't seen her tiny, flibbertigibbet sister very much since becoming queen. There were dragons in charge of her education and training, and Snowfall assumed they'd carried on since Queen Glacier's death the same as they had before. Mink's life shouldn't have changed very much at all.

"Well. Thank you," Snowfall said, aware of the guards' eyes on her. "Now, I'm very busy, so —"

"Oh, can't I please come in?" Mink pleaded. "I miss M-Mommy's room."

Snowfall frowned at her. "You miss her *room*?"

"I s-slept in there sometimes when I c-couldn't fall asleep," Mink explained.

That figured. Snowfall would never have dared to crawl into her mother's room in the middle of the night. It was highly against the rules and would almost certainly have gotten her knocked down a few spots on the wall. Training herself to go back to sleep alone was part of being a First Circle kind of dragon.

But that wasn't the kind of thing Mink worried about. If she weren't everyone's beloved princess, she'd probably be stuck in the Sixth Circle her whole life.

"You can't sleep in there now," Snowfall said. "It's my room." She had enough trouble sleeping without adding a fidgety little snuggle lizard into the situation.

"I know," Mink said, her wings drooping. "I just w-want to see it again."

Snowfall sighed. If she sent Mink away now, these guards would probably tell everyone in the palace that she'd hurt her sister's feelings. Not an excellent queen move, for sure.

Besides. She should probably know about the Forbidden Treasury.

Queen Glacier had taken Snowfall down there only once, when she was four years old, and she'd done the same with Crystal, three years before that. *But not Mink. She was still too young.*

I should show it to her. With Crystal gone, if anything happens to me . . . this secret could be lost forever.

Snowfall shivered. It was extremely strange to think of little Mink as her sole heir; even stranger to think that Snowfall should teach her how to be queen, just in case. Snowfall wasn't cut out to be a patient teacher — and Mink definitely wasn't cut out to be a ruthless queen.

"All right, come in," Snowfall said grumpily.

Mink squeaked happily and bounded into the room ahead of her.

"Nobody else is allowed in for the rest of the night," Snowfall ordered the guards. (Did that sound cool and calm, or strange and paranoid? Wasn't this a perfectly normal thing for a queen to command? The guards' expressions were impassive, unmoving. What were they thinking about her? Did they find her queenly, or ridiculous?)

In the main chamber, the bed dominated the center of the room, a block of ice carved into whorls and drifts where a dragon body could fit perfectly. As Snowfall shut the doors, Mink leaped onto the bed and wriggled around, looking ridiculously comfortable.

The truth was, Snowfall still hadn't slept in her mother's bed — she couldn't stop thinking of it *as* her mother's bed. She wasn't sure how she ever would. Most queens killed their predecessor on a battlefield, or in an arena, or before the whole court in a bloodstained throne room. They didn't watch them slip away into darkness in the very spot where they then had to fall asleep for the rest of their lives.

It was just as comfortable up on top of the jewel cabinet anyway. Or on the polar bear rug by the window. Or in the icy bathtub in the next room.

Fine, nowhere at all was comfortable, but that was FINE. Queens didn't complain about their sleeping quarters! Real queens probably didn't need as much sleep as regular dragons anyway!

"Off," she ordered her sister. "I have to show you something." Mink hopped off the bed immediately, her eyes wide.

Snowfall braced her talons against the spot at the foot of the bed, the one her mother had shown her, and pushed. The bed slid aside soundlessly, revealing a hole underneath that plunged into endless darkness.

"Wow," Mink breathed. "Wow oh wow. Why is there a hole in the floor? I never ever *knew* there was a big hole under the bed!"

"It's a secret for queens," Snowfall said.

Mink's face fell. "Oh," she said. "Not for m-me, then."

"Well," Snowfall said reluctantly. "It could be for you, one day, if anything happens to me and you have to become queen."

"What?" Mink cried. "No! I don't want to be! What's going to happen to you?"

"Nothing!" Snowfall said. "I'm going to be queen for AGES and ages. But you should see it anyway, just in case. Hang on to your light globe and follow me."

She clasped her own light globe in her front talons, spread her wings, and dove into the chasm. The walls glittered around them as they spun down and down and down, until soon all she could see above and below them was darkness.

Finally her light reflected off a smooth glassy surface at the bottom of the hole, several heartbeats away. She banked her wings and slowed to a gentle drift until she felt her claws touch down. A little thump behind her announced the arrival of her sister as Snowfall released her light globe to drift over her shoulder once more.

"Oh my gosh oh my gosh," Mink whispered, trying to crawl under one of Snowfall's wings to press against her side. "What is this place?"

Teaching her little sister about royal secrets was one thing; snuggling was quite another, and definitely not on her list of queen responsibilities. Snowfall wiggled away and took a step into the dark corridor before them.

"This is the Forbidden Treasury," she said. "You must never tell anyone where it is or how to get here. There are secrets down here, and magic that only a queen can use." She realized she'd slipped into her mother's voice, echoing the words Queen Glacier had said to her on this very spot.

"I won't tell," Mink breathed. "I promise promise."

The walls around them were blackest ice, gleaming with silvery filaments and bubbles when the light hit them. Snowfall led the way through the passage's spiral; it coiled in on itself like a snail shell, with alcoves cut into the ice at eye level every few steps. Well, eye level for an older dragon; they were slightly above Snowfall's head, but she could stretch her neck up and see into them. Everything was too high for Mink to reach without flying.

The first two alcoves were empty — they had been when Snowfall visited with Glacier, too. She didn't know what had been in them, or if they'd been left empty in anticipation of gifts that had never arrived (thank you, NightWings).

Her light glittered off something shimmery in the third alcove and she paused. It was a tiara, delicate and elegant. Much lighter and smaller than her hideous crown, and prettier, too. *Hmmm.* She nudged the light globe closer to the wall, where words were carved into the ice.

THE GIFT OF STRENGTH. USE CAUTIOUSLY.

Oooooo. Strength sounded promising. This would definitely be useful! Would it make the whole kingdom stronger somehow, or specifically just whoever wore the tiara?

Snowfall thought for a moment, then lifted out the tiara and placed it carefully on her head.

Nothing dramatic happened. She felt the same. It fit so comfortably she could hardly tell she was wearing it. She glanced down at Mink.

"What do you think?"

The little dragon's eyes were shining. "It's so pretty," she breathed. "Can I try it on?"

"No, no, definitely not," Snowfall said quickly. "Everything down here is only for queens. You can look, but you can't touch, all right?"

Mink's face fell and her wings drooped on either side of her. Snowfall turned away quickly before she could see any tears in her sister's eyes.

"Come on, let's see what else there is," she said briskly. She trotted forward, and she heard Mink's tiny claws scrambling on the ice to keep up.

The next alcove held a scepter, carved from some dark blue rock with little diamonds set into it. Snowfall disliked it immediately. It reminded her of NightWings.

THE GIFT OF COMPROMISE, read the inscription.

NO, THANK YOU, Snowfall thought furiously. She didn't read the rest of the carved words, which covered half the wall under the alcove. Compromise was NOT what the IceWings needed! They needed a strong queen who could do impressive giant scary magic things, like maybe shoot lightning bolts from her claws, or suddenly grow to three times her size, or flick her tail and make it rain poisonous scorpions! Compromise INDEED.

Mink fluttered her wings to get high enough to see the scepter, but Snowfall was already whisking away.

"Not useful!" she called, striding to the next alcove.

This one held a ring — a weird-looking ring. It had a milky pink-gold-white-green opal set into the center of it, and the rest of the ring looked like silver dragon tails, winding around the opal and the space where a dragon's claw would go.

Snowfall studied it for a moment. The opal was kind of mesmerizing. The more she looked at it, the more flecks of different colors she could see in it.

This one said: THE GIFT OF VISION.

No other notes. Well, that was pretty straightforward. Better vision? Snowfall would take that. It wasn't as useful as strength or scorpion hail, but maybe it would help her see the mystery dragons from much farther away. Maybe she'd be able to identify them long before they hit the shores of the Ice Kingdom.

She lifted it out and slipped it on one of her front left claws. It was a bit too big, as if it had been designed for a bigger, older dragon. *A real queen.* Snowfall sighed. *SHUT UP, BRAIN. STOP THINKING LIKE THAT. This is MY gift now; that MAKES me a real queen!*

She stormed on to the next alcove, which was empty. Whatever had been written underneath had been violently scratched out sometime long ago. Snowfall wondered if there was any explanation in one of the old IceWing history books. Not that she had time for HISTORY right now. Three MOONS.

After that was an alcove that seemed to have been added

later; it wasn't at the same distance from the others, and it looked hacked out of the ice instead of beautifully carved. The item inside looked like an unwearable mystery piece of silver. The scribble-scratch writing underneath said PART OF THE GIFT OF UNDERSTANDING, which was weird (part of? where was the rest?) and not helpful either (bah humbug understanding!).

Snowfall was getting nervous. The walls were spiraling in tighter and tighter; soon they'd be at the end. Wasn't there ANYTHING down here that could destroy an invading army with one swoop if she wanted to?

Absolutely useless animus idiots.

The next treasure, though, looked a lot more promising. Pale silver wristbands set with diamonds . . . and underneath . . .

Snowfall read the inscription and smiled.

Well. It's not exactly what I wanted.

But it'll definitely give those invading dragons quite an unwelcome surprise.

CHAPTER 4

Snowfall arrived at the front gate at dawn with five guards, because she was the queen and she did what she liked and Lynx didn't get to decide all the things, so there.

Lynx was waiting at the gate, looking unfairly well rested. She kind of rolled her eyes at the five guards, but she didn't say anything, so Snowfall didn't have to threaten her face first thing in the morning.

They flew south and west along the coast, out toward the farthest peninsula that reached into the ocean. The ocean that was *supposed* to be so big no one could cross it, so even if there was a continent full of dangerous dragons on the other side, they'd have to stay over there. If Lynx was right, how had they gotten here? And why now?

Why would they arrive right when I've just become queen? Did they hear about me and decide to invade because they think I'm young and useless and I'll be easy to defeat?

She gnawed at these questions as they flew and the sun rose higher, setting the snow below them into a dazzling blaze of sparkles. It was so beautiful and pure out here, all these untouched snow drifts stretching out below them. No murder plots or magic plagues or untrustworthy dragons anywhere to be seen.

"You look tired," Lynx said after a little while.

"That's treason, and no, I don't," Snowfall snapped.

"Did you sleep at all?" Lynx asked.

Did Snowfall ever actually sleep? Or did her brain just slide a little underwater, where the worries were blurrier and NightWings stalked around in the dark trying to kill her? Did it count as sleeping when she woke up more tired than she'd been before? Could she even call it waking up, when it felt more as though all her worries suddenly became so pressing that her eyes flew open? The arrival of dawn only seemed to shove her from a drifting haze of nebulous problems straight into a blistering ice storm of them.

Last night she hadn't even tried. "No," she answered Lynx. "I was very busy."

Lynx tilted her head. "Doing what?"

"You might find this hard to imagine," Snowfall said, "but QUEENS have A LOT TO DO, ACTUALLY."

"But . . . when everyone else is asleep?" Lynx asked again. "What did you do, specifically?"

Snowfall tipped her wings to catch an air current. "Last night, *specifically*, I visited the treasury." She knew Lynx would think she meant the regular royal treasury. "And then I spent absoLUTELY forever trying to make a certain pathetic seal-eyed princess go away, but she ended up falling asleep on MY bed in the MIDDLE of my lecture, which was VERY RUDE."

"Ooooooh, the *treasury*," Lynx said. "I thought you looked extra-sparkly today. Is this to impress the strange dragons?" She flicked her tail at Snowfall's accessories.

"Sure," Snowfall said, rolling her eyes. "Wow oh wow, I really hope they think I'm extra-sparkly, too!"

"All right, sarcasm face." Lynx flicked her tail at Snowfall again. "Then what's all this about?"

Snowfall held out her front talons, where the diamond-crusted wristbands glittered alongside sleek, fitted knife sheaths. The tiara of strength was perched on her horns. The ring of vision was still on the front left claw where she'd put it, but so far, she hadn't noticed any improvement in her eyesight. Maybe she had to activate it somehow.

If Lynx couldn't guess why she was wearing all of this, maybe she wasn't cut out for the new council Snowfall was thinking about, after all.

Just as she had that thought, Lynx's eyes widened.

"Wait," she said, lowering her voice even though the guards were flying a perimeter around them, just out of ear-shot. "Snowfall! You don't mean the Forbidden Treasury, do you? Are those jewels animus-touched?"

Snowfall smiled slyly, letting the sun catch on the opal in her ring. "I'm glad to see your brain does work sometimes."

"But — you can't go to the Forbidden Treasury! It's

forbidden! It's right there in the name! And you definitely can't take things *out* of it!"

"Of course I can!" Snowfall snapped. "I'm THE QUEEN, even though you can't seem to remember that! I'm literally the only dragon allowed in the Forbidden Treasury! It's MY treasury!"

"Yeah, but — isn't all that stuff forbidden for a reason?"

"It's *forbidden* to dragons who would be too weak to use it properly," Snowfall said. "Not queens. And besides, this is an emergency, and why would we keep stuff like that around if not for exactly this?"

Lynx tilted her wings, looking puzzled. "An emergency?"

"You are a very poor listener!" Snowfall shouted. "Animus magic is BROKEN! No one can cast any more spells! We can't make anything to protect ourselves from the invaders!"

"But . . . hasn't that been the case . . . for, like, two thousand years?" Lynx asked. "IceWings haven't had an animus dragon since Prince Arctic."

Snowfall didn't want to tell her about Jerboa, the difficult SandWing animus that Queen Glacier had found and formed some kind of alliance with. Glacier had told Snowfall to go find Jerboa in the hopes that the animus could stop the plague, but they were too late. And, of course, now it turned out the SandWing was perfectly useless. *Now*. Right when Snowfall *needed* her.

Maybe the invading dragons somehow know that, too. Or maybe THEY froze everyone's animus magic!

"Irrelevant! And classified!" she hissed at Lynx. "The important part is that I realized we can use something we *already have*. The Forbidden Treasury is where we keep our ancient magic from thousands of years ago, before we lost our animus bloodline. Back then every animus dragon made a gift for the tribe. I realized, because I am a genius, that there's a chance one of those could save us, and I could find it in the Forbidden Treasury."

"I never saw Queen Glacier wearing any of that," Lynx said cautiously.

"Maybe my mother was not as brilliant as everyone thinks," Snowfall said. "Maybe if she'd thought of this, she could have found something in the treasury to protect us all, and *maybe* she'd still be alive."

She tipped her head up until her eyes stopped watering. The thought of magic lying under the palace, forgotten, unused, going to waste . . . it made her claws itch to stab something.

"All right, so what do all those jewels do?" Lynx asked.

"I'm not telling you," Snowfall snapped.

"But . . . you do *know*?" Lynx asked nervously. "I mean. You understand each of the things you're wearing? You can control them?"

Snowfall cast her a withering look. "Of course," she said. "Most of them were stored with notes from the queens who used them." She squinted at a shape moving below them, but it was only an arctic hare — and it looked the same as arctic hares always did from up in the sky. She'd kind of expected the gift of vision to actually, you know, DO something to her vision. Maybe that one was broken. Lynx didn't need to know about that.

"*Most* of them?" Lynx squeaked as Snowfall whisked ahead of her. She flapped her wings to catch up. "Snowfall, what if they're dangerous?"

"They'd BETTER be dangerous," Snowfall said. "That's the whole point! There's an invasion on its way here, remember? We need all the protection we can get. This is why facing them with an army would be the best idea."

"I think you're just as scary as any army all on your own," Lynx said. "Without any magic."

"HA," Snowfall snorted. "*I* only have, like, seven nonmagical weapons on me. We need THOUSANDS of weapons to drive these dragons away!"

Lynx glanced down at her claws, as if she'd only just noticed that those were the only weapons she'd brought. "Really? Seven weapons?"

"Yes, of course!" Snowfall said. She pointed to the spear on her back. "Spear." Then to the knives in the sheaths at her wrists. "Knife, knife." Then to the sheaths under her wings, the concealed pockets of her chain mail armor, and the pouch around her neck. "Knife, knife, throwing stars, poison."

She didn't mention the other three hidden weapons, just in case Lynx was actually working for Crystal or the

NightWings or had her own ulterior motives and was maybe planning to attack Snowfall as soon as she had her away from the castle unprotected. Well, ha ha, Snowfall had foiled her with those five guards! And the extra secret weaponry. And the totally being onto her!

"Headache again?" Lynx said sympathetically.

"No," Snowfall snapped, jerking her claws away from her temples. *More like headache always*, she thought. *And you're not helping, potentially untrustworthy dragon!*

She spotted a cluster of ice structures below them, along the cliff that overlooked the ocean here. "What's that?"

"One of the outer villages," Lynx said. "Where-the-Terns-Fly, I think."

"I should royally decree that all IceWing villages must have one-word names," Snowfall said grumpily. Her claws still hurt from years of writing out the list of villages, over and over again, and labeling them on maps, and writing essays about them. The time she could have saved if Hamlet-That-Worships-the-Whales-Who-Sing-at-Night had just been called Whales! Not to be confused with Where-the-Whales-Leap-at-Dawn, of course.

"That would be a GREAT royal decree," Lynx said fervently. "At least for maps and lists and essays by exhausted dragonets!"

"Your puny little estate is out here somewhere," Snowfall remembered.

"It is." Lynx cast a wistful glance to her left. "It overlooks

Among-the-Evergreens. My father lives there but . . . I haven't been back in a while."

"What is he — Fifth Circle? Sixth?"

"Fifth, for the last couple of years," Lynx said. *Because Lynx's success at court has raised him up*, Snowfall guessed. "But hang on, isn't there some kind of rule that no one is allowed to talk to the queen about the wall?"

"It's fine if *I* bring it up!" Snowfall said, bristling. "But you can't ask me to change anything! Not that I would anyway! No one else makes my decisions for me!"

"Oh, good," Lynx said. "I was wondering why Tundra and Permafrost had stayed up so high lately when they're always so awful, but now that I know it's entirely your decision, I feel much better."

Snowfall glared at her. "That sounded like SARCASM."

"Did it?" Lynx gasped.

"Your Majesty," one of the guards interrupted, swooping back toward them. "We think we see something."

Snowfall pumped her wings to shoot ahead of Lynx, catching up to another guard who'd been flying out in front. She squinted at the horizon, where the ocean took over from the snowy cliffs.

At first she thought she was looking at clouds — ordinary clouds, nonthreatening puffs of fluff in the sky. And then she realized that the clouds were flickering and shivering with movement. Flashes of green and gold and rose and aquamarine caught the sunlight.

They were clouds of wings, a whole fog of dragons descending on her kingdom.

The jolt of terror that ran through Snowfall's veins was like being stabbed with a SandWing tail. It was like six NightWings attacking her at once.

It was like the moment a cobalt-blue hybrid dragon had bowed in front of her, held out a garish earring, and said, "I am so sorry I didn't get here sooner, Queen Snowfall. I am too late for your mother, but I can at least save your life, if you put this on. This plague — it's a spell. It was sent by an animus NightWing named Darkstalker to wipe out the entire tribe of IceWings."

"They're coming to kill us," she said, whisking around in the air and nearly colliding with Lynx. Hearing her words, the closest guards faltered in the sky; they looked as scared as she felt.

"They're *not* coming to kill us," Lynx said. "I mean, we don't know that they're coming to kill us. They're *probably* not coming to kill us. We're going to find out!"

"This is a terrible way to find out!" Snowfall protested as Lynx turned her around. "It would be much smarter to attack them with my whole army the moment they land!"

"No, no," Lynx objected, alarmed. "That would start things off on completely the wrong talon! Listen, it won't take long to get your army if we need it. If these dragons do seem danger-ous, we can retreat to my father's estate and use the mirror signal system to summon backup. See? No need to panic."

Snowfall hissed at her. Yes, fine, she should probably act less terrified in front of the guards. Queens weren't supposed to freak out about anything. Queens never panicked.

Mother was never scared, not once, not during the war and not even when the plague came.

But WHY NOT, is my question. There are SO MANY THINGS to be scared of! Was she secretly this close to falling apart all the time, like I am? Did she wonder how she was going to hold the whole tribe together in this large cold kingdom after a war with so many deaths? Didn't she spend all her time worrying about how we could possibly survive against a tribe of dragons who hate us and who by the way have ALL the magic powers?

Stop thinking about NightWings. Deal with the brand-new mysterious scary thing.

"Nobody is panicking," she said, flicking her tail. "You're an impertinent gnat. Stop annoying me." She pushed Lynx aside and flew on ahead. There was an alarming heartbeat of stillness from the guards, but then she sensed them moving into place around her, flying in formation just as though she were exactly the right queen doing exactly the right thing.

Instead of making this all up as I go.

She led them to a cliff that overlooked a grove of snow-covered pines and a rocky beach. Below them, dragons were swooping down to land.

They were not NightWings — the scout was right about that.

They were not SeaWings or RainWings either.

The green dragons — actually green and brown and sometimes flecked with gold scales, Snowfall noticed — had wings elegantly shaped like leaves, no phosphorescent markings, and no webs between their claws.

The other tribe was much stranger. Their scales were all over the color spectrum — shimmering pinks, dark violets, pale lavenders, blues and oranges and summery yellows. They each had four wings instead of two, and even at a distance, Snowfall could see delicate antennae curling from their foreheads.

"Weird creepy dragons," she hissed, crouching close to the ground and peering over the cliff edge. "They must be evil! They look totally different from us!"

"So do SandWings, but we managed to ally with a bunch of them during the war," Lynx pointed out from beside her. "Every tribe looks a little different, but none of them are completely *evil*."

"Wrong," Snowfall snapped. "Objectively wrong. Night-Wings are NINE THOUSAND PERCENT evil."

Lynx gave her that curious sideways look again. "Didn't that empathy spell work on you at all?" she asked. "Didn't you feel what they were feeling, during our battle with them? It made the rest of us IceWings hate them way less. Why not you?"

Snowfall didn't answer. That moment — in the middle of the battle, when an animus dragon had connected all the minds of the fighting dragons, IceWings and NightWings together — that had been one of the worst moments of her life.

Because threaded through the IceWings' fear, in dragon after dragon, she'd found one particular whisper: *What are we going to do without Queen Glacier?*

How can Snowfall possibly save us from this?

She's not ready.

She's a smug little monster.

Our new queen is a spoiled dragonet who has no idea what to do.

Why would Glacier pick her?

Up until then, she'd thought maybe the tribe was proud of her. Maybe they were glad she was the sister who'd been chosen; maybe they knew how fiercely she would fight for them. Maybe when Glacier chose her, it had convinced everyone that she was truly a worthy queen.

Apparently not.

And over on the other side, she felt the NightWings' triumph, too — *look at their queen! She's barely old enough to fly! She doesn't know anything!*

We can destroy her easily.

It wasn't the biggest feeling the battling dragons were all having — that was fear. And now that fear was all anyone talked about: NightWings, hey, maybe they're just like us! Maybe they're scared of stuff, too! We can totally understand them!

Snowfall seemed to be the only one who remembered

those layers of doubt under everything else. At least, no one had ever dared to ask her, "Hey, did you happen to hear me thinking about what a terrible queen you'll be?"

And she was still afraid of NightWings. The other IceWings were delusional not to be.

"Do you want me to go talk to them first?" Lynx asked. Snowfall realized the other dragon had been studying her face for the last few minutes.

"No," Snowfall growled. "I'll go. We'll leave two guards here in case they have to fly for help." She flicked her tail at the three biggest guards to signal them to follow her.

The closer they got, the more Snowfall noticed how bedraggled all the invaders looked. Some of them had singed tails or wings; all of them were wet and crusted with salt from the spray. Most of them were very thin. Almost all the colorful dragons had heavy-looking metal wrist cuffs around their front talons. *Why would anyone wear something like that for a long flight?* Snowfall wondered suspiciously. *They'd drag you down the whole time. They must be some kind of powerful weapon.*

Some of the green dragons looked oddly lumpy, until she realized they were each wearing several woven pouches. *And what's in those?* she wondered. *Cursed objects? What if they have something that can enchant us to hand over our whole kingdom?*

She touched the diamonds in her armband, sharp-edged and cold. It was comforting to know she had magic of her own.

Most of the dragons looked up wearily as Snowfall and the others landed, pebbles and ice crunching under her claws.

One of the green dragons stood up, frowning, but then another green dragon tugged her back down, and a third green dragon climbed to her feet and came to face Snowfall.

"Who are you?" Snowfall demanded. "What are you doing in my kingdom?"

The green dragon sat down and spread her wings with her front talons raised, palms up. "I am Pr — um, Queen Hazel of the LeafWings. The other dragons traveling with us are SilkWings. We come from the land of Pantala, across the sea."

"Seems like a lot of dragons to bring with you for a neighborly visit," Snowfall said.

"I'm afraid we need help," Hazel said, sorrow flickering across her face. "We were forced to flee our home very suddenly. Our jungle was burning and our queen was gone. There is a terrible danger back on our continent, and if we hadn't escaped, it would have destroyed us all."

Snowfall could FEEL the waves of sympathy radiating off Lynx, who was standing a little too close to her left. No surprise that *she* would fall for any sad-snout story she heard. But Snowfall was smarter than that. She had a kingdom to protect.

"It sounds like you should have stayed and fought for your land," she said. "We don't have any room for you anyway. You're going to have to leave. Right now."

Hazel's face fell. "Just — wait, please. Let me tell you the whole story."

Something suddenly charged at them across the sand, shrieking alien syllables. Snowfall spun toward it, drawing her knives, and was a tail flick away from throwing them when she realized the attacker was a tiny dragonet.

Like, *really* tiny. It skidded to a stop with a terrified yelp, staring up at her glittering weaponry. Big, black-rimmed eyes blinked in a warm golden face. Her four wings were a little more shimmery and thinner than most of the others, and her scales alternated in black and yellow stripes.

The dragonet burst into tears.

"Oh, well done, Your Majesty," Lynx whispered to Snowfall. "Excellent self-defense."

Another yellow-and-black dragon came hurrying over and wrapped her wings around the baby. She wore crooked spectacles and she looked absolutely exhausted.

"It's all right," she murmured. "Don't cry, Bumblebee! Look, we made it to the Distant Kingdoms! Can you believe it's real? Isn't this amazing? We're here! We're safe now!"

Lynx shot Snowfall a "you're going to crush this moment, aren't you?" look.

"Pribbishimmy," Bumblebee sniffled into the other dragon's shoulder. "BuTEETH! ARROARAWR!"

The spectacled dragon looked up and met Snowfall's gaze. Her eyes flew wide, and suddenly she didn't look tired at all.

"Oh, wow!" she cried. "Our first new dragon in the

Distant Kingdoms! Isn't she *beyond* amazing? Oh my gosh, she looks like she's made of ice! I had no idea — hello, hi, are you actually made of ice? I mean . . . you can't be, right? No, you're clearly biological, but how are you *so* shiny? It is very cold here; is this some kind of arctic adaptation?"

"Cricket," the one called Hazel said in a warning tone. "I am trying to negotiate with this dragon queen."

"She *is* the queen?" Cricket burst out, so excited her words started tumbling over each other even faster. "Of the whole continent? Wow! How many dragons is that? Do you think this place is as big as Pantala?"

"Of the Ice Kingdom," Snowfall interrupted coldly. "I am Queen Snowfall of the IceWings."

"But no, we're not actually made of ice," Lynx whispered to Cricket. Snowfall glared at her.

Beyond Cricket and Hazel and Bumblebee, Snowfall could see even more dragons arriving, staggering onto the beach. There really were hundreds of them. And they landed with such . . . *relieved* expressions, as though this was exactly where they wanted to be. As though it were just the kind of territory they'd been hoping to steal.

One of them collapsed, digging his claws into the snow-dusted soil. *Is he sick?* Snowfall wondered. *Is he contagious?* Another movement made her spin to her right, but it was only a pair of young, strong LeafWings helping to drag a SilkWing out of the water. *Do they have magic? Are they going to suddenly turn violent?*

"You must leave," she said to Hazel. She realized she was still holding the knives she'd brandished at the dragonet. She lifted her head regally and sheathed them. "You are not welcome here. Go invade Thorn's kingdom instead."

"We have several dragons who can't possibly fly any farther right now," Hazel pleaded. "They're injured or elderly or too small, and we've been traveling for days. Please. They need to rest."

"That's not my problem," Snowfall said. "They're not my dragons."

"Snowfall," Lynx said meaningfully.

"They're not!" Snowfall protested. "I have a tribe to protect!"

"We're no threat to you, I promise," Hazel said. Snowfall realized the LeafWing queen was shivering. Was that fear or exhaustion or cold? Hopefully cold — maybe the temperatures would drive them out of the Ice Kingdom even faster than she could.

If so, maybe letting them stay for one night would be all right, if they promised to stay on the beach . . . and left first thing in the morning . . .

"That's everybody!" a brash, familiar voice announced. Someone large and blue bounded out of the ocean. "I mean, except Turtle, but he'll come wheezing up soon, don't worry."

Snowfall gasped.

"*You*," she spat.

It was that awful SeaWing "dragonet of destiny" who ran the Jade Mountain Academy! So this WAS a SeaWing invasion! Somehow! And wasn't she friends with Glory? The NightWings were probably lurking nearby, waiting for Snowfall to be distracted by the weird-looking dragons, and then they would POUNCE! An ambush! An attack! Just as she'd suspected!

"Oh no," Tsunami said, wrinkling her snout and giving Snowfall a disgruntled look. "We hit the Ice Kingdom? I thought we were way farther south." She sighed and shook out her wings, scattering salt water and kelp and tiny sea snails everywhere.

"What are you doing here?" Snowfall demanded furiously. "How DARE you come into my kingdom? Bringing an enormous throng of suspicious, weird-looking strangers?! Get out at ONCE!"

"We're not suspicious," the one named Cricket protested. "We're just tired and scared and running away from a really scary bad thing. What do you think we could possibly do?"

"It's all right, Cricket," Hazel said, taking a step back toward her other green dragons. Snowfall noticed that the first one who'd moved was standing up again, frowning menacingly. "I'd be alarmed if this many dragons suddenly showed up in my jungle, too."

"You wouldn't be SUPER RUDE to them, though, I bet," Tsunami snapped.

"Oh, I know!" Cricket said. "Wait, Queen Snowfall, we're

not total strangers! Bumblebee and I had an ancestor from your continent, hundreds of years ago. Doesn't that help to know? You must have heard of her — we're descendants of Clearsight!"

Out of the corner of her eye, Snowfall saw Tsunami wince.

Snowfall had a strange moment of vertigo, as though the ground under her had suddenly cracked and sent her sliding into the dark ocean. A pulse of fury stabbed through her temples and out to the tips of her wings.

The black scales. The secretive, smarter-than-you expressions. She should have seen it. These dragons were *part NightWing*.

And worse than that, they were related to *Clearsight*. Clearsight, the dragon who'd helped Darkstalker rise to power in the first place. The true love of that mass murderer.

Seething with rage, Snowfall lifted her wrists and smashed the diamonds together. Once, twice, three times, just as the instructions had said.

Behind her, along the top of the cliff, the entire IceWing army appeared.

CHAPTER 5

Lynx jumped away from her, startled. The other dragons — Hazel, Cricket, Bumblebee, Tsunami, and the hundreds of invaders — froze in place, staring up at the glittering ranks of soldiers.

"Three moons — how did you do that?" Lynx hissed.

Snowfall tipped the wristbands toward her, smirking. "The gift of stealth," she said. According to the notes in the Forbidden Treasury, she could use it to hide herself or anything else she wanted to. So she'd gathered her army in the night and prepared them to fly, weapons at the ready. She'd tested her new magic toy to make sure she could hide them, soaring along behind her. And there they were, as though she'd pulled them from thin air.

Now she felt strong. She felt like a queen. The strange dragons all looked terrified — of *her*. SO BRILLIANT. Everything she'd hoped for! Between the army and the magic, she'd proven her power. They wouldn't dare argue with her anymore.

Why didn't Mother ever dig these out? she wondered. *We could have used some impressive IceWing magic during the war. She could have hidden her army or spies or an assassin to go after Burn and Blister. The gift of stealth could have made us the most dangerous tribe in the war!*

Well. It's time for an IceWing queen who's not afraid to use all her resources.

She lowered her voice to its coldest, iciest tone. "I said," she hissed softly. "Get. Out."

Hazel's gaze flickered hesitantly from her to the army to Lynx. "Of course," she said. "We'll — we'll go." She took another step back.

There was one dragon who didn't look terrified, Snowfall realized. The frowning LeafWing behind Hazel was bristling like an angry polar bear about to charge. Her tail lashed as she glared back at Snowfall. The sooner Snowfall got *that* one out of the Ice Kingdom, the better.

"What *was* that?" Cricket breathed, adjusting her glasses to squint up at the army. "Can all dragons here turn invisible? What else can you do? Bumblebee, did you see that?"

"Sprkltoothy," Bumblebee murmured, burying her head in Cricket's shoulder.

"All right, all right," Tsunami grumbled. She spread her wings. "I might have known we'd land in the worst kingdom and the first dragon we'd see would be the queen of grumps."

Before Snowfall could bite Tsunami's head off, Lynx unexpectedly spoke up.

"She's not grumpy!" Lynx said. "She's a GREAT queen and this is the best kingdom and nobody invited *you* here to insult us."

Hazel had been giving quiet orders in the background, sending dragons to gather everyone, but now she paused and touched Tsunami's shoulder before the SeaWing could argue with Lynx. "Can you lead us somewhere else?" she asked.

"Yeah, south to the Kingdom of Sand," Tsunami said. "We'll find Luna and Moon there. And I'm sure *Queen Thorn* will know how to treat a group of harmless, tired, sad dragons who've lost their home."

"She's welcome to keep you!" Snowfall snapped, throwing her wings back. Tsunami tossed her a disgusted look and turned to help organize the dragons for departure.

South, Snowfall thought suddenly. *If they follow the coast . . . which they probably will, so they can rest often . . . they might end up flying within range of the Great Ice Cliff.*

Which will promptly shoot them all with ice spears, even though they'll be flying over it from the other side.

She hesitated. That *would* get rid of the problem completely. Those descendants of Clearsight would be gone and she wouldn't have to worry about any of this anymore, and her kingdom would be safe again. She would be safe again.

But sending them off to be massacred was exactly the kind of thing Darkstalker would do.

Snowfall was about to speak — she was pretty sure she was about to say something — when Lynx got there first.

"You have to be careful," she said to Hazel. "There's an ice cliff at our southern border that attacks dragons who fly over it if they're not IceWings. You'll have to circle out to sea to avoid it — pretty far out to sea, I think."

This news made Hazel look so tired (and Cricket so fascinated) that Snowfall almost *almost* melted.

But she couldn't. She had to be strong. Outside dragons were dangerous; that was all there was to it.

"We'll fly with you," Lynx said, with absolutely NO EFFORT TO RUN THIS PLAN BY SNOWFALL AT ALL. "We'll take you to the southern border of the Ice Kingdom and make sure you get across safely."

"All of you?" Hazel asked, glancing up at the army again.

"Just me and Queen Snowfall," Lynx said.

"AHEM," Snowfall interjected. "And ten of my personal guard."

She wasn't quite sure why she was agreeing to go along at all. Perhaps she just wanted to make sure they were really gone. Yes, that made sense. Best to see them well over the border and definitely out of her life forever.

Should she re-cloak her army and have them follow? Or would that be overkill . . . a sign of fear instead of strength? Hmmm.

She considered her options while she sat up on the cliff and watched the dragons below prepare to leave. They

moved VERY SLOWLY. If it was true that they'd been fleeing some enemy, Snowfall thought it must have been a rather
lethargic one, or else it could have caught them easily. An
enormous sloth, perhaps. An elephant seal on land. A malevolent glacier.

Lynx was down there trying to help. Snowfall could see
her moving between the dragons, bringing them bowls of
melted snow to drink. She'd also asked one of the soldiers
to fly to the nearest gift of subsistence and bring back a few
seals to share among the dragons. Snowfall had considered
ordering him not to, but she decided it would be queenlier
not to get involved. And after all, the gift of subsistence was
magic, producing as many seals as the dragons needed, so
they couldn't exactly run out.

Apparently the SilkWings didn't eat meat, though, which
added to Snowfall's suspicions, because wasn't that true of
RainWings as well? Was anyone sure that these weird dragons weren't working for Queen Glory?

Anyway, there was nothing growing in the pine grove
that they could eat. *See, the Ice Kingdom would be all wrong
for them*, Snowfall told herself, freezing over any twinges of
guilt inside her. *Too cold, no plants, dragons who want them
gone. They should move right along and become some other
queen's problem.*

The strange dragons had some kind of large makeshift
thing that floated on the ocean, made of palm trees lashed
together with vines, as far as Snowfall could tell. Tsunami

had left it out at sea when she came crashing in, but she swam back out to get it and a few of the healthier dragons, plus Lynx, helped her drag it onto the shore. Snowfall watched them narrowly as they guided some of the oldest, weakest, and smallest dragons to climb on top of it. Evidently the idea was to haul them over the top of the ocean, because they were incapable of flying that distance on their own.

Then they shouldn't have left their own stupid continent, she thought. *What did she call it? Pintala? They should have stayed there and dealt with their own problems, instead of bringing them to me.*

She flicked her tail to summon her favorite general. Ivory came over immediately, bowing with exactly the amount of respect Snowfall was looking for.

Ivory had been in that battle with the NightWings. But she hadn't thought, *Queen Snowfall, ugh, what a terrible choice*, like so many of the dragons in her army. Her thoughts had been more like: *I hope she can do this. If we survive this, I'm going to help our new queen however I can.*

It wasn't exactly "Hooray, Snowfall, she's the best!" but it was one of the only supportive things Snowfall had heard in the chaos. That's why she was Snowfall's favorite, and would stay in the First Circle forever, as far as Snowfall was concerned.

"I'm putting you in charge while I'm away from the kingdom," Snowfall said.

"Me?" General Ivory looked surprised for a moment. "Yes, Your Majesty. May I ask — what if Tundra objects?"

"Then she can eat her own tail," Snowfall snapped. "Tell her if she complains I'll be happy to move her down to a different circle." *Oh*, she thought with a sudden surge of something almost like joy. *If I escort the invaders out of here, I definitely won't make it back to the palace by nightfall tonight. I'll have to camp overnight somewhere. Which means I won't have to do the wall!*

Perhaps it was a bad sign that this moment was literally the happiest she'd felt since becoming queen.

Lynx waved up to her, and the dragons below rose from the beach in a whirlwind of wingbeats. Snowfall summoned the ten guards she'd chosen and leaped into the sky to join them. Not *with* them, obviously; more like off to the side, where she could see them but not get bumped by any of them.

Her plan to stay apart was thwarted, though, when Queen Hazel soared over to fly next to her.

"What are you doing?" Snowfall asked, banking away slightly.

"We'll be out of your kingdom soon," Hazel said. "I was just hoping . . . you're the only queen I've ever met, besides my great-grandmother. And you're not at all ancient. I mean, you seem about my age, and I just . . . I'd love to know how you do everything, because it's really new for me and it's a lot . . . a lot harder than I thought it would be. You know? My great-grandmother has been queen for the longest ever time, and I thought I'd have so much longer before I'd have to do this."

Snowfall was certainly not going to feel sympathy for a weird invasive dragon from across the sea. They were NOT the same at all.

"How long have you been queen?" Hazel asked.

Less than half a year, but if she told Hazel that, the invading dragons wouldn't take her seriously. She needed them to stay afraid of her.

"A long time," she answered. It actually felt very true as she said it. Maybe when you barely slept, all the days and nights seemed a thousand times longer.

"Oh," Hazel said. "So you must find it really easy by now."

Snowfall hoped her face didn't give her away. "There are . . . challenges, of course," she said. "But the IceWings have a lot of traditions in place that I'm responsible for upholding. They help keep the kingdom safe and orderly, so as long as I follow them, everything stays in its place and everyone will be safe."

"Safe would be so great," Hazel said sadly. "We lost our home and our trees before I even hatched. If we had traditions like that once, they're gone now." She paused for a moment, gazing off west as if the horizon was lined with the ghosts of everything her tribe had lost. After a few heartbeats, she asked, "How did your last queen die?"

"Evil magic plague," Snowfall said. "Yours?"

Hazel hesitated. "Well . . . I don't think she's dead. But I don't know for sure. We were fighting this enemy who can take over dragon minds and control them, and it got control of Queen Sequoia. So it might have killed her, I guess, but I think it would keep her alive, to use her against us." She sighed, and then noticed the way Snowfall was staring at her. "What?"

"An enemy who can take over dragon minds?" Snowfall asked. "Was his name Darkstalker?"

"N-no," Hazel said cautiously. "That is, we always thought it was Queen Wasp, but it turns out maybe it's a plant?"

Snowfall narrowed her eyes. "A plant."

"A very evil plant," Hazel added.

What was more likely — an evil plant, or that Darkstalker's terrible NightWing powers somehow reached across the ocean to ensnare a mythical continent full of Clearsight's descendants?

Snowfall pondered this for a moment. Nothing really seemed beyond Darkstalker's magic or malevolence, in her opinion.

Or maybe it was some other magic, malevolent NightWing. There could definitely be others.

"So if she is still alive, are you going back to save her?" Snowfall asked.

"Definitely. Yes. If I can figure out how," Hazel said. "How to stop the mind control, I mean."

"But then wouldn't you have to give your throne back to her?"

"I'd do that in a heartbeat!" Hazel said fervently.

Would I? Snowfall thought. *In exchange for my mother back?*

Yes . . . but they still weren't the same. Hazel, for instance, probably didn't have a nefarious missing sister lurking around.

"Is there anyone else who wants to be queen?" Snowfall asked. "I mean, someone who might take the throne from you?"

Hazel cast a glance over her shoulder, and Snowfall followed her gaze to the LeafWing who'd been frowning at her before. She was flying close to her green friend, almost close enough to twine their tails together, and it looked like they were arguing.

"No," Hazel said. "I mean, there are dragons who would probably be better queens than me. But they don't want it."

"Ha! They *say* they don't want it," Snowfall burst out. "You want some advice on being a queen? Watch your back. Don't trust anyone. Someone is always plotting to take your throne, or murder your subjects, or steal your territory!"

Hazel blinked, shading her eyes from the bright reflection off the snowy cliffs to their left. "Always?" she said faintly. "Even here in the Distant Kingdoms?"

Snowfall snorted. "*Especially* here. And especially the NightWing tribe — watch out for any dragons with black and silver scales. They can read your mind and see the future and they want to wipe out all the other tribes so they can be the only ones left."

"That sounds like Clearsight," Hazel said thoughtfully. "I mean, not the mind reading. I've never heard that she could do that — can dragons here really do that? But she could see the future . . . and her descendants nearly wiped out my tribe."

"See?" Snowfall batted a seagull away from her with her tail. "NightWings. Evil. Untrustworthy. And yes, totally mind readers."

"She doesn't sound evil in her book, though," Hazel offered. "I read it a few times on the journey and she sounds much kinder than, say, Queen Wasp. I don't think she would have wiped out a tribe or hurt anyone if she could help it."

Snowfall rolled her eyes. This green dragon wasn't going to rule much longer if she kept trying to see the best in dragons like Clearsight.

"I'd better go check on the raft," Hazel said, squinting down at the dragons towing their contraption through the waves. "I hope we can talk more later!" She whisked away, leaving Snowfall to her unending circle of anxious thoughts.

It was a much longer flight than Snowfall had anticipated, partly because the strange dragons had to stop to rest, like, ALL the TIME, and partly because they had to detour so far out over the ocean to stay out of range of the Ice Cliff, and partly because the raft was unwieldy and awkward and the dragons towing it kept switching places and once a surprise wave flipped the whole thing over and everyone had a massive panic attack and dove into the water to rescue the floundering swimmers, even though Tsunami and Turtle were right there and everything was totally fine and all the overreacting was completely unnecessary.

But by late afternoon, they finally reached the far side of the tundra that was the disputed territory between the Ice Kingdom and the Kingdom of Sand. (Territory that was DEFINITELY Snowfall's! As far as Snowfall was concerned, the land belonged to the Ice Kingdom, and Queen Thorn could stick a cactus up her nose if she thought she had any right to it!)

The pebbly beaches gave way slowly to a coastline of yellow-white sand, and the temperature grew warmer and warmer as they flew. Just as the sun brushed the western edge of the orange-flooded sky, Tsunami came flying out of the water, waved at Hazel, and pointed to something down below.

A hut with a palm-frond roof, tucked into a small cove where the water was calm and clear. And standing outside the hut, on the sand: four dragons, gazing up at the sky.

Snowfall narrowed her eyes, wishing again that the stupid gift of vision ring actually worked. IceWing eyesight was sharper than that of most other tribes, but she couldn't see their faces clearly from this distance, like she wanted to.

She could see, though, that one of the dragons down there was pale green with bits of blue and gold and white, and that it had four wings, like some of the strange dragons from across the sea — the SilkWings, Hazel had called them.

Also, it was standing next to what was CLEARLY a NightWing. A NightWing! With one of the weird rainbow dragons! They WERE working together! Snowfall was right all along!

She felt a shiver of fear run along her scales and tried to tamp it down. There were ten well-armed IceWing soldiers with her. She had the gift of stealth and the gift of strength. That NightWing was the one who should be scared.

The other two were SandWings, boring, nothing to . . . wait.

Snowfall swooped lower and let out a hiss.

One of the SandWings was *Jerboa*.

Jerboa, HER animus dragon! Her animus who was supposed to live in a hut all alone and never talk to anyone but the IceWing queen! (Maybe that wasn't exactly what Queen Glacier had said, but something like that!) She wasn't supposed to help other SandWings and weird dragons from across the sea and she DEFINITELY SHOULDN'T BE HANGING OUT WITH A NIGHTWING.

NightWings had their own animus dragons! They didn't need Jerboa, too! Why was she helping one of them? Or ALL OF THEM MAYBE ACTUALLY?

So maybe Jerboa WAS lying about animus magic being broken, because she didn't want to help IceWings anymore, because now she was working with Snowfall's enemies!

Snowfall's wings were vibrating with stress and anger and nerves as she crashed onto the beach ahead of the other dragons.

The SilkWing bounded toward her with her whole face alight. "Is Blue with you? And Swordtail? Wait, you're not a SilkWing, sorry — but — oh! Sundew!" She hurried past Snowfall and threw her wings around the frowny LeafWing, who, it turned out, had other expressions besides menacing, such as startled.

"Sundew!" the SilkWing cried again, letting her go. "I can't believe you all made it here! Where's Swordtail? And Blue?"

Sundew's pleased look fell away and she dug grooves in the sand with her claws. "They're not here, Luna. I'm so sorry."

Luna pressed her talons to her face, but before she could burst into tears, Sundew's companion jumped in.

"They're still alive, as far as we know," she said. "But Queen Wasp has them. It's a long story."

"We're going to get them back," Sundew said fiercely. "I promise you that. Even that slugs-for-brains Swordtail. We'll figure out how to save them."

"Yes!" Luna said. "I'm so ready! If you know how to cross the ocean, I'll do it right now!"

"Crossing the ocean isn't the hard part, unfortunately," Sundew said.

Luna's eyes drifted to Cricket, standing behind the Leaf-Wings and holding Bumblebee. She beckoned the yellow-and-black dragon forward and hugged her, too. "Come tell me all about it," she said, and the five of them went up the beach into the hut.

Snowfall had only been half listening. Her focus was on

Jerboa, and if she could freeze dragons with her eyeballs, the animus SandWing would have turned to ice all the way to her bones. The force of the rage in her glare was so strong, she couldn't *believe* how long it took Jerboa to finally turn and meet her eyes. And then Jerboa didn't even look guilty! She looked . . . annoyed? Tired? SOMETHING AGGRAVATING!

Snowfall stormed up to her. The NightWing and the other SandWing had gone down to the water to help the SeaWings drag the raft ashore, with lots of yelps and chirps and gleeful reunion noises. There was a small oasis of silence around Jerboa and her little patch of sand.

"What are you doing here?" Snowfall growled at her.

Jerboa arched one eyebrow. "*I* live here. What are *you* doing here?"

"Are you working with these dragons?" Snowfall demanded. "Did you give them some magic to help them invade my kingdom?"

Jerboa gave her a withering look. "As I am quite sure I have mentioned before," she said, "no one wants to invade your kingdom."

"Wrong," Snowfall snapped. "These dragons tried to, and I have driven them out. BY MYSELF, I might add, without any help from *you*."

"See," Jerboa said flatly. "I knew you could do it. You just had to believe in yourself. Rah rah."

"Why are you helping a NightWing instead of me?" Snowfall asked in a low hiss.

"I'm not helping anyone," Jerboa said. "I've fulfilled my purpose. All I did here is provide some shelter and make an introduction, although providing shelter to three dragons is quite different from sharing my cove with two entire tribes."

She wrinkled her snout slightly as she looked around at the chaos of dragons engulfing her beach. Tails and talons were churning up the sand. Several dragons were wading in the shallows of the cove, catching fish and crabs and clouding the water with silt. Others had collapsed all along the beach, wings flung out to either side, soaking up the sun. The relieved expressions were back on most of their faces, and some of the SilkWings were already gathering coconuts to eat and debating placidly about how to open them.

The NightWing came floundering back up the beach and Snowfall finally recognized her. It was that interfering little one with the visions, the one Winter liked so much. Moonface, or something like that. The one who had been Darkstalker's very best friend when he first came out of the mountain.

According to Winter, she'd also been instrumental in stopping Darkstalker, but given the lack of actual evidence (or a body, specifically; Snowfall would have liked a specifically clearly dead body to examine and yell at and stomp on), Snowfall couldn't help but still find her very suspicious.

This was a particularly bad NightWing to find with *her* animus.

"Hello," Moonface said breathlessly. "You're Queen Snowfall, aren't you?"

"You know perfectly well that I am," Snowfall said coldly. "Mind reader."

The black dragon had the grace to look a little abashed. "It's Moon, actually," she said. "Just Moon, not Moonface."

Snowfall wished one of the IceWing animus gifts had been an invulnerability to NightWing powers. That would have been EXTREMELY useful. WHY didn't anyone ever think of that?

Because they weren't our mortal enemies until they stole Arctic, she remembered. *And after that, there were no more animus gifts.*

Moon winced and touched her temples. "This is a lot of noisy dragons," she said to Jerboa.

"It certainly is," Jerboa said, eyeing a pair of LeafWing dragonets as they tumbled and wrestled along the beach with squeals of joy. "Is this what your vision showed you?"

"Sort of," Moon said. "But it's only the beginning, I think."

"Only the beginning?" Jerboa looked nearly as annoyed with Moon as she was with Snowfall. "Are there a lot more coming? *Here?* To this beach in particular?"

"No . . . wait, actually; I don't know," Moon said.

"They can stay for now," Jerboa said with a sigh. "Until

they're ready to move on, which had better be soon. But where do you expect them to end up?"

"I know!" cried the other SandWing, jumping over the dunes toward them in little flying-hopping leaps. "I have an idea! Moon, we can take them to Sanctuary!"

"Yes, of course," the NightWing said, her whole face relaxing. "That's perfect. They'll be safe there."

"That's where Winter is, right?" Lynx asked.

Moon gave her a curious look. "Have we met?"

"I'm Lynx," the IceWing offered. "A friend of Winter's. Buuuuut an even more loyal subject to my excellent one true queen Snowfall right here, of course," she added quickly.

Snowfall flicked sand in her face with her tail and Lynx sneezed.

"Do you want to come with us? To Sanctuary?" Moon asked. "I'm sure Winter would be happy to see you, and we could use a few more strong wings to help these dragons get there."

Lynx gave Snowfall a hopeful look.

"We can't sit here for days and days," Snowfall pointed out.

"It won't be that long," Moon said, catching the look on Jerboa's face. "Maybe one day to rest and we leave the day after tomorrow? Or tomorrow, maybe tomorrow."

Night was falling swiftly around them, but for once, Snowfall could watch the stars come out without a sense of suffocating dread. For once, her scales weren't crawling with the knowledge that Tundra was tip-tapping toward her on cold, judgmental claws. The wall was far, far away, and Snowfall did not have to worry about it for one blissful night.

Which could be two nights. Maybe three . . . maybe even four, if Sanctuary required inspecting or anything like that.

The wall wasn't going anywhere. Snowfall would face it again when she returned to the ice palace. There was no need to rush back. Queen Glacier had often gone on diplomatic trips or battle missions for days, and the kingdom didn't collapse.

Maybe that was why she'd gone away so often, come to think of it.

"Fine," Snowfall said to Lynx. "We'll go to Sanctuary. But only so I can make sure my weird scavenger-obsessed cousin isn't up to anything with all his new other-tribe friends." Snowfall shot a glare at Moon, just to clarify exactly who she meant.

The tribes settled down to sleep early. The SilkWings, it turned out, could produce some kind of strange silvery stuff from their wrists, and several of them made little hammocks out of it to hang from the trees, then slept in them. It was very weird and didn't seem like a normal dragon ability to Snowfall at all.

Snowfall ordered the other IceWings to choose their own section of beach, some ways off from the other tribes, but still within sight. She set a rotating guard schedule and gave them instructions to keep an eye out for the NightWing especially.

It was mercifully cooler after the sun went down, but still a little too warm for Snowfall's comfort. She stabbed her claws into the sand, digging down and down until she found a cold layer of sand far below the sun-warmed layers on top. This was better. It was no slab of ice, but it would cool her off enough to sleep.

She curled into the hole and felt her weapons jab her in the side. The animus-touched wristbands weighed down her talons, and the tiara was quite uncomfortable to sleep in. But she wasn't about to take any of it off, of course. She might need those knives or throwing stars or other knives or magic strength if someone attacked her in the middle of the night. She was surrounded by enemies here, after all. (Well, technically she was surrounded by ten IceWing soldiers, and THEN a bunch of enemies. Still.)

But she could take off the gift of vision, at least, since the stupid thing didn't work at all.

She tugged on the opal ring to slide it off her claw.

It didn't move.

Which was odd. Hadn't it felt loose when she first put it on?

Snowfall frowned at it. The opal caught the starlight and twinkled cheerfully at her.

She tugged on it again. It was definitely stuck.

Weird and annoying.

With a sigh, she gave up. She was too tired for a wrestling match with an accessory tonight. Tomorrow she'd rub palm oil all over it or something, and then it would slide off easily. Stupid useless frustrating stupid thing.

She tucked her nose under her tail, and for the first time in months, she fell asleep within moments.

— CHAPTER 6 —

She is flying, although her wings feel so heavy, she thinks they might drag her down into the ocean any moment. She has been flying for days and days, and below her there is nothing but treacherous water in every direction, restlessly waiting to swallow her up.

Each island is so far away, and some of them are so tiny it's a miracle anyone spotted them at all. There was one island that was big enough she'd hoped it was the Distant Kingdoms — but it was empty, and the map said it was only halfway to the other continent.

Every morning she lifts into the sky on a new wave of terror, afraid that this *will be the day they run out of islands and everyone will drown.*

They can't turn back. Nobody can. There's only one map. She wouldn't know how to follow the chain of islands all the way back home on her own. And what's behind them is even worse than this . . . the burning jungle, the white-eyed dragons, the mind control you can catch as easily as breathing in the wrong smoke, someone said. Her wings shiver with terror.

She thought she was joining an army. She'd thought the time for rebellion had finally come — that it was time to be brave and heroic! Io said the Chrysalis was going to rise up, join the LeafWings, and fight Queen Wasp for freedom and a better future.

But they never had a chance.

"Aren't we going to fight them?" she'd asked.

No. By the time they reached the Poison Jungle, everything had changed. Queen Wasp could control SilkWings and LeafWings now. They'd lost before lifting even a single claw.

All they could do was run.

She couldn't even stop to get her little brother or her placid, perpetually confused grandparents. She'd left them in Yellowjacket Hive, thinking she'd be home within a day or two to free them with a triumphant LeafWing army. She didn't even say good-bye.

Where are they now? Have their minds been taken by the HiveWing queen?

Are they even less free now than they'd been before?

And will she ever see them again?

Her tears blur the shapes of the dragons around her before they're swept away by the cold wind.

"Two more days until we reach the Distant Kingdoms," says a LeafWing flying beside her, his voice kind. Gentle LeafWings — she'd had no idea such a thing had ever existed,

before all this. "We're almost there. Then we can rest and be safe."

Safety. Rest. Those both sound impossible. All she wants is to lie down on solid ground and feel, for even a moment, that she doesn't have to be completely terrified.

She rubs her face dry and flies on.

Snowfall jolted awake, her heart pounding. Her wings flared up and flung sand in all directions.

Her wings, her own wings. White and curved and only two of them, as there were supposed to be. She touched her claws to her skull: nothing strange growing out of her head. She checked her wings again, but they definitely hadn't turned peach-orange with sapphire spots during the night.

She was on a beach. A beach with waves pounding nearby, everything pale and pearly gray in the early morning light. Dragons slept all around her.

I'm Queen Snowfall, she reassured herself. "I AM Queen Snowfall," she said out loud, because the universe had a whole skeptical vibe about it that was very aggravating.

Lynx lifted her head from a nearby sandpile, squinting blearily. "Who said you weren't?" she mumbled. "I'm-a kill-em, sure yes. Later-ish. Now's too early, no stabbing before breakfast." Her voice rambled off into nonsense as she slid back down to sleep.

Snowfall considered making her wake up, which was a thing a queen could certainly do, except then the queen would have to explain that she'd been freaked out by a bad dream and just wanted company, which didn't seem very regal at all, really.

It wasn't so much the content of the dream, although it had been unsettling. But she'd spent the whole day with that nervous, forlorn tribe of meek rainbow dragons. It wasn't all that weird that she might dream about their situation.

The freaky part was that she'd *really* felt like she was *someone else*. In the dream, she'd completely been one of those homeless SilkWings, completely *inside* another dragon. Not even a thought of the Ice Kingdom. No hint of Snowfall left at all.

She did NOT LIKE THAT, NO SIR.

And now there were all these lingering FEELINGS. The terror skittering along her scales was one thing; she was used to worrying about dangerous things out there. Not these specific dangerous things, but she could slide that all into one compartment.

It was the boring exhausting SADNESS she didn't like. How could she be feeling this depressed about a continent and a few dragons she'd never seen? Dragons who didn't exist, mind you, because her brain had conjured them out of nothing!

Snap out of it. I'm fine. It's just these stupid pathetic dragons messing with my head.

She glared balefully up the beach at the slumbering forms

around Jerboa's hut. Wait, what if that was LITERALLY true? Maybe this was some kind of sinister dragon magic from across the sea! Maybe they'd given her a sappy nightmare to trick her into feeling sorry for them!

Which was an unimpressive bit of magic, if that was all they could do. If *she* had the power to give dragons specific dreams, she'd make them all dream about how strong and amazing she was, so they'd be totally in awe of her and do everything she said and never have any doubts about her ever.

Snowfall leaned over and poked Lynx in the shoulder. "Hey," she said. "Lynx. Lynx. LYNX. Wake up, I have an important question! Did you have any weird dreams?"

"Arrrrrgrmph," Lynx said in a muffled voice, trying to roll away from Snowfall's claw. "Go away."

"You can't tell your queen to go away," Snowfall pointed out. "Your queen demands that you answer her question! It's a royal command!"

"Whaaaaaaaaaaaaaat?" Lynx protested without opening her eyes.

"Did you have any weird dreams last night?" Snowfall said impatiently.

"No," Lynx mumbled. "Slept great. Would still be sleeping great if it were up to me. Unless I'm dreaming that my queen is waking me up at a horrifying hour to ask about my dreams, in which case, yes, this one is a bit weird."

"You are a useless minion," Snowfall observed.

"Frieeeeeend," Lynx enunciated clearly before edging

away and burying herself farther into the sand. Her voice came sleepily over the dune. "The word you're looking for is *friend*."

"Hrmph." Snowfall stabbed a hole in the beach and shoved a passing crab into it. Come to think of it . . . she'd slept well, too. Really, truly slept. Despite the dream, she felt rested for the first time in forever.

OK, so. Shake it off. It was just a dream. Time to get these dragons to Sanctuary and make them some other queen's problem so I can go home.

Two of her guards jumped to their feet and followed her as she marched up the beach. Most of the Pantalan dragons were still asleep, but the one who'd been here before the rest, waiting with Jerboa, was gathering wood into a pile, and a few others were helping her.

Snowfall slowed down as she approached, her eyes drifting over the strangers. She knew her brain had simply jumbled together a bunch of ideas from her subconscious, but —

She felt her heart do a startled little spasm in her chest.

There: asleep with her back pressed against one of the green dragons. Peach-orange scales, sapphire-blue spots. And the LeafWing beside her . . . wasn't he the one who'd spoken to her in the sky?

Except I MADE THAT UP. In my head! In a random dream!

She must have seen the two dragons flying together yesterday, even if she hadn't thought about it consciously.

Her subconscious brain probably saw them being friendly and stuffed that image into a box labeled GROSS! INTERTRIBE FLIRTING! NOT OK! DREAM ABOUT THIS LATER!

And if it *did* turn out that the SilkWing's name was Atala, that was *also definitely* a coincidence with a reasonable explanation and so she did not at all need to find that out.

Snowfall sat down and watched the dragons building the fire instead. As far as she'd seen yesterday, neither SilkWings nor LeafWings could breathe fire, so she expected the NightWing or one of the SandWings to emerge and light it for them.

But once the woodpile was high enough, the first SilkWing stepped forward and held out her front talons. Their peculiar dragon silk started spiraling out from her wrists . . . except . . .

Snowfall shot to her feet and paced closer.

This dragon's silk was the color of gold, and where it touched the wood, licks of flame growled to life.

Whoa.

"What is that?" Snowfall demanded of the nearest SilkWing. He was smaller than her, all pale gray and brown with hints of purple. He blinked, yawned, stretched, yawned again, and finally about three hundred years later answered her question.

"Oh," he said. "Right. Luna's a flamesilk."

He started to yawn again and Snowfall was tempted to throw a lobster at his face. "That means nothing to me," she snapped. "Use MORE WORDS that CONVEY ACTUAL INFORMATION, if you please."

"Um," he said, swallowing his yawn nervously. "Like, her silk can be fire? If she wants it to be?"

Snowfall narrowed her eyes at him. "Can you all do that?"

"No, no, no," he said. He shook his head and flicked his tail toward Luna. "Flamesilks are very rare. That's why she ran away, you know, before any of us, because Queen Wasp keeps them all trapped and she escaped and —"

"OK, that's enough words," Snowfall said, waving him away. He blinked a few times, and then resumed his stretching. The sound of clanking drew Snowfall's attention back to the fire.

Luna had taken one of the threads of her flamesilk and twisted it into a long wire, which she held between her talons.

She can hold fire?

Snowfall watched as Luna bent over a SilkWing's talons and carefully traced the flame thread across the metal cuff on the SilkWing's wrist. A singed line appeared on the metal, and then, as Luna traced it over and over, the fire burned through the cuff and it *thunked* into the sand.

Luna and the SilkWing grinned at each other, and then she turned to the next dragon's cuff to do the same.

As strange powers went, this one wasn't the scariest. Snowfall had fought plenty of dragons who breathed fire; the flamesilk was just a weirder, slower-moving version of that, basically.

Which probably means they can do something else, but they're hiding it, she thought huffily. *Even the RainWings aren't as harmless and mellow as these twits. The SilkWings probably have secret venom, too, and they're just waiting for a chance to spring it on us!*

Snowfall rubbed her own wrists under the gift of stealth. In her dream last night, she'd been wearing a wrist cuff like all the SilkWings. It was horribly heavy, she remembered now. She — dream her — had felt as though it might drag her down into the ocean. There was an inscription on it that allowed her in and out of Yellowjacket Hive.

Yellowjacket Hive. What a melodramatic name my dream brain came up with.

Or probably I heard someone say it yesterday and just don't remember it.

She glanced around, but the sapphire-spotted dragon (Atala?) was still asleep. Snowfall felt an irrational desire to run over and shake her, to yell "Luna's burning off the wrist cuffs! You can finally be free of it! Hurry, get it off!"

Wait, there had been letters carved into her palm, too. Letters that signified her parents and her own name . . . *why would I KNOW that?*

Her scales prickled uncomfortably.

"Hey," she said to the same SilkWing she'd interrogated before. He was now standing in line to get his cuff burned off, and he jumped when Snowfall accosted him again. "Show me your right talon."

"Um," he said, but he held it out agreeably. Sure enough, three letters were carved into his palm, a triangle of old, deliberate scars.

"What do these mean?" Snowfall asked.

"The big one is an *L* for my name," he said. "Which is Lappet, if that's not too much information. Then the two little ones are my parents' initials."

"Why would your parents do this to you?" Snowfall frowned — the cuts must have been deep and fairly painful to leave permanent marks like these.

"They didn't," he said. "The HiveWings did this." Something flashed in his eyes, the first strong emotion she'd seen from him. "They do this to all the SilkWing dragonets. It's one of the ways they keep track of us."

"So they can control us. YOU, I mean, obviously you," Snowfall corrected herself quickly. "The HiveWings and Queen Wasp. They control your whole tribe."

He pulled back his talon and clenched it into a fist. "They *did*," he said. "But we were going to fight them. We've been planning to change things, we just — didn't know how."

"That's what the Chrysalis is," Snowfall realized. "Your resistance group."

Lappet gave her a very confused, slightly suspicious look. "How do you know about the Chrysalis?"

That is a REALLY EXCELLENT QUESTION, Lappet. "I must have heard someone talking about it yesterday," she said.

Or.

Or her dream was actually real, after all. And she'd actually been inside one of Atala's memories.

She didn't want to ask, but she kind of had to. "Do you know that dragon?" she asked, pointing at the SilkWing with blue spots. "What's her name?"

"Atala," he said cautiously.

ARRRRRRRRRRRGH NO. It could still be a coincidence! Maybe I heard someone say it! Maybe my subconscious gathered a whole heck ton of information without my realizing it.

Or theory two: giant magical conspiracy. Equally possible!

"What else can you do?" she demanded. "Do SilkWings have other powers? Like sharing dreams or possessing other dragons or anything like that?"

"N-no," Lappet said, edging a step away from her. "Flamesilk is the only 'power' SilkWings have, if you'd call it that."

"Shooting fire from your wrists? Yeah, that counts as a power, butterfly — dragon," she amended before she could say "butterfly-brain." Would that even be an insult to a SilkWing? "What about the LeafWings? Do *they* have any dream powers?"

"Not that I know of," he said. "Why? Did, uh . . . did something happen?"

"NO!" she barked. "Three moons! Stop BEING SO NOSY,

LAPPET." She turned in a flurry of sand and stomped down the beach toward the water.

If he was telling the truth, and she'd had a real inside-another-dragon's-head dream, and it really really wasn't sent by one of the weird new tribes, then this was someone else's fault.

Or rather, some*thing* else's fault.

Theory three: The most annoying one, because of the FACE Lynx will give me if it's true.

If something else had sent her that dream, Snowfall had an awful suspicion that she knew exactly which smug little accessory was to blame.

~ CHAPTER 7 ~

"Everything is fine," Snowfall muttered to herself. She glowered at the silvery fish flickering around her talons. The ocean was unpleasantly warmer here than it was up around the Ice Kingdom. "There's nothing to worry about. I'm definitely not wearing a piece of haunted jewelry. It'll slide off easily any moment and then I'll feel silly."

The gift of vision . . .

"NO," she barked at the ring. "It's not possible! How could an ICEWING object give me WEIRD DREAMS about WEIRD FARAWAY DRAGONS THAT WEREN'T SUPPOSED TO EXIST?"

The *last* thing she needed was mystical visions of total strangers. How was that supposed to help her be a strong, powerful, excellent queen? Who was the idiot animus that would come up with something like this?

If she had to have a magic "vision," couldn't it be of someone useful? Like, say, a certain scheming sister who might be plotting to take her throne?

And even if it was the source of the dream, that didn't explain why it wouldn't come off now.

She soaked the ring until her claws started to feel numb, and then she yanked on it as hard as she could.

Ow. It wasn't even *budging*.

"Great Ice Spirits," she hissed at the opal. "What is wrong with you?" She tried wedging a claw underneath the band, but it was on too tight. She tried wiggling it furiously, but it wouldn't even spin around her claw. She tried smashing the opal into a rock sticking out of the water, but that just made her talons hurt, and the opal twinkled saucily at her, completely intact.

"What ARE you doing?" said Lynx's voice behind her.

"Nothing!" Snowfall called over her shoulder. She stuck the ring back in the water and turned around with her most serenely regal face on.

Lynx did a thing with her eyebrows that meant something like, "I *know* you're lying but I can't *say* you are because you're the queen but maybe you should just *admit* it because my *eyebrows* are so onto you."

"Well, you were doing that nothing very vigorously," Lynx said. "So I wondered. You know. A whole lot of vigorous nothing before breakfast."

"Maybe I have had breakfast," Snowfall observed. "You wouldn't know, since you've been asleep half the morning."

"I *do* know that you have not," Lynx said, "because I asked your guards and they said you've been out here for ages, doing battle with either your own claws or an invisible shark."

Snowfall bristled and shot a dark look at her guards, who were lined up on the beach with concerned expressions. "Is that what they said?"

"No," Lynx admitted. "They just said you haven't had breakfast yet. I interpreted the rest by watching you for a few minutes."

"I am having a swim," Snowfall said, lifting her chin. "There is nothing unusual about that."

"I've seen you swim!" Lynx said. "You don't usually look quite so much like an agitated squid."

"I'm just going to start making a mental list," Snowfall informed her. "So that when we get home, I can execute you for all your treason at once."

"Once would probably be enough," Lynx said, laughing. She flicked a spray of water at Snowfall with her tail. "Come on, Snowfall. Even queens need someone to talk to. Tell me what's wrong."

"Nothing is wrong!" Snowfall protested. "I'm just having a *small* problem with this ring I can't get off, but it's not important. I mean, not compared to 'what are we going to do with all these homeless dragons and the bad things they're running away from,' like, seriously."

Lynx tilted her head and studied Snowfall for a moment as though she were a palm tree that had suddenly sprouted in the middle of the Ice Palace. "They'll be all right now that they're here," she said finally. "Let me see that ring."

Snowfall grudgingly held out her talons, and Lynx gripped the ring between her claws. She pulled and wiggled it and tried sliding her claws under it and yanked some more, until Snowfall finally got fed up and snatched her arm back.

"Well, YOU'RE no use," Snowfall hissed. "No surprise there." She dunked her claws in the water again.

But now Lynx looked worried, which meant she was about to get very annoying. "It's really not moving at all," she said. "Snowfall . . . was that ring from the Forbidden Treasury? Is it animus-touched?"

Snowfall frowned and shook a piece of seaweed off her tail. "Yes. But it doesn't work."

"Are you sure?" Lynx asked. "What is it supposed to do?"

"It's . . . supposed to make your eyesight sharper," Snowfall said. "But it didn't make any difference at all, which is why I want it off."

"Were there any notes?" Lynx pressed. "About how to use it or what it did for other queens or who made it?"

"No!" Snowfall said. "Nobody wrote an encyclopedia about it! It's not that complicated! Put on the ring, get better vision!"

"But that isn't what happened," Lynx said. "Wait, were there *any* notes?" Her expression shifted to the most absolutely irritating wide-eyed alarm. "Did you just put it on without knowing anything about it?"

"Why not?" Snowfall snapped. "Better vision would be helpful!"

"But what if there's a catch?" Lynx cried. "What if there's a secret downside to the spell? What if the animus dragon who made it added a curse to the magic?"

Or what if it does something entirely different than I thought it did? Snowfall shoved that thought away.

"Then we wouldn't have kept it!" she snarled at Lynx. "It wouldn't still BE in our treasury if it was evil! Some cursed queen before us would have destroyed it!"

"Unless it was enchanted so it could never be destroyed!" Lynx yelped, sounding uncomfortably like Snowfall's inner monologue. "Maybe it magically shows up in the Forbidden Treasury once every hundred years to ensnare some new hapless queen!"

"I'm not HAPLESS!" Snowfall shouted. "Who's being paranoid now? It was a *gift* for IceWing queens! So it's supposed to make us stronger and safer! Like the wall and the Ice Cliff!"

"Personally, I don't think it makes our tribe stronger for us all to be constantly pitted against each other," Lynx cried. "And I don't think cutting us off from the other tribes makes us safer either!"

"Wow," Snowfall said with a hiss. "Questioning the most fundamental gifts that hold our tribe together? You really don't belong in the First Circle! What kind of IceWing are you?"

"The kind who actually thinks for herself sometimes," Lynx said, flinging up her wings and accidentally splashing a small fish into Snowfall's face. "The kind who wants you to be a better queen than the ones we've had before, because I know you and I know you can be. But feel free to keep living your life by the rules of that oppressive wall, if that's all you want, and feel free to move me down to the bottom of the list when we get home." She took a step toward the beach, then turned back for one more shot. "*If* that mysterious magic ring even lets you get home. After everything animus magic has done to us, I can't believe you'd throw yourself into its talons again!"

She splashed away furiously. Snowfall threw herself under the water and screamed out her rage in a flurry of bubbles.

This was why she didn't tell anyone her problems! Because they would definitely make them worse!

Lynx was *not* right. It was just a *stupid broken ring*.

Snowfall had definitely *not* misinterpreted what a gift of vision might mean and this had NOTHING TO DO WITH HER DREAM LAST NIGHT. NO. She WOULD NOT STAND FOR IT.

When she surfaced again, Lynx was with the strangers by the fire, where some of the littlest dragonets were building a kind of treelike termite mound out of the sand. Snowfall squinted at them as two young LeafWings pounced on the shape and stomped it flat.

The opal ring winked gold-blue-lavender in the morning light.

I'm not afraid of you, Snowfall thought fiercely. *I'm getting rid of you today, even if I have to cut off my own claw to do it.*

She would get this ring off and throw it into the ocean, and then she would make sure the strange dragons went to Sanctuary, and then she would go home and everything would go back to the normal, everyday anxiety festival her life was supposed to be.

Snowfall splashed her way back onto the beach, waving regally at her guards. Nothing to see here. No queens losing their royal minds. Certainly not.

She waited until she was sure Lynx wasn't watching her, and then she tried smothering her claws in palm oil from one of the jars outside Jerboa's hut. That didn't work either; it only left Snowfall's talons feeling greasy.

"Oh, please," Jerboa said acidly from the doorway. "Help yourself. My stuff is everybody's stuff, evidently."

"This is your fault," Snowfall said, brandishing the now extremely shiny ring.

"That you're wearing too much hideous jewelry?" Jerboa said. "Makes sense. I do have that effect on dragons."

"I wouldn't need this if your stupid magic worked," Snowfall said with a flick of her wings. "Have you checked today? Is it working now?"

The frown lines in Jerboa's face deepened. "No. It's not

working for anyone." She glanced back into the hut; Snowfall wasn't sure why.

"Really definitely?" Snowfall asked. She held out her front talons. "Let's test it. Tell this ring to slide off my claw."

Jerboa sighed and cast another glance around, but no other dragons were close enough to pay attention to them. The SandWing reached out and tapped the ring twice. "Come off the queen's claw this instant," she said.

The ring didn't move. Snowfall tried pulling on it again, but it was just as stuck as before. She growled softly.

"Is it animus-touched?" Jerboa asked, finally sounding curious.

"I thought so," Snowfall said. "But it seems to be flipping broken."

"Animus-touched by who?" Jerboa frowned again. "When?"

"Like thousands of years ago," Snowfall said with a sigh. "By the worst IceWing animus in history, I'm guessing! Some kind of worm-brained sand-snorter! WHY would ANYONE enchant a ring to STAY ON SOMEONE'S CLAW? What kind of stupid waste of magic is that?"

Jerboa scratched her jaw thoughtfully, but her tense expression had relaxed. "Maybe it's enchanted to frustrate easily annoyed queens into learning some patience."

"BOO HISS!" Snowfall shouted. Several of the SilkWings jumped and turned to see what the noise was. She lowered her voice again. "I don't need an ancient accessory to teach me anything! I'm *very* patient! I have been queen for *months* without stabbing *anybody* in the face with an icicle, despite lots of dragons *highly deserving it*."

"Well," Jerboa said, "if my magic comes back, I'll make removing your ring my top priority, how about that?"

"No need," Snowfall said. "I have another plan." She narrowed her eyes at Jerboa and added in a whisper, "But if it does come back, tell me right away!"

Jerboa's expression was quite far from reassuring, but she ducked into her hut without saying anything else. Snowfall caught a glimpse of the NightWing inside, still fast asleep. She moved away as quickly as she could — the last thing she needed was that dragon poking around inside her head! It was bad enough to have Lynx making worried eyes at her all the time; she didn't need any NightWings thinking she was weak (or cursed by weird jewelry).

Over by the fire, Luna was finally alone, more or less, surrounded by a mound of discarded wrist cuffs. Most of the other SilkWings had gone off to gather coconuts or lie quietly on the warm sand, and Lynx was up in the sky, flying with one of the LeafWings.

Snowfall sidled up to Luna. The SilkWing dropped the cuff she'd been holding and eyed Snowfall with alarm.

"Hey," Snowfall said gruffly. "That fire thread thing. Can you try that on my ring? It's stuck and it's annoying me."

"You're the queen of the IceWings, right?" Luna said, lifting her chin. "The one who kicked my tribe out of your kingdom yesterday?"

"Lucky for you," Snowfall pointed out. "Or they wouldn't be here, having this touching reunion with you."

Luna rolled her eyes and held out her claws. "Show me."

Snowfall gingerly offered the talon with the ring on it. Luna picked up a filament of fire from the sand beside her and bent over their twined claws.

The burning filament brushed the silver curve of the ring once, twice, three times, without even leaving a trace on the metal. Luna frowned and tried again. The heat was enormously uncomfortable that close to Snowfall's scales, and she didn't like the feel of this SilkWing gripping her talons either. But she held still, glaring into the opal's shimmering depths, until Luna finally said, "That's so weird. Sorry, Your Majesty. It's not working."

Snowfall lifted the opal to eye level and hissed at it. How could *fire* not work? "Don't tell Lynx," she said to Luna.

"Uh . . . sure," Luna agreed. "You're welcome."

"For what?" Snowfall snapped and stomped away.

She found a large boulder in a shaded spot near the tree line and perched on it to brood for a while. Her guards fanned out in a discreet circle around her, and one of them brought her a fish to eat, and she even remembered to thank him for it. *So at least I did one excellently queenly thing today.*

The other animus-touched things came off easily, no problem. The stealth wristbands and the tiara of strength, off and back on, nothing sinister about them at all.

Snowfall had always assumed that if something was

made by an IceWing animus, it would be something great. Something good and helpful and smart and clever. Like an IceWing! An IceWing animus wouldn't make a secret evil spell like a NightWing would. Surely. Right?

The ring was not a big deal, she told herself. It was Lynx's fault that she was even worrying about it at all. But really, if she thought about it, she felt fine; better than usual, in fact. Probably because she hadn't had to see Aunt Tundra's smug face for a whole day.

Moreover, if there *was* a secret spell on the ring, it hadn't given her a terrible illness (*yet*) or turned her into a different dragon (HA, it could TRY; she was ALWAYS SNOWFALL AND ALWAYS WOULD BE). It hadn't tricked her into letting strange invader dragons into her kingdom. She was the same as always. Everything was normal.

Even the lingering sadness from the dream lifted a little as the day went on. She could see Atala from her spot, and the SilkWing didn't *look* totally miserable, so that helped. Atala got her wrist cuff burned off, ate a talonful of dates, laughed at a LeafWing when he tried to catch a crab and it tweaked his nose, and took several naps. The SilkWing also spent a while staring out at the ocean. *Thinking about the family she left behind*, Snowfall guessed. *I hope they're safe.*

No, I don't! I don't care at all! She shook herself vigorously. *I don't know them! Why would I care?*

Stupid dream. Or vision. Or whatever.

Shortly before sunset, Snowfall heard the cracks and

snaps of talonsteps in the trees behind her. She turned and spotted the frowny LeafWing pacing between the palms, throwing fallen coconuts into a sack. Another green dragon followed her, this one with pinkish streaks on her wings and horns.

"We *just* got here," said the pink-tinted LeafWing languidly. "Why are you acting like such a frustrated panther already? Wasn't this the goal?"

"But we can't stay, Cobra Lily!" cried the other one. "We can't just find a nice safe spot to settle down and get comfortable! That's not the plan! I *won't* give up on our whole continent and everyone there!"

Cobra Lily shrugged, an elegant lift and fall of her wings. "You can't be that upset about losing Nettle and Belladonna and a few silly SilkWings," she said. "Seems like an upside to me. No more Nettle annoying us. No more Belladonna telling you what to do."

The scowly one fixed her with a particularly ferocious scowl. "Queen Sequoia is back there, plus half the dragons we grew up with. A monster has stolen our home! And by the way, those 'silly' SilkWings risked a lot to help us."

"Don't get excited," Cobra Lily said. "I'm just saying, this place is already significantly nicer than a jungle full of carnivorous plants or a land full of mind-controlled bug dragons. Maybe we could stay here. Make a new home. One queen over both the SilkWings and the LeafWings. I bet most of these dragons wouldn't mind following a Queen Sundew."

"No," Sundew growled. "Stop saying that. Hazel is our queen." She half turned and finally spotted Snowfall lying on her boulder. Her tail lashed for a moment, and then she spread her wings and lifted off into the sky.

That's interesting, Snowfall thought. *Sundew. She is a threat to Hazel's rule. Even if she doesn't mean to be, other dragons want her to be.*

Just like the dragons who probably still want Crystal to be queen instead of me. How many of them are there? Are they hiding her? Are they planning something? Gathering an army? Conspiring with NightWings?

Where IS she?

Snowfall brooded about this until one of her guards came over to inform her that the strange tribes had decided to stay one more night, before setting out for Sanctuary in the morning. Snowfall could tell that Hazel would have liked to stay longer — the LeafWing queen kept leaning wistfully on the palm trees and gazing up at their swaying leaves. But Moon was bustling around reassuring everyone that Sanctuary would be even better, with more trees and lots of space and food for them.

Highly suspicious. Possibly some kind of nefarious plan at work, if a NightWing was all excited about it.

As the sun set, Snowfall dug her sleeping hole with extra vigor, throwing all the excess sand in Lynx's direction. She was not going to worry about this ridiculous ring. She REFUSED to have another "VISION" of mystery dragons she didn't know. She was the queen, and she would simply order her brain to have an ordinary night with perfectly ordinary dreams. Yes.

She curled up, closed her eyes, and dropped almost instantly into another dragon's scales.

— CHAPTER 8 —

She is alone in the kitchen, rolling antelope meatballs, trying to keep her claws busy.

She is trying not to think about Cinnabar, or how she should be with the rest of the Chrysalis, finally trying to change the world.

She is trying not to hate her misshapen wing.

"I'm sorry, Tau," Cinnabar had whispered, clasping her front talons between her own. "We talked about this. You knew if there was fighting, you wouldn't be able to join us. It would be too dangerous for you."

"You mean I couldn't keep up with you," Tau had answered ruefully.

"Think about who we're fighting, though," Cinnabar had pressed. "What if you saw Treehopper on the battlefield? All white eyes and zombie brain? What if he attacked you — or me? You're better off not having to face him like that. You'll be safe here until we win and come back for you."

"You'd better win." Tau had hugged her, her heart beating fiercely.

Being left behind was worse than she'd expected, though. Not knowing what was happening. All her friends off fighting a battle without her. Wondering if they really did find an antidote to the mind control.

Is Treehopper finally free of Queen Wasp?

Or is he killing SilkWings right now, dead-eyed and soulless?

She shivers. How will he ever forgive himself if Wasp forces him to hurt Tau's friends?

There hasn't been any sign of the HiveWings since every single one of them suddenly froze, pivoted to the nearest window, and flew away north. It's peaceful with all of Jewel Hive nearly empty, but also unsettling.

"Tau!"

Right — not every HiveWing.

Lady Scarab marches into the kitchen and eyes the meatballs so intently she practically sticks her nose into one of them. "What is this?" she demands. "What herbs are you using? Why does it smell like that?"

"Antelope meatballs," Tau says patiently.

"I have the only good recipe for antelope meatballs," Lady Scarab announces. "If you didn't put chives in it, these won't be worth eating."

"I did put chives in it," Tau says.

"Probably too many," Lady Scarab sniffs.

Something crashes in the hall behind them and they both

turn toward the sound of galloping talonsteps. Lady Jewel bursts into the kitchen, and the sight of her face sends Tau straight into full-blown panic.

"Cinnabar was just here," Jewel gasps. "With a message — the HiveWings won. They're burning the Poison Jungle, and when they're done, they'll come here, and now they can mind-control SilkWings as well."

"What?" Tau clutches the counter, her talons slippery with grease. She can't process any piece of that information, let alone all of it. She latches on to the first thing. "Cinnabar is here? Is she all right?"

"She only had time to give me the message," Jewel says. "They have to get to the other Hives as fast as they can, to warn the rest of the SilkWings. I told her we'd get everyone here to safety." She glances around the room wildly, as though she's considering trying to fit every SilkWing in the Hive into one of her potato barrels.

"But how?" Tau asks. "Where can we go?" Her heart feels like it's squeezing inward, shrinking into a nest of fear and spikes. They weren't supposed to lose. It wasn't supposed to get worse.

"Well, this is a fine mess," Lady Scarab hisses. "NOW who's going to take down my dreadful niece? Certainly would be nice if I had a daughter willing to fight for the throne that should actually be ours."

"Not NOW, Mother," Jewel says. "Cinnabar said to bring everyone to Lake Scorpion. There's somewhere we can go from *there, she said, but we have to all go together."* She presses her claws to her temples for a moment. *"We need messengers to check every level of the Hive. Someone to go to the webs. Dragons to carry the cocoons of any SilkWings in Metamorphosis right now, others to carry all the SilkWing and HiveWing eggs in the Hatcheries."*

"No," Scarab says. *"Not the HiveWing eggs, Jewel."*

"We can't leave them behind!" Jewel protests. *"All those tiny dragonets —"*

"They're already infected," Scarab says bluntly. *"As soon as they hatch, Wasp will be able to see through their eyes, and then she'll find us. You can't bring them along, or you doom everyone else."*

Jewel curls her talons and takes a deep breath. Tau knows she is thinking of her own children, who are out of reach now, summoned along with everyone else. Jewel had thought they were free of the mind control until they flew away with all the other HiveWings.

Lady Scarab must guess Jewel's thoughts, too, because she says, with unaccustomed gentleness, *"I miss them, too. But it's better that we know, at least. She could have used them against us if she'd left them here."*

"She still can," Jewel says quietly.

"Only if she can find you to threaten you," Scarab points out. *"They'll be safer if you vanish."*

Jewel doesn't answer, but her tail lashes across the floor, knocking over a stack of lemons.

"Maybe we can bring some of the HiveWing eggs," Tau suggests. "The ones who have only been stabbed once — remember, Cricket said that Wasp has to inject each egg twice to be able to control them."

"That was her theory," Scarab growls. "She could be wrong. It's too risky."

"But if we can save some of them, we have to," Jewel says. "I'll think about it — in the meanwhile, you two go bring as many SilkWings here as you can, and then we'll split into teams." She hurries out of the kitchen again, murmuring lists of tasks to herself.

Tau doesn't stop to hear any more of Scarab's grim warnings. She runs out of the kitchen, through Jewel's mansion, her talons skidding on the floor. She'll start with the other servants and the prisoners in Jewel's dungeon. How many SilkWings are there in the whole Hive? Will they all listen to her, or to Lady Jewel? How fast can they escape?

Only as fast as our slowest dragons — which includes me.

The terror drives her onward, calling dragon after dragon to the ballroom. She can't get the images out of her head: images of her friends with white eyes like the mind-controlled HiveWings, images of Treehopper slicing ruthlessly through any SilkWing who tries to stop him, images of Queen Wasp burning the jungle, killing all the LeafWings, laughing her merciless laugh.

But Cinnabar got away from her. So it's possible, if we can move fast enough.

We have to escape. We *have* to. Or none of us will ever be free again.

Snowfall woke up EXTREMELY grumpy.

That is, first she woke up in a state of heart-pounding panic, confused and terrified about how she was suddenly asleep on a beach when she should be gathering dragons to escape Jewel Hive. But as her heart rate gradually slowed to normal and she remembered who she *actually* was, her natural grumpiness returned to the power of ten.

What. The Moons. Was THAT.

She glanced down and saw that her claws were shaking. She shoved them as far into the sand as she could until they stopped.

"I said no more visions!" she hissed at the ring under her breath. And this time she couldn't even pretend she'd just happened to dream about someone she'd seen. She'd never laid eyes on Tau in her life and probably never would. So either she'd conjured an entire imaginary dragon (with a forbidden love and revolutionary friends and an entire Hive and about a MILLION more dragons to worry about!) or the stupid magic had dragged her brain *all the way across the ocean* to torture her with scary things she could do nothing about.

WHAT IS THE POINT OF THIS?!

Snowfall heard someone floundering through the sand toward her. She lifted her head out of her hole and of course it was Lynx, looking all kinds of wound up.

"I have a theory!" Lynx cried as soon as she spotted Snowfall's face. No "good morning" or "hello, Your Majesty" or "sorry for being a judgmental walrus yesterday."

Snowfall shook out her wings irritably. "Marvelous," she said. "Let me guess, it involves me doing something wrong."

"You woke me up to ask me about weird dreams yesterday," Lynx said, pointing at her. "Because *you* had a weird dream. And that ring you can't get off is called the gift of vision, isn't it? That's why you thought it was about eyesight. But it's not! I think it's giving you weird dreams! Because they're not dreams! They're *visions*. Get it? See what I mean? Gift of *vision*?"

"Great Ice Spirits, stop talking already," Snowfall growled. "I figured that out about a hundred years ago. But even if that's the case, it does not explain why the ring is stuck on my claw. I still think it's broken."

"But it is doing *something*!" Lynx flicked her tail, and now her expression was definitely veering toward excited. "Maybe it's important! Did you have another vision last night? What was it about?"

"I thought you didn't trust animus magic and wearing this was a terrible idea," Snowfall said accusingly.

"I'm still right about that," Lynx said, "but as long as you're stuck with it, we should figure out what it's trying to tell us."

"It's not trying to tell me anything!" Snowfall protested. "It's a ring! An inanimate object! With no agenda or feelings!

Except maybe smugness. You're very smug," she snapped at the opal.

"Arrgh, Snowfall, tell me what you saw!" Lynx lashed her tail, sending up gusts of sand. "Something happening back in the Ice Kingdom? Something that's *going* to happen?"

"No!" Snowfall barked. "Nothing useful! Nothing about my tribe or my problems! Nothing important at all! If this is stupid MAGIC, then it's REALLY STUPID magic! Why would *I*, queen of the IceWings, need to know about all the inner emotions of a bunch of rainbow dragons from a completely irrelevant continent that I'll never see?"

"Inner emotions?" Lynx asked. "Like — you could feel what the SilkWings were feeling?"

"First I was one of those sad-snouts," Snowfall said, pointing up the beach. "Her name is Atala. Total tragedy face. And then last night I was some RANDOM dragon named Tau who is stuck back over there and freaking out. Why would I need to see that? It's not like I can do anything to help her!"

Not that she would have, even if she could! She wasn't going to invite MORE invasive, strange-looking dragons here!

"Hmmmm," Lynx said. "Maybe you can? Somehow? Maybe we just need to lay out everything you learned from your visions and figure out what to do about them."

"That's not a gift, that's homework!" Snowfall snapped. "I've had quite enough of that, thank you! I'm queen now; other dragons should have to do the things I don't want to do!"

"So tell me about it," Lynx said eagerly. "And everything

about the first one, before you forget it. And *I'll* figure out what they mean."

Snowfall pointed one claw at her. "No. I am going to ignore this nonsense. Are these slow-slug dragons ready to fly to Sanctuary yet?"

Lynx looked as if she wanted to keep arguing, but she stayed quiet as she followed Snowfall up the beach to investigate.

And no, of course nobody was ready to go. Of course it took the foreign tribes the entire morning to get organized. And then they decided to leave half the dragons behind so the stronger ones could go ahead and make sure there was a place for everyone. So then they had to resettle the ones they were leaving behind, and then they decided to take a break to eat something. By the time their wings finally lifted into the sky, the sun was high above them.

Snowfall was stalking back to summon the rest of her guards when she heard someone say Queen Thorn's name. Her ears pricked, and she turned to see Moon talking to the SandWing who wasn't Jerboa.

"I'll fly ahead and visit Thorn on the way," he said. "You know, in case she wants to know why there's a flood of unusual-looking dragons flying over her kingdom. Seems like something she might want a heads-up about."

"Tell her where they're going," Moon suggested. "Sanctuary is technically on the border of SandWing and SkyWing territory, so she should know that they're there."

Ha, Snowfall thought to herself, pacing forward again. *Let's see how SHE likes it! If Thorn lets all these dragons flap around over her desert and settle on her border, maybe she isn't as strong a queen as everyone thinks!*

She wondered how Queen Ruby would feel about these new dragons living on the edge of SkyWing territory. Sanctuary was supposed to be a small enclave where dragons who couldn't go home to their own kingdoms could live. Dragons like Snowfall's cousin Winter, who'd been banished, or the remaining Talons of Peace who wanted to stay with one another more than they wanted to return to their tribes. Snowfall didn't think Ruby or Thorn had ever imagined it as a refuge for hundreds of strange dragons when they agreed to let the Talons of Peace build it.

And what happens if even more dragons follow them here from Pantala? Is Cinnabar trying to bring all the rest of the SilkWings over, too? ALL of them, from all the Hives?

Where else can they go, with Queen Wasp and her brainwashed HiveWings controlling all of Pantala?

Snowfall cut off that train of thought with a hiss. *That's THEIR problem. Not MY problem. I have IceWings to take care of! I'm not responsible for anyone else and I don't care about them!*

The terror seemed to still be lingering in her veins, though, and she couldn't shake the urgent, panicked feeling that she had to get an entire city of dragons to safety before it was too late. She wondered how old the vision was — had that scene happened last night, while Snowfall dreamt it, or days earlier, like her vision of Atala?

If it happened days ago . . . where were Tau and Jewel and Scarab now? Safely hidden, or captured?

DON'T CARE. STOP THINKING ABOUT THEM.

"Let's go," she ordered her guards. They took up their positions in formation around her and followed the SilkWings and LeafWings away from the ocean, east into the desert sky. Snowfall glanced back and saw Jerboa sitting outside her hut, watching them leave.

Why doesn't she seem to care more that her magic isn't working? Snowfall wondered. If *she'd* been an animus dragon, and then suddenly her power was gone, she'd have absolutely freaked out. Jerboa, on the other talon, seemed mostly amused by how much that annoyed Snowfall.

It was still possible she was lying to Snowfall. But if animus magic was working, wouldn't Tsunami's gang of righteous do-gooders have used it to bring all the Pantalan dragons to safety? Or to stop Queen Wasp?

They definitely would. They used it to end the plague and stop Darkstalker. They could solve all the Pantalan dragons' problems with a snap of their claws if they had magic right now.

So why don't they?

Why would magic just . . . stop working?

Snowfall eyeballed the opal ring. "Do you know anything about this?" she growled at it. "Why do YOU work and actual useful magic doesn't?" She shook out her talons grumpily and glared at it again. "You know what, how about instead of filling my head with sympathy and nonsense, you give me some information I really need? Like a vision that explains what happened to magic?"

Maybe that's what she was doing wrong. Maybe she needed to tell the ring what vision she wanted. Oh, that would be simple and SO great! Visions of anything she wanted! Why hadn't she thought of this earlier?

"Yes," she said firmly. "You hear me, ring? Tonight, no more SilkWing nightmares. Just a nice, uncomplicated scene where I find out why animus magic isn't working. This is a good plan."

The opal caught the light and sparkled rainbows at her. Snowfall couldn't tell if those were "absolutely, Your Majesty, anything you say" rainbows or "ha ha ha! I'll give you whatever I want to give you and there's nothing you can do about it ha ha!" rainbows.

I guess I'll find out tonight.

She flew after the ribbon of dragons stretched across the sky, trying to feel confident that she'd solved her problem.

But it was hard to shake the ominous feeling that maybe, just perhaps, she'd stumbled into a more dangerous magic than she'd expected.

~ CHAPTER 9 ~

The IceWings, LeafWings, and SilkWings flew in their weird, mismatched crowd over the desert, which, incidentally, was a DREADFUL place. The sun beat down mercilessly, drying the scales on Snowfall's back until she felt as if they might crack off. How could anyone live in a place like this? It was SO HOT. BLEH.

The LeafWings looked almost as unhappy about the heat as she was. Their wingbeats slowed as they flew farther and farther from the ocean and the vast, treeless landscape spread out below them. Rocks and sand and sand and rocks and a whole lot of nothing.

Jerboa kept saying that nobody would want the Ice Kingdom, but who would prefer THIS? Of course dragons would rather live in a cool, beautiful, snowy, crystalline place full of polar bears and walruses. What did they have to eat here? Tiny brittle lizards? Bony, gross-smelling camels? It made much more sense that dragons would want to invade the Ice Kingdom than here. Snowfall was absolutely right to worry about defending it.

Moon had some kind of map from her SandWing friend that showed each oasis along their route, so they were able to stop twice for water. Snowfall waded all the way into the tiny springs, trying to soak every drop into her scales. It suddenly seemed slightly insane to her that her tribe had ever fought with the SandWings, when this territory was the absolute worst and they couldn't possibly want anything here.

It was late in the afternoon when they caught their first glimpse of the mountains ahead, like a long, giant dragon spine curled across the horizon. They were mostly green and brown, but dappled with glorious snow at the peaks.

Tau has never seen mountains, Snowfall thought, and then caught herself thinking that and was furious.

So WHAT? she demanded of her brain. *I've never seen one of these "Hive" cities and I'm PERFECTLY HAPPY ABOUT IT.*

She put on a burst of speed to catch up to Hazel, who looked a little surprised to be approached, but too tired to have much more of a reaction.

"Hello, question for you," Snowfall said. "How many dragons did you leave behind?"

"On Jerboa's beach?" Hazel asked. "About —"

"No, no," Snowfall interrupted. "Back on Pantala. How many dragons did you leave there?"

"Oh." Hazel blinked. "Well, the . . . the LeafWing army,

I guess you'd call it — everyone who went with Queen Sequoia to fight. They must have been exposed to the breath of evil right away . . . they're probably under Wasp's power now." She bit her lip and furrowed her brow and did some more odd things with her face, which Snowfall eventually realized were all Hazel trying not to cry. "I hope some of them managed to escape, though. And then there's the rest of the SilkWings in all the Hives. Hundreds of them, but I don't know exactly how many. The ones who flew over with us are only from three of the Hives, and they were in a group called the Chrysalis. They'd come to the jungle to help us fight the HiveWings."

"But that went horribly wrong," Snowfall said. "And now all the SilkWings you left behind are in danger."

"Yes . . ." Hazel trailed off and gave her a sideways, confused expression. "You sound kind of worried about them?"

"I'm not!" Snowfall cried. "I'm definitely not!" *Maybe just a little worried about Tau. But not really! Only because of a dopey magic spell giving me weird dreams!* "No," she added firmly. "If I am at all WORRIED, it is because I am WONDERING whether all THOSE dragons are going to end up floundering into my kingdom sometime soon as well."

"It is very hard to get across the ocean," Hazel said. "I — I mean, we hope they'll try . . . but I can't predict how many, or if they'll succeed, or when, if that's what you're asking."

"NIGHTWING!" Snowfall bellowed, startling Hazel into losing her flight rhythm for a moment. Up ahead, Moon twisted around, looking puzzled. Snowfall beckoned to her, and Moon came soaring back to fly on the other side of Hazel.

"Yes?" Moon said cautiously.

"You can see the future, can't you?" Snowfall demanded. "Winter told me you had some prophecy about Darkstalker, not that it helped anyone at all. Are you ever useful? Can you predict if the other SilkWings are going to make it to this continent?"

"I — that's not —" Moon stammered, flustered. "My visions aren't specific like that. I caught a glimpse of this group arriving, but I haven't seen any other Pantalan dragons. That doesn't mean they won't make it, though."

"And we can't poke your head to find out?" Snowfall asked. "Like, summon a vision, or whatever?"

"I thought you could," Hazel admitted. "I mean, I thought Clearsight could, from what I've read. So I thought you all could see whatever you wanted."

Moon shook her head. "Clearsight's power was unusual. All I get is flashes whenever the universe feels like giving them to me, and the occasional cryptic prophecy." She shut her mouth quickly, but Snowfall had already caught the shift in her eyes.

"AHA!" she said. "You had a 'cryptic prophecy' about all this, didn't you?"

"That's right, Tsunami said you did!" Hazel's eyes lit up. "Did it mention the breath of evil? Did it tell you how we can rescue everyone and save Pantala?"

"Not exactly," Moon admitted reluctantly. "I mean, the key word here is 'cryptic,' remember?"

"Tell us anyway," Snowfall commanded. "We will un-cryptic it for you."

Moon sighed, and then recited:

"Turn your eyes, your wings, your fire
To the land across the sea
Where dragons are poisoned and dragons are dying
And no one can ever be free.
A secret lurks inside their eggs.
A secret hides within their book.
A secret buried far below
May save those brave enough to look.
Open your hearts, your minds, your wings
To the dragons who flee from the Hive.
Face a great evil with talons united
Or none of the tribes will survive."

There was silence for several wingbeats after she finished. Hazel stared off into the sky ahead of them, her brow furrowed, her mouth moving as she repeated the prophecy quietly to herself.

"Well," Snowfall said finally. "I do not like that. No, I do not. Darkstalker was quite enough great evil for me." She saw Moon flinch when she said Darkstalker's name, which was interesting. Did the NightWing feel guilty about everything that had happened with him? Or did she feel guilty because she was totally lying about him actually being gone?

Wasn't it possible that HE was the "great evil"? After all, how many "great evils" could there possibly be?

"Hang on," she said, her thoughts swerving onto a new track. "Did you say *none* of the tribes will survive?"

"That's the prophecy," Moon said, spreading her front talons in an "I have no idea" gesture.

"But you mean none of the *Pantalan* tribes," Snowfall clarified. "Right? Just those three. Not the seven tribes on this continent. It has nothing to do with us. Right?"

"I think it might mean all of us," Lynx said, suddenly and very unwelcomely. Snowfall hadn't even noticed her pop up below them. "I mean, it starts off talking to us — 'turn your eyes to the land across the sea,' right? And then 'face a great evil with talons united' — that sounds like it's talking about all the tribes, here *and* there."

"Bosh," said Snowfall. "We can't unite to face an evil that's all the way across the ocean, even if we wanted to. Which, to be clear, the IceWing tribe DOES NOT."

"There are seven tribes here?" Hazel asked Moon. "Each with its own queen?"

Moon nodded. "Yes. We should call a council and see if they'll all come," she said. "They should know about you and Pantala and everything happening over there."

Oh, marvelous, Snowfall thought grouchily. *All the queens who annoy me in one place, arguing and telling me what to do.* On the plus side, staying in Sanctuary for a queen council would mean avoiding the wall for a few more days. But listening to Thorn and Ruby and Moorhen and Coral and worst of all Glory go on and ON about unity and working together and "mutual trust" and all THAT sort of nonsense was basically Snowfall's NIGHTMARE. BLERGH.

"I'll tell Tsunami," Moon said, tilting her wings. "I'm sure she can organize some dragons from Sanctuary to take messages to the queens." She flew off toward the pair of SeaWings.

"It's amazing that all your queens get along so well," Hazel said wistfully. "I wish we could have three tribes peacefully coexisting on Pantala."

"HA!" Snowfall said. "Peacefully coexisting! We just got out of a war!" *Two, technically, if you count the IceWing-NightWing war I TRIED to have before that busybody animus interfered.*

"You did?" Hazel said, wide-eyed.

"Long story," Snowfall added with a snort.

"I'll explain it," Lynx offered, and then spent the rest of the flight telling Hazel about the War of SandWing Succession and how it started and all about the prophecy and how the shiny heroic dragonets finally ended it. Personally, Snowfall thought they got an awful lot of credit considering the real heroes were a deadly snake and an old enchanted orb. If there'd been an IceWing in the prophecy, she probably would have ended the war way sooner and more neatly. But whatever, not Snowfall's problem.

As they started their descent into Sanctuary, Snowfall

was startled to see how much bigger it was than she'd imagined. The new dragon village was built along a stream trickling downhill from a lake in the foothills of the Claws of the Clouds mountains. Some of the new dragon buildings were in the wildflower meadows, while some were under the trees of the forest. It was VERY disorganized, as far as Snowfall could see. Each dragon home looked completely different from the next. Here there was a weird mound of clay with a hole at the top, then right beside it there'd be a rough cabin made of logs and leaves, while over by the lake there were a couple of crooked structures poking half in and half out of the water.

Upon landing, Snowfall noticed that there were also more dragonets than she'd expected, and some of them were really odd-looking. The first one she saw was a tiny thing playing in the stream, pouncing on fish. Its scales were a deep mahogany brown like a MudWing's, but speckled with phosphorescent bluish scales along its spine and wings, and as far as she could tell its talons were webbed like a SeaWing's.

Nearby, a little cluster of orange and red dragonets were gathered around a SkyWing, listening as he read them a scroll. But two of the red dragonets had scorpion-like tail barbs, and one of the orange ones had a scattering of black scales across its nose.

Snowfall's brain was still contorting itself around this information when a sky-blue SeaWing came bounding out of the trees toward them.

"Tsunami!" he cried as though the sun itself had arrived to visit him. His whole FACE was full of joy, which made NO sense, because who could possibly be that excited to see the very absolute most annoying member of the dragonet prophecy?

"Hey, Riptide," she said in a voice that *sounded* as confident as she usually did, but didn't quite match the funny look on her face. The two SeaWings awkwardly tried to hug and their wings all went in the wrong directions and they ended up bonking heads and then jumping back and flapping about for a bit.

Snowfall guessed there was something she could infer from their strange interaction, but she wasn't all that interested. She was looking around for her cousin Winter.

Was that a flash of white scales in the trees? Snowfall squinted, but whoever it was had vanished again. Or maybe it had been a trick of the light.

"It's so great to see you!" Riptide was saying to Tsunami. "I was hoping you'd come see all the changes we . . ." His voice trailed off as his eyes followed the line of dragons behind her up into the sky, where more and more dragons were arriving as the slowpokes caught up. "What —" Riptide tried. "What — um —"

"Surprise!" Tsunami said buoyantly. "New dragons for Sanctuary!"

"New — all these — but —" Riptide sputtered.

"Are those RainWings?" asked a new voice from Snowfall's

right. She turned and saw Winter splashing through the stream, staring up at the arriving SilkWings. Hmm. So that couldn't have been him in the woods.

"Winter!" Lynx cried with delight. He jumped and dropped his gaze to her, and then to Snowfall standing right next to her.

"Lynx?" he said in a wondering voice. "Snowfall? What are you doing here?"

Lynx cleared her throat and bobbed her head meaningfully in Snowfall's direction.

"I mean — apologies — Your Majesty," he said to Snowfall. "Welcome to Sanctuary." He even bowed properly, which was mollifying.

"I have come to inspect this new city," Snowfall informed him. "And to make sure these peculiar dragons settle here and don't try to come back into the Ice Kingdom."

"Not that they can," Lynx observed. "Given the cliff and everything."

"Are they hybrids?" Winter asked, tilting his head at a LeafWing who was burying her snout in the stream. "We have a lot of those here. SeaWing-RainWing, maybe? But there's so many —" His eyes widened as a SilkWing landed, stumbling, beside Tsunami. "That dragon has *four* wings," he whispered to Lynx. "Wait, so does that one! And that one!"

"They're from the other continent!" Lynx burst out, flinging excitement in all directions. "It's real, Winter! It's full of dragons! Totally different tribes! The colorful ones are SilkWings and the green ones are LeafWings. And there are also two . . . there, see the yellow-and-black ones? Those are HiveWings."

Snowfall had almost never seen her cousin look confused, let alone this discombobulated. It kind of made the whole trip to Sanctuary worthwhile.

Something caught her eye in the trees again — a flash of reflected light in the bushes, a shimmer of scales behind the leaves. But when she turned toward it, there was nothing but wind aimlessly stirring the forest floor.

She trusted her instincts, though. Another IceWing was hidden over there, watching her.

And whoever it was, they did not want to be seen.

CHAPTER 10

"Are there other IceWings here?" Snowfall asked Winter.

"A few," he said with a guarded expression. "Didn't you know that?"

She looked down her snout at him. "Of *course* I know that. I merely wish to know how many, and who exactly."

"I think I . . . shouldn't be the one to tell you that, Your Majesty," he said. "I don't know their reasons for being here. But I'm sure they'll tell you, if you want to ask them."

Snowfall considered finding this irritating enough to yell at him. She could do that now that she was the queen, and he wouldn't be able to argue back at her or run away, the way he sometimes did when they were dragonets.

She missed her chance, though, because while she was thinking, that awful NightWing landed and sucked up all the air around Winter's head.

"Moon," he said in a quiet, wondering voice.

"Hey, Winter," Moon said nervously. She batted one of

her wings at him without actually touching him. "We really miss you at Jade Mountain."

"I miss you, too," he said. "All of you, I mean, everything, I miss — I miss everyone."

"So why aren't you still there?" Lynx asked.

For some reason, they all looked at Snowfall. She waited a beat to see if that was a mistake, and then, when everyone kept looking at her, she said, "What?"

"You're the one who said he couldn't go back to the academy," Moon offered.

"I did?" Snowfall considered this news for a moment. She couldn't remember making a royal decree like that, or even thinking about it at all. She knew two new IceWing dragonets had been chosen to go to the academy, and now that she thought about it, those were probably replacing Icicle and Winter. But she had no recollection of anyone asking her whether Winter could keep being a student there or not. She had decided he was still banished from the Ice Kingdom, but she didn't particularly care what he did outside the Ice Kingdom.

"I don't actually care," she informed Winter. "You can go ahead and study hugs and whatever nonsense happens at that school if you want to. I have much more important things to deal with, like these homeless dragons and all the ones they left behind." She waved her wings at the tribes that were still landing around them. The meadow was starting to get a bit crowded. Riptide was starting to look slightly panic-stricken.

"The ones they left behind?" Lynx echoed, giving her almost the exact same puzzled look Hazel had given her earlier.

As if it was SO WEIRD for Snowfall to feel even a HINT of concern for all the SilkWings still trapped with the creepy evil thing over there!

"I'm not saying they should come here!" Snowfall snapped at her. "But I don't expect these dragons to just *give up* on them."

One of the LeafWings by the stream looked up and gave her a fierce, intense stare. Snowfall recognized her from the day before — she was the one who might be a threat to Hazel's crown. Sun-something. The one who was always frowning and glaring and looking ready for a fight.

"WHAT?" Snowfall demanded.

"We're not giving up on them!" the LeafWing said with a hiss. "We won't abandon them!"

The LeafWing beside her brushed her wing gently. "No one is saying we will," she said.

"This pile of icicles just did!" snapped the first LeafWing.

"No, love," the second one said calmly. "Actually, if you were listening, Queen Snowfall is saying exactly what you've been saying for the last three days. That we need to make a plan to go back and save everyone."

Yes. Exactly. That is what I meant, Snowfall thought.

Not because I care about any of those dragons over there. Just because I want all of these ones to be able to go away again.

"I'm Willow," the second LeafWing said to Winter. "And this is Sundew. We're very worried about the dragons who are still stuck back on Pantala."

"We should go back now, right away," Sundew said. "Even if it's just you and me and Cricket. We should take them by surprise, before the breath of evil gets any stronger."

Moon shuddered and Winter turned to her quickly. "No, not a vision," she said before he could ask. "Just those words . . . breath of evil. They scare me every time."

"Imagine how you'd feel if you were stuck on the same continent with it," Snowfall said. And then half of them gave her the weird look AGAIN. Maybe the ring was also turning her horns bright pink or something; otherwise it made no sense that everyone kept reacting as though she'd vomited miniature caribou each time she spoke.

Fortunately Tsunami and Riptide and Hazel arrived to create a distraction.

"Riptide has plenty of room here," Tsunami announced briskly. "Everyone can stay."

"That's not what I said!" Riptide objected. "*I* said, I don't know where we can possibly put them all, but they can stay for a few nights while we figure this out."

"Ha!" Snowfall flicked her tail at Tsunami. "See? Even

your precious friend and his heartwarming togetherness project don't want all these sad-snouts! I'm NOT the bad guy! My reaction is the normal one! No offense," she added to Hazel.

Tsunami shot a glare at Riptide and he backpedaled quickly. "Of course I want them!" he said. "We can make this work. I mean, this more than quadruples the number of dragons living here, but — but, um, I just have to — and maybe if we — but then the — I mean, yes, yes, of course they can stay."

"Great!" Tsunami said, now beaming at him. "I knew we could count on you."

"We can help," Hazel promised. "LeafWings prefer to build our homes in the trees anyway, so we won't take up any extra ground space. And the SilkWings can make their own webs. Maybe their silk could be useful." Snowfall could tell that Hazel was trying really hard not to glance pointedly at some of the more ramshackle buildings around them.

"Besides, we're not staying long," Sundew cut in. "We're going back to Pantala just as soon as we figure out how to defeat the breath of evil."

Hazel and Willow exchanged a glance that made even Snowfall feel all bristly; she wasn't surprised when Sundew let out a hiss and stalked off toward the lake.

"Queen Snowfall," Hazel said. "Would you be able to stay with us a few more days?"

"Me?" Snowfall said, fluffing out her wings. "Here? Why?"

"So we can summon the other queens, of course," Tsunami said. "For a big old queen summit. Not because we want you around, don't worry."

"Don't be rude to my queen," Lynx said sharply.

"I'd really appreciate it, Your Majesty," Hazel interjected, her eyes wide. "You're the only one I know. I'd feel so much better if I had a friend among the queens."

Three moons, Snowfall, tell me you are not melting into a puddle just because this strange green dragon called you a friend. She doesn't know you at all, and vice versa! Why would I even WANT a friend from another tribe? What good can she possibly do for the IceWings? It's not like an alliance with her would make us stronger.

But there are other perfectly logical, queenly reasons to stay. I mean, I don't want all the other queens meeting without me! Who KNOWS what they would say about me if I wasn't here! They might plot! And scheme! And make smug faces!

Staying is the right thing to do for the IceWing tribe. I need to know what everyone is up to anyway.

"Very well," Snowfall said, trying to sound bored. "We can stay until the other queens arrive. But tell them to make it snappy. I can't be gone from my palace for too long."

"Let's go choose the messengers," Riptide said to Tsunami, tugging her away before she could say whatever snarky thing was building up inside her snout.

"Show me around?" Lynx said to Winter. "I want to see everything!"

"Of course," he said, and then, after a moment of hesitation, added, "Moon, do you want to come, too?"

The NightWing nodded a little vaguely. She had a kind of distracted air about her most of the time, as though invisible dragons were whispering in her ears while everyone was talking.

Oh, Snowfall realized. *Because she's listening to our thoughts. I KNOW YOU CAN HEAR MY THOUGHTS, NIGHTWING! HERE'S ONE FOR YOU: I THINK YOUR ENTIRE TRIBE IS A BUNCH OF MALEVOLENT FIRE-SNORTING TOADS!*

Moon jumped slightly, gave Snowfall a wounded look, and followed Winter and Lynx off into the meadow. Hazel and Willow stood around for a moment, as though they weren't sure that Snowfall was done with them, and then finally went off in the same direction Sundew had gone.

Snowfall waded into the stream, which was brilliantly cold, like melted snow. She stood there, letting her scales cool down, as she studied the dragons scattered across Sanctuary. From where she stood, she could see dragons from almost every tribe: SandWings, SkyWings, SeaWings, MudWings, even a couple of RainWings, although at first glance she mistook them for SilkWings.

But no IceWings, as far as she could see. She was about to think, *Well, ha, that makes sense, because our kingdom is so amazing, why would anyone want to leave it?* But then she had to admit she didn't see any NightWings either, which sort of undercut her theory. And Winter said there *were* other IceWings here. So where were they? Why hadn't they come out to see the giant throng of new visitors?

The Sanctuary dragons seemed curious rather than afraid of the strange tribes. Snowfall wondered if that was because some of them were so odd-looking themselves, or because they were used to living with other kinds of dragons already. She watched the little brown dragon with phosphorescent blue scales dart up to a SilkWing, circle his talons slowly, and then sit down to gawp up at his four indigo-and-orange wings.

And then another flicker of white caught her gaze. Moving through the trees on the other side of the meadow — that was *definitely* an IceWing!

Snowfall bounded out of the water and charged across the grass, scattering clumsy dragonets in her wake. In the shadows of the trees, there was a whirl of white wings as the IceWing turned and fled.

Fled! From HER, Queen Snowfall! The indignity!

Snowfall doubled her pace as she plunged into the trees. Pine needles slipped under her talons and the smell of damp leaves filled her snout. Squirrels shouted angry chirpy things at her as she raced past, dodging tree trunks. Ahead, she could see her prey's white tail flickering. A shady forest at twilight wasn't exactly the best place for an IceWing to hide.

The best place is the ICE KINGDOM, Snowfall thought irritably. *Why would any sensible dragon ever leave it?*

Because of me, her brain offered with an awful jolt. *Because they think I'm a terrible queen. Just like all the dragons in that NightWing battle. Maybe IceWings are sneaking out of the kingdom in droves because they're afraid I'm going to ruin the whole tribe or do something dreadful.*

She shook her head fiercely. It was unlikely she'd catch this dragon with speed, since she was tired from flying all day. She could try throwing a spear or a knife, although that would be kind of a violent way to find out who it was. But wait . . . she had magic!

Snowfall skidded to a stop and banged the wristbands of stealth together, imagining herself invisible. And then she was. She couldn't even see her own talons. The bushes behind her seemed to shiver in a nonexistent breeze as she flicked them with her tail.

She carried on after the fleeing IceWing, but now she moved more slowly, trying to sneak up on whoever it was. It was hard to be quiet in such a noisy, crackly, yippy place, but soon she heard someone gasping for air up ahead. The IceWing thought Snowfall had lost its trail. It had stopped, panting, next to a giant boulder half covered in poison ivy.

Snowfall crept toward it, one talon, then the next, keeping her eyes fixed on the shimmering white scales beyond the foliage. And then . . . she POUNCED!

Debris flew up in all directions as she slammed into the

IceWing, tumbling talons over wings until they both crashed into the bare side of the boulder. Snowfall recovered first. She shook out her wings and leaped to pin down the other dragon.

"Ack!" her captive shrieked. "I'm sorry! I'm sorry!"

Snowfall blinked down at the pale blue eyes, the long graceful neck, and the unmistakable face of her missing sister.

PART TWO

SANCTUARY & SCAVENGERS

── CHAPTER 11 ──

"Crystal?" Snowfall blurted. She sat up and used the bracelets to turn herself visible again. Her sister's eyes widened as Snowfall shimmered into view. "Did you follow me here?"

"Follow *you*?" Crystal said indignantly. "You're the one who chased *me* through the woods!"

"Because you were lurking! Suspiciously!" Snowfall cried. "How long have you been watching me?"

"I have *not* been watching you," Crystal objected. "I don't have any desire to watch you. I've been staying far away from you. *You're* the one who came to *my* nice quiet place. What are you doing here?" She pushed ineffectively at Snowfall's talons. "Also, can you please get off already?"

"Wait," Snowfall said, backing up so Crystal could climb to her feet. "You mean — you've been *here*? In Sanctuary, this whole time?" She was having about eighty thousand emotions at once and it was VERY OVERWHELMING. Did this mean Crystal hadn't been skulking around the Ice Palace at any point? But what about her nefarious plots? And why would she come here? Was Snowfall in danger? Was this all a trap?

Admittedly even she couldn't quite imagine how Crystal could have engineered an invasion of mystery dragons just to get Snowfall to visit Sanctuary. But her pounding heart and shaking claws were having some trouble coming up with any other explanation for this. Crystal! Here! Lying in wait!

Crystal glanced around as though she hadn't ever thought about where she was. "I mean, I suppose I've been here since Mother died, more or less," she said.

"Doing what?" Snowfall demanded. "Plotting? Gathering an army? Hiring assassins?"

Her sister looked faintly amused. "If I wanted to hire an assassin, I wouldn't start in a community of scavenger-huggers like this. I'd go straight to the Scorpion Den."

"So you *have* thought about it!" Snowfall said accusingly.

A sudden crashing in the undergrowth warned Snowfall just in time. She spun as a dragon threw himself out of the trees at her head. He flew past, clipping her on the nose with his wings, and ricocheted off the boulder. She ducked again as he lunged back toward her, but this time he was able to pivot and slam her into a tree.

I knew it! I knew Crystal was planning to kill me!

Crystal was shouting something, but Snowfall couldn't hear the words over the grunts and snarls of her opponent as she kicked him in the chest. He had brown scales and a flat, square head and heavy talons — a MudWing. Crystal had formed an alliance with the MudWings! Did she have Queen Moorhen on her side? Snowfall had always found Moorhen the least annoying of the other queens, but maybe her quiet demeanor was all an act while she conspired with Crystal!

With a hiss of rage, Snowfall summoned the strength magic. She sank her talons into the MudWing and threw him off into the forest.

He hurtled out of sight, smashing a path through the branches. A moment later, there was a resounding thud in the distance.

Crystal shrieked and pelted after him, and Snowfall chased her into the trees.

"That's what happens!" she shouted at her sister. "I'm not as easy to kill as you think!"

Crystal didn't even look back. She ran full tilt along the path of destruction until she found the MudWing lying flat on his back at the other end, wings flung out to either side.

"Gharial!" she cried, crouching beside him. "Gharial, are you all right?"

"Saving . . . you . . ." he wheezed.

"Not very well, you great hippo," Crystal scolded. "She wasn't even attacking me!"

"But . . . dangerous," he managed to gasp.

Crystal looked over her shoulder at Snowfall, who had paused at the edge of the glade, puzzled by the tableau. Crystal was clutching the MudWing's front talons in her own, and he had this bonkers moony expression on his face as he gazed up at her. He must have hit his head *really* hard to be making that face, especially at Crystal, of all dragons.

"Are you here to kill me?" Crystal asked Snowfall.

"No!" Snowfall said. "I mean, not unless you're planning something. Should I?"

"Kill me? No, thank you," Crystal said. "Snowfall, how could I possibly be plotting against you or trying to kill you? We swore an oath to our mother, remember? I promised not to try to take the throne from you."

"Yes," Snowfall said, "but — you — but still, what if you . . ." She trailed off. Somehow it had never occurred to her that Crystal would take that oath so seriously. "I mean, if you're *not* plotting something, why did you disappear?" she demanded.

"Well," Crystal said, "to be honest, I was pretty sure *you* were going to kill *me*. The oath said not to fight for the throne. It didn't say anything about keeping your sisters and possible threats alive."

"*Pffft,*" Snowfall snorted. "I'm not the kind of queen who kills all her heirs just to feel safe! That's pure stupidity."

"I also . . . I had somewhere else I wanted to be," Crystal said, looking down at the MudWing again. "Or rather, someone else I wanted to be with."

Snowfall tilted her head at them. This still made no sense to her. Where else would anyone want to be besides the Ice Kingdom? Here, in this noisy fluttery forest full of dragons from other tribes? Why?

"Snowfall, this is Gharial," Crystal said. "We met during the war, when his troop joined our army to fight Blister. Once I was home again, I couldn't stop thinking about him."

"Oh," Snowfall said. *"Ohhh."* Now Crystal was making the same schmoopy face as he had, and she didn't have a head injury as an excuse. Crystal was in love with this MudWing! Of ALL THE ABSURD BRAINMELT.

This is the secret Lynx guessed she had.

"I think — I think Mother knew, actually," Crystal said. "Or guessed, at least. I think that might be partly why she didn't give me the crown."

"Because she was so horrified?" Snowfall supplied.

Crystal whipped her head up and frowned at her. "No! Because she knew it would tear me apart if I had to choose between the IceWing throne and the dragon I love. He could never come to the Ice Palace. If I were queen, there'd be no future for us."

This was the silliest thing Snowfall had ever heard. Choosing a romance over being queen of an entire kingdom? A romance with a MUDWING, no less?

For the first time since the battle with the NightWings, Snowfall felt a brief shining moment of *You know what — my mother* did *pick the right dragon to be queen.*

All that worrying. The endless nightmares and stress and peering around corners, thinking Crystal was lurking in every shadow with murderous intent. And the whole time, Crystal was *here*, throwing away her kingdom and being a total sap about someone who was, frankly, a very ordinary-looking brown dragon.

"Well," Snowfall said, sitting down, folding her wings neatly, and letting out a yawn. "You could have TOLD me instead of SNEAKING OFF and giving me a months-long PANIC ATTACK."

"Could I have told you?" Crystal said skeptically. "Wouldn't you have made that exact disgusted face and tried to forbid me from leaving?"

Snowfall made an effort to rearrange her expression, but she could tell it wasn't working. "Probably," she agreed. "Because what are you thinking? A *MudWing*?"

"I'm right . . . here," Gharial said weakly.

"You don't know anything about love," Crystal said haughtily, flicking her tail at Snowfall. "Or MudWings, for that matter."

"Yeah, and I'm way better off that way!" Snowfall pointed out. She got up and turned back toward the center of Sanctuary. "Very well, then. If you're really not planning to assassinate me, I'm going to bed."

"Nice to meet you," Gharial wheezed as she left.

Snowfall's wings ached from flying all day, but she felt lighter than she could remember feeling in forever. As though her scales were made of moonlight, shining through the dark clouds that had been around her.

Mother knew I'd be a better choice than Crystal. Because I care about the kingdom more than anything.

She glanced up at the two moons that were already visible in the twilight sky, and her talons stumbled over a fallen branch.

Or . . . she knew Crystal's secret, so she was forced to choose me. Maybe she would have picked her, but she was stuck with me instead because she knew Crystal might leave.

Snowfall sighed. That shining moment hadn't lasted very long.

She found her way back to the Sanctuary lake and waded in to wash off all the dirt of the forest and clean the scratches that MudWing had given her. Her guards looked surprisingly pleased to see her, although she guessed that was because they'd have a hard time explaining how they'd lost the queen to everyone back home. They followed her to a spot on the lakeshore, a fair distance away from all the other dragons, and formed a perimeter around her while she tried to scratch together enough moss for a comfortable sleeping spot.

Snowfall wondered where Lynx was. Having a jolly marvelous time with Winter and Moon, no doubt. Romping around Sanctuary, telling stories about everything Snowfall had already done wrong as queen, laughing at her. *Can you believe she was dumb enough to get an animus-touched ring stuck on her claw?* That sort of thing.

She tried once more to pull it off, and when that didn't work (*of course*), she lay down and stared gloomily at the ring in the darkness. It had nothing to say for itself. Not even a smug twinkle tonight.

Remember what I told you, she thought at it fiercely. *I demand a specific vision! I want to know what happened to animus magic! If you must haunt my dreams tonight, that is the vision I choose to summon. I am your queen and that is my command. You hear me?*

Impudent silence from the ring.

Snowfall sighed, closed her eyes, and drifted uneasily toward sleep.

CHAPTER 12

Her wings are green and they miss the sun. Her claws hurt from walking on stone instead of dirt for days. She is hungry; there is not enough food for all the dragons they are hiding, but every time someone goes out to get more, they fly back with terrifying stories of HiveWing swarms hunting the savanna.

For them — the dragons who burned Bloodworm Hive? Or for Sundew and her allies? She's not sure.

A gray dragon is curled beside her, asleep with his head resting on her shoulder and his tail twined around hers. He is the sweetest dragon the world has ever seen. He thinks she's a hero for destroying his home. He loves her when she's angry just as much as when she's cheerful. She has no idea how she fell in love with a gentle SilkWing, but she will murder anyone who hurts him.

Another LeafWing enters the cave and she motions for him to whisper so he won't wake Grayling.

"Strange happenings above," he says quietly. "Pokeweed

just got back, and he says he saw SilkWings flying with the HiveWings."

"What's strange about that?" she asks. "SilkWings have been working for HiveWings for so long. I'm sure some have been forced to help with the hunt, that's all."

"No," Hemlock says with a sigh. "All flying the same way. In formation. Exact wing movements. All in sync." He took a deep breath. "And they had white eyes."

She blinks at him. "That's impossible. Wasp's power doesn't work on SilkWings."

"I guess it does now." He rubs his face.

"Where's Pokeweed?" she asks. "I want to know exactly what he saw."

"He went deeper into the caves," Hemlock answers. "Still trying to catch those monkey-looking creatures."

They've seen the underground monkeys scurrying out of sight a few times, but none of the three LeafWings have managed to eat one yet. They're either faster than they look or surprisingly clever.

"There's something worse," Hemlock says reluctantly. "One of the SilkWings said she saw LeafWings up there, too."

She flinches so hard she knocks Grayling awake. He sits up, yawning and brushing her wings with his. He's too thin. She wishes she could protect him better — from the hunger, and from this news.

"That can't be right," she says to Hemlock with a low hiss.

"We saw all that smoke in the north," he says bleakly.

"Maybe Queen Wasp burned the Poison Jungle to punish us for burning Bloodworm Hive. Maybe our tribe lost and now —"

"No. They're out there somewhere," Grayling interrupts. He gives her a look with more trust in it than she's ever felt about anything. "The LeafWings have survived terrible things before. They'll fight back. The HiveWings won't win; they can't."

She wants to feel that way so badly. She doesn't know what will hurt more: to believe the worst, so if it's true she can't feel any lower . . . or to hold on to hope, but run the risk of being crushed.

"I wish we could do something," she says. "I wish we knew what was happening. I thought Belladonna would have sent us a message by now."

"Maybe we should go fight the HiveWings," Grayling suggests. "With all the SilkWings from Bloodworm Hive, there are so many of us down here — couldn't we fight them?"

"Not if Queen Wasp can control SilkWings and LeafWings now." She doesn't add that SilkWings are kind of useless fighters. She takes Grayling's front talons as his face crumples. "Don't worry. Wasp is never getting you. Never, never, never."

But what is she going to do? They can't hide underground for the rest of their lives. But if they can't go back to the Poison Jungle either . . . is there anywhere they can possibly be safe?

When Snowfall awoke, there was another dragon lying close beside her, one wing resting on hers, and she had to stare at the dragon's soothing white scales for entirely too long before she realized it wasn't Grayling.

Of course it wasn't Grayling. Grayling was stuck on the other side of the ocean. Grayling was a SilkWing in a cave under a continent Snowfall was never going to see, which was great news because that continent sounded more and more dreadful every time she visited it.

No, the impertinent dragon sleeping next to her was Lynx.

Snowfall poked her face until Lynx's eyes fluttered open.

"Ow," Lynx grumbled. "Rude." She turned her face away and buried it under her other wing.

"What's rude is sleeping on the queen's tail," Snowfall barked. "Get off!"

Lynx rolled away, still muttering, and then suddenly shook herself and sat up. "What happened last night?" she asked, blinking. "Did you have another vision?"

"Yes," Snowfall admitted reluctantly, even though this was exactly why she'd woken Lynx in the first place. "I was a stupid LeafWing this time."

"One of the ones here?"

"No." Snowfall shook her head. "Her name is Bryony. She knows that Sundew dragon, though."

Lynx slammed her talon down on something small and furry that was scurrying through the undergrowth. "Ooooh, maybe that means you're supposed to tell Sundew about your vision."

"BLECH. NO. I do NOT need a thousand more dragons

having opinions about my magic head trips. One is FAR MORE THAN ENOUGH." Snowfall glared at the ring. She was starting to feel a little more like herself, but the quiet, worried Bryony personality was still shifting under her scales, and it was SO UNSETTLING.

"You stupid broken thing," she hissed balefully at the opal. "That vision had nothing to do with animus magic."

Shimmer shimmer shimmer, the opal winked back serenely.

Snowfall stood up and flapped her wings, trying to shake off the lingering strands of affection for the adorable gray SilkWing. He was different from the others. He was special and beloved and WHAT WAS HAPPENING TO HER? Melting like a snowball in the desert over a strange dragon she'd never met who was definitely not her type even if she did?!

Was this how Crystal felt about that MudWing? Snowfall shot another suspicious glance at the ring. Was it trying to hit her over the head with a lesson about *sympathy* and *understanding*? YUCK.

Am I going to have dreams like this for the rest of my life? Will I still be me if I spend every night as an entirely different dragon?

"I saw Crystal yesterday," she informed Lynx abruptly. "She lives here now."

Lynx's eyes widened and she put down her half-eaten prey. "No way! She was here the entire time?" She grinned. There was a tuft of mouse fur caught in her teeth. "So, wait . . . doesn't that mean she was *not* plotting against you, after all?"

"She ran away to be with a *MudWing*," Snowfall said with a snort.

"Hmmm," Lynx said. "Sounds like maybe you were being extremely paranoid and anxious about nothing, then? And just possibly that might apply to other things you are extremely paranoid about?"

"You are the most aggravating dragon in the world," Snowfall observed. She had a sense that normally she would be furious with Lynx, and that she should be yelling and perhaps throwing her in the lake, but it was hard to get worked up about a little insubordination when Bryony was stuck underground and Grayling was in danger of being mind-controlled and she had no idea if Tau had escaped Jewel Hive or whether any of them would ever find one another.

Lynx studied her for a moment with a crease of worry along her forehead, and then she shook herself vigorously. "Come see what our lunatic friend Winter has done."

"Friend" seemed like a bit of a stretch in Snowfall's opinion, but she was definitely up for a distraction, so she followed Lynx along the lakeshore, back through Sanctuary. Not far from the water's edge, in an area that had been cleared of trees, there was an odd space surrounded by a tall fence. The fence was made of entire tree trunks lashed together, so it was very high, and Snowfall had to crane her neck to see over it.

Inside, there was a dragon-made pool of water, a pile of leaves and pine needles with a small leaf canopy over it, and something that darted around so energetically it took Snowfall a moment to figure out what it was.

"Great Ice Spirits," she said to Lynx. "I thought he was over his scavenger obsession!"

Winter poked his head out of a hut near the fence. "I'm not," he said huffily. "Why would I be? Scavengers are fascinating!"

"You are so weird!" Snowfall said. "Nobody else keeps their lunch in a pretty cage for months to 'study' it!"

"She's not LUNCH," he said, outraged. "My scavenger is a *research subject*. I'm learning so much about them! They're really smart!"

Snowfall rolled her eyes. "What happened to that droopy one Mother let you have when you went off to school?"

"Bandit. I had to let him go," Winter said tragically. "I have no idea what was wrong with him. But this one is different!"

"This one has bitten him *five times*," Lynx whispered to Snowfall.

"She's very brave," he said with a hint of pride. "She's come up with all kinds of ways to escape."

Snowfall peered over the top of the fence again. The scavenger had a long tail of dark fur on her head, tied up with a scrap of fabric that might have been bright yellow at some point. She was now marching up and down the length of the fence, shoving each of the logs and testing them for footholds.

"Moon says she's really mad," Lynx told Snowfall.

"What?" Snowfall said. "Why would Moon be mad about this?"

"No, I mean, the scavenger is mad. She *really* wants to get out of there."

Snowfall frowned at Lynx. "Are you trying to suggest that that NightWing can read scavenger minds as well?"

"Not exactly," Winter answered. "It's not as clear as reading dragon minds, but she gets a sense of their emotions. She says they're just as strong and complicated as dragon emotions," he added with a little smile.

"I'm not going to dignify this conversation with any more of my attention," Snowfall said. "That is the MOST RIDICULOUS THING I'VE EVER HEARD."

"Winter's being ridiculous?" a new voice suddenly chimed in. "If so, that's me, I did that! All credit to me! I built his entire sense of humor from the ground up!"

The IceWings whirled around to find a pair of SandWings emerging from the trees. The one speaking was in front, bounding toward Winter with an irrepressible grin on his face. He was the one from the beach, Snowfall was pretty sure — Moon's friend.

"Oh no," Winter said drily. "There goes the neighborhood."

"Aw, I can see it in your eyes; you missed me so much!" said the SandWing. He threw one wing affectionately over Winter's shoulders and nudged the side of his neck with his snout. "I missed you, too, best friend."

Snowfall raised her eyebrows at Winter, who said, "I have no idea who this scruffy-snout is."

"His favorite dragon in the world," the SandWing said with genuine delight. "Did we ever officially meet, Your Majesty?" he asked Snowfall. "I'm Qibli. Queen Thorn's second-in-command, basically."

"Ha!" said the other SandWing, and then started actually laughing as Qibli gave her an offended look.

Lynx nudged Snowfall in the ribs, but she had already recognized the laughing dragon. Snowfall had made a diplomatic trip to each of the kingdoms soon after becoming queen, very much against her will, but apparently it was one of those things a queen was required to do.

"Queen Thorn," she said, inclining her head exactly the right amount.

"Queen Snowfall," Thorn replied, doing the same. "I'm glad you're still here."

"Oh?" Snowfall said. The spikes along her spine ruffled up as she braced herself for a lecture about how real queens behaved. No, wait — that was more Queen Coral's style. Queen Thorn didn't care much for rules and traditions. But that also meant she could be horribly direct about sharing her opinions.

"I don't like the sound of that thing across the ocean," said Thorn. "Thank the moons Pyrrhia's at peace, so we can all talk about it together like sensible dragons instead of snarling hyenas."

Pyrrhia's at peace. Snowfall had never thought about it that way. Sure, the War of SandWing Succession was over, but her mother had been murdered *pretty recently* by a NightWing. Snowfall wouldn't describe her feelings about *that* tribe as exactly *peaceful*.

That didn't make her a snarling hyena, though! Seriously!

"Are the other queens on their way?" Snowfall asked.

"Riptide said they could be here by tonight," Qibli answered cheerfully. He gave Winter another hopeful smile, and his earring caught the light of a sunbeam.

That earring — *the* earring. Or at least, it looked exactly like the earrings that had saved her tribe from Darkstalker and the plague. She remembered them arriving, sacks and sacks of them, brought by IceWings who lived in Possibility, sent by Queen Thorn in the Sand Kingdom. Snowfall's very first task as queen had been making sure that every IceWing in her kingdom received one, to reverse the effects of the plague.

For a long time, they weren't sure if it was safe to take them off again. Every IceWing had gone around for months wearing them, and then one day someone took theirs off, to see what would happen, and the plague didn't come back, so gradually they had disappeared off the dragons. But everyone kept theirs tucked away into safe spots just in case . . . just in case they were needed again.

Just in case he wasn't really gone.

Snowfall had been the last IceWing to remove her earring. She still carried it with her, in the pouch around her neck.

It was so strange to see the exact same earring on this enthusiastic SandWing, just a regular little accessory instead of the thing that had saved her entire tribe.

"Are you all right?" Lynx whispered in her ear.

Snowfall pulled herself up and folded her wings regally. "Yes. Always."

And then something flashed behind her eyes like a bolt of lightning, and her head split in two, and everything around her — Sanctuary, the scavenger enclosure, Queen Thorn, Lynx, Snowfall herself — all vanished into thin air.

CHAPTER 13

His claws are shaking. They are his claws and they are not his claws.

His claws would never seize a fleeing dragonet from the webs and drag her into the Hive. His voice would never shout orders at terrified SilkWings; his talons would never threaten them with this spear. Where did this spear even come from? How long has he been like this? The days are blurring together, and he hasn't been his real self for so long.

The queen is in his head, in his muscles, in his talons. It's worse than he ever imagined, any of the times he tried to imagine how the HiveWings must feel as she takes over. If he pulls himself all the way back inside and stares inward, he can lose time, knowing his body is moving without him.

But right now, he can't do that. He's in his own Hive. The place he fled with Cricket and Swordtail not so long ago. He is storming through familiar hallways, smashing displays in the market, rounding up all the SilkWings who were peacefully lying in the sun in the Mosaic Garden. He sees dragons he knows from school, who stare at him in paralyzed terror.

They know he would never do this, so this is how they discover the queen can control SilkWings now, as well as HiveWings. Except it's not the queen . . . it's even worse. But they don't know that yet.

They look at their own talons, wondering when it will happen, if they'll remember it — all the things Blue wondered, too.

But there's a process. The new, stronger breath of evil plant is needed for the process, and the dragons who were supposed to make it grow faster escaped.

Sundew. *No one has found her yet, or Cricket, as far as Blue knows. She might be safe . . . maybe they're even in the Distant Kingdoms now, far from all of this.*

Carelessness, *Wasp's voice hisses in his head. This was a strange discovery, that although she can't read his thoughts, he can hear hers, sometimes very clearly.*

She's furious about the SilkWings that have slipped through her claws already. Hundreds of them vanished during the two days while her army was rescuing every last scrap of the breath of evil plant from the burning jungle.

The jungle she made me burn, *he thinks, but has to stop himself from thinking.*

They were hunting for LeafWings at the same time, but found none.

None.

How did they ALL ESSSSSSSCAPE?

Where could they have gone?

I will find them. And destroy them.

At least I have their army and their queen. *Inside his head, the queen is thrilled and the queen is furious at the same time. Wasp wants to kill Queen Sequoia and all the LeafWings in her power, but the breath of evil won't let her.*

It controls her just as completely as she controls the HiveWings.

And it needs the LeafWings; it needs any hint of leafspeak they have, to grow more of the plant as fast as they can.

Once there is enough, they can take over the SilkWings — but only if they can find all the SilkWings. And most of them went into hiding while the jungle burned. Blue was with Queen Wasp's army as they searched Hive after Hive. Yellowjacket Hive: empty, except for Wasp's mean, bewildered sister, Lady Yellowjacket. Wasp Hive: empty. Jewel Hive: empty, and Queen Wasp was especially furious about that, because where did Lady Jewel and Lady Scarab go? Did they run off WITH the SilkWings?

I knew I should have killed them years ago.

That's when she realized they needed to get ahead of who-ever was warning the Hives, if there was any chance left to do that, and she sent warriors out to all the Hives. That's how Blue ended up here, in his own home. He'd hoped it would be empty, too — but whoever was coming to warn them was already too late.

He'd seen his mothers, Burnet and Silverspot, but he didn't think they saw him, which was a small mercy. They were in the crowd being shoved into the Hatchery; that's where the SilkWings were to be kept until the breath of evil was ready for them.

And *I* have to stand guard, *Blue thinks*. Over my own friends and family. I can't even talk to them or tell them I missed them or that I'm sorry about this.

When tears come, as they often do, he can't wipe them away, because his claws are not his claws.

They're my claws.

All their claws are my claws.

She enjoys looking through this little SilkWing, the flame-silk who dared to defy her, but she has a lot of dragons to wield and can't stay entangled in any one for too long. The traps are set in Cicada Hive and Hornet Hive. Whoever has been warning the SilkWings will arrive to save them, and then her toothy leaves will snap shut and they'll be caught like flies in a plant's jaws.

Wasp frowns. That was not her metaphor.

"Get out of my head," *she says with a hiss, but it doesn't bother answering.*

This will all be worth it. **Sometimes you have to work with monsters to get the power you want.**

Three tribes, all bowing to her. It's what she's wanted all along, isn't it? She knew the SilkWings and LeafWings were a threat from the moment she saw them, as a young dragonet. They were different; dangerous; strange and terrifying.

Those tribes would have attacked me first if I hadn't attacked them.

If everyone is evil, the only way to survive is to be the most evil.

SilkWings and LeafWings are different from us and need to be controlled.

As long as she controls everything, she'll be safe. Everyone will be safe. No one can threaten her when they can't even lift a claw against her.

Everyone was out to get me but I showed them, and now they are all mine.

This is what it means to be a true queen: complete control. Nothing to fear. No one to stop her or argue with her or complain about her. They fear HER, and that is how it should be.

She is pacing, and she realizes her thoughts are spiraling down an uncontrolled path again. She'll have to kill something to calm herself down.

Snowfall was wrenched very suddenly out of Wasp and landed hard, painfully, back in her own mind. It felt as though she had just plummeted from a great height, and midway she had turned from one dragon into another, completely different dragon.

Or more like a third dragon. Blue to Wasp to me.

Blue was the most opposite of herself she'd ever been, and

the most powerless. It was AWFUL and she HATED it and she would never never forgive the ring for doing this to her.

But Wasp . . . Wasp was worse, because Snowfall had heard echoes of her own fears inside Wasp's head.

I'm not like her, am I? I would never make the choices she's made . . . would I?

Such as accepting a strange magic I don't know enough about in order to make myself more powerful? asked an uncomfortable part of her brain.

She realized she was lying on grass, and her face was wet, as though someone had flung part of the lake over her head. The air smelled like scavengers and pine trees and distant snow. She was definitely on her own continent again.

I'm not Wasp or Blue. I am me. I'm Snowfall. I've always been Snowfall.

I don't WANT to be anyone else! Ever again!

Someone was shaking her shoulder.

"Wake up, please wake up," the someone said. "Snowfall? Snowfall?"

That must be Lynx, disrespectfully forgetting how a queen should be addressed, again.

Snowfall cracked her eyes open. Her skull hurt as though she'd whacked it on something when she fainted. Well . . . not fainted, exactly. Got taken over by a stupid magic vision.

Oh NO.

That wasn't supposed to happen! A vision in the middle of the day, when she was wide-awake? She'd thought they only came at night, like normal dreams. Could she be attacked by visions *anytime?!*

She shoved herself up to a sitting position and seized the ring, trying to yank it off.

Lynx let out a yelp that sounded like joy and threw her wings around Snowfall. "That was terrifying!" she cried. "Please don't ever do that again!"

"Do . . . what exactly?" Qibli's voice asked. Snowfall looked up and realized there was a whole circle of dragons around her, expressions ranging from puzzled to curious to worried. An entirely oversized audience for her collapse. Qibli, Winter, Queen Thorn, and Lynx were all there, but at some point, they'd been joined by Sundew, Luna, and Cricket, who was holding the squirmy little HiveWing.

Cricket. Snowfall's heart did a hideous little jump-stutter thing at the sight of her. She could almost feel Blue leaning through her scales, shooting out beams of love at the bespectacled dragon. UGH HORRIFYING. Cricket was perhaps a *scale* closer to Snowfall's type than Grayling, but still several continents off!

"I'm fine!" she snapped. "It's nothing! I'm fine! Stop looking at me like that!"

Queen Thorn and Winter politely took a step back and pretended to study the clouds. But Cricket couldn't seem to

pull her eyes away; she was giving Snowfall the most fascinated look through her glasses.

"S-sorry, b-but your expression —" Cricket stammered.
"Something about your face, for a moment when you were
still unconscious — it was so weirdly familiar."

"She looked like Moon does when she has visions of the
future," Luna suggested. "Can you see the future, too? What
did you see?"

Snowfall shook her head, crouching a little lower to the
grass. Her claw hurt from her violent attempts to pull off
the ring, and her head still ached from being yanked out
of Wasp, and she had a weird flippy feeling in her stomach
that had no reasonable explanation, except maybe that turning from one dragon into another all of a sudden might have
some physical side effects.

Had she seen the future? Or was that the past? Or was it
happening right now?

"Maybe she's just hungry," Lynx said, trying to cover for
Snowfall. "Dragons faint from hunger all the time, right?"

"IceWings don't have the power of foresight," Winter said
to Luna. "Only NightWings."

"But that looked like magic," Qibli said. He glanced at
Thorn, as if she had the eyes he trusted the most. "Didn't it?
Like something magic just happened to Queen Snowfall. Do
you feel all right?" he asked her. He sounded genuinely concerned, his voice suddenly gentle instead of playful. Snowfall

saw him reach up and instinctively touch his earring. She wondered if he was thinking of Darkstalker, and the plague, and what had happened to the last IceWing queen, and other unknown evil spells that might be lurking about.

Was it possible the ring had been secretly spirited into the palace by Darkstalker? Could this be one of *his* curses that was doing this to her?

In a panic, Snowfall fumbled for her pouch, pulled out the earring that had cured her of the Darkstalker plague, and stabbed it into her ear.

Everyone was staring at her again as she grabbed the ring and tried to wrestle it off her claw.

It didn't budge. If it had been a Darkstalker spell, it should have lost all its power over her the moment she put on the earring. She should have been able to pull it off easily.

With a sigh, she took the earring off and tucked it back in her pouch.

"*What* is going on?" Sundew said into the silence.

"Do you have magic besides seeing the future?" Luna asked, her gaze going from Snowfall to Lynx to Qibli and Thorn.

"They do — like the invisible IceWing army! Remember I told you about that?" Cricket said. "I've been wondering about how she did that for days. It seems to be . . . jewelry-related?" She studied Snowfall's bracelets and the ring that sat obstinately on her claw.

Qibli gave her a surprised, approving look. He held out one talon to Snowfall. "May I see?"

Snowfall wasn't sure why she placed her talon in his, letting him bend down to peer at the opal ring. Maybe it was the smoky haze of Blue's brain inside hers, wanting to trust everyone. Which was still better than the sharp teeth of Wasp's brain that wanted her to bite him instead.

Is that right? Am I being all Snowfall right now? Would Snowfall normally want to bite him, too? Are any of my feelings real?

"Invisible army?" Winter murmured to Lynx. She tugged him a few steps away from the group and whispered in his ear.

At the same time, Qibli was tapping on the opal and trying to wiggle the ring around Snowfall's claw.

"This isn't an ordinary stuck ring, is it?" he said. "What's the spell on it? Do you know who cast it?"

Sundew drew in a sharp breath behind him. "Spell?" she echoed. "You can cast actual magic spells?"

Part of Snowfall really REALLY wanted to tell these other-tribe dragons nothing. This was IceWing business! Nothing to do with anyone else!

But there was Cricket, and her curious face that Blue loved so much, and Blue would never hide anything from her. And even the parts of Snowfall that weren't all blurry from being Blue couldn't help thinking, *she should know that he's still alive, or at least he was whenever that vision happened . . . is going to happen? Arrgh it would be HELPFUL to KNOW THINGS, you stupid ring.*

"It's an old animus-touched object from way back in

IceWing history," she told Qibli. "I found it in our treasury. It gives me visions of other dragons, like I'm inside them, thinking their thoughts, feeling their feelings." She scowled. "It's THE WORST, if you want to know the truth."

"Wow," Cricket breathed. "Blue would *love* that."

Snowfall rubbed her head. "The one I just had . . . I was Blue, actually." She didn't want to tell them the Wasp part. Maybe she could keep that to herself, and by keeping it to herself, forget it ever happened.

Cricket and Luna stared at her with a whole new light in their eyes. "Blue?" Luna gasped, and "You saw him? He's all right?" Cricket blurted at the same time.

"I didn't *see* him," Snowfall explained snippily. "I *was* him. I was stuck *inside* him. He is the *sappiest little butterfly of a dragon* I have *ever encountered*."

"That's Blue," Luna said affectionately.

Tears were running down Cricket's face. "What was he doing? Is he safe?"

"Not even remotely," Snowfall said, and then "OW!" as Lynx kicked her tail and gave her a significant look. "I mean, he's ALIVE. But that evil queen of yours is controlling his talons and he's trapped with her army and they were just forced to round up a bunch of SilkWings in Cicada Hive, including his mothers, and he was feeling really guilty about that. WHAT?" she barked as Lynx kicked her tail again.

"It's all right," Cricket said to Lynx, although her tears hadn't stopped. "I want to know the truth."

"SEE?" Snowfall glowered at Lynx.

"Have you had visions of other Pantalan dragons?" Sundew interrupted. "Any LeafWings?"

"Yes. One named Bryony," Snowfall said.

Sundew's eyes narrowed, but less like she was mad at Snowfall and more like she was trying not to have some other expression. "Was she . . . did Queen Wasp have her? And the other LeafWings with her?"

"No, she's in hiding," Snowfall said. "With Hemlock and all the SilkWings from Bloodworm Hive."

"All the *SilkWings* from Bloodworm Hive?" Sundew echoed, confusion taking over her face.

"Yes," Snowfall snapped. "I know your plan was to leave them all to die with the HiveWings, but Bryony didn't let that happen."

Sundew blinked, and it was Cricket who jumped in to defend her. "Sundew didn't want them to burn the Hive at all," she said. "And she's the one who made sure they contacted the Chrysalis first."

"This is so weird," Lynx said. "I mean, listening to you talk about all this Pantala stuff and those dragons over there as if you know them," she added to Snowfall. *As if you care about them*, her puzzled eyebrows seemed to say.

"It's not great!" Snowfall lashed her tail. "It's pretty aggravating, in fact! I have enough problems to handle in the Ice Kingdom! I don't want to worry about problems on a whole other continent, too!"

"Thank you for telling us, though," Cricket said, wiping her eyes. "It means a lot."

"Who else?" Sundew demanded. "How long have you been having these visions without telling us?"

Snowfall hissed at her. "Just since you came barging into my kingdom," she said. "The other two times were SilkWings. In the first vision, I was Atala while she flew over the ocean with you all, but she's here now and totally fine. The other is named Tau. She was trying to escape Jewel Hive before the HiveWings got there."

"Tau," Cricket said softly. "Did she make it?"

"I don't know!" Snowfall threw her wings up in the air, scattering pine needles. "Wait, yes, I do, sort of, because Blue was thinking about how Wasp's army found Jewel Hive empty. So I think she did, but I can't be sure because I don't even know if I was seeing the past, present, or future! There's no *reason* for any of this! And now they're happening during the *day*?" She growled low in her throat. "I can't be collapsing and getting infested with other dragons' emotions in the middle of a council of queens. Let's cut off my claw," she said abruptly to Lynx.

"That might be a bit drastic," Qibli said, and she realized he was still holding her talon, studying the ring. "I mean, let's make that plan B. Or, like, plan F."

"WHAT'S PLAN A?" Snowfall shouted at him.

"Can you communicate with the dragons in your visions?" Qibli asked. "Like, to let them know where everyone has gone or that they should come across the ocean, too?"

"No!" Snowfall cried. "WHAT IS WRONG WITH YOUR EARS? I'm not Snowfall when I'm inside them! Snowfall disappears! I have no way of telling them anything! I can't even remember what Snowfall knows! It's like I never existed at all!" She took a deep, shuddering breath.

Queen Thorn nudged Qibli aside and took his place beside Snowfall. "The queen needs a moment," Thorn said with authority. "Everyone who's not me, go away."

"But —" Qibli and Sundew both started to protest at the same time.

"Now," Thorn said with a forbidding look.

The other dragons melted away like magic. *Real queen magic*, Snowfall thought wistfully. *The magic of saying things and being instantly obeyed. The magic of being so queenly that everyone listens to you. Because they trust you and know you're a great queen.*

"*Whewf*," Thorn said when they were gone, her voice suddenly, surprisingly normal. "Have you noticed that it's awfully hard to get any peace and quiet when you're queen?"

Snowfall thought of her empty, echoing palace and the way dragons vanished when they saw her coming. The long, long nights that were *too* quiet, and yet not peaceful at all. But also the constant pressure inside her head, knowing the wall was always waiting for her and feeling as though dragons were watching her every move.

I wonder if Tundra has changed any of the rankings while I've been gone. Narwhal used to, when Queen Glacier was away. Snowfall didn't think she'd officially authorized that, but maybe Tundra would just assume that power because Snowfall hadn't told her *not* to.

"Let's go flying," Thorn suggested. "We can figure out what we think before the other queens get here."

"I don't know how to figure out what I think," Snowfall said, standing up. "Should I get my guards?"

"Nah. Just you and me," Thorn said. "I mean, who would dare attack *us*? Brain-dead beetles who want to be crushed, maybe!"

Snowfall laughed despite herself. Flying away from everyone was exactly what she wanted to do right now anyway.

They lifted up into the sky, letting the late-morning sun wash over them, and soared toward the peaks. Snowfall inhaled the smell of distant snow . . . along with the scent of not-so-distant scavengers.

More than one scavenger? She glanced down at Winter's little enclosure. The creature in there was sprinting around the space again, making lots of funny squeaking noises. But Snowfall's nose told her that wasn't the only scavenger nearby. And . . . were those tree branches moving in more than the wind?

Snowfall shrugged. She had never cared about scavengers, and she wasn't about to start now. She tilted her wings and followed Queen Thorn into the clouds.

CHAPTER 14

Queen Thorn didn't make Snowfall talk or ask a bunch of questions or lecture her on queenliness. They just flew, and hunted when they got hungry, and flew some more, until the sun was high in the sky, warming their chilled wings.

Snowfall felt her head clearing of the post-vision Blue haze. Her own thoughts sharpened and felt real again.

Thoughts including, *is that going to keep happening? Visions in the middle of the day?*

What if one happens while I'm flying? Will I just fall out of the sky and die?

Will they ever stop, or will they start coming more and more frequently until my mind is never my own anymore?

She shivered. What was the *point* of this magic? Was it set to get worse and worse gradually . . . maybe so the original animus would have had time to escape the kingdom before the queen went mad?

And what was happening with Blue now? Or Bryony, or

Tau? If only she could compel the ring to give her visions she actually WANTED. USEFUL visions, instead of walking nightmares she couldn't do anything about.

"Ready to go back?" Thorn asked, swooping up beside her.

Snowfall made a face. "I can't wait. More interrogation! How thrilling!"

"You just shut them down whenever you need to," Thorn suggested. "You are a queen. But remember that of course they're curious and worried about their friends, so that's why they want to know more."

"Yes, yes," Snowfall grumbled. If Blue had *known* Snowfall was inside him, he would have been over the MOONS to give her a message for Cricket. The least she could do for that poor trapped dragon was reassure the HiveWing he loved.

Another intertribal romance, she thought, shaking her head. Were they more common than she realized? She'd always assumed IceWings would NEVER choose to be with dragons outside their tribe. But then, the dragon who'd brought them the first two earrings had been a hybrid IceWing-SeaWing from Possibility. And now there was Crystal and Gharial . . . so it did happen.

Hybrids. Winter mentioned them. In the chaos yesterday, she hadn't really registered it, but now she remembered. He'd said, *we have a lot of hybrids here.* That meant dragonets whose parents were from two different tribes — like the ones she'd spotted yesterday. *Probably a MudWing-SeaWing, and at least two SkyWing-SandWings, and maybe a SkyWing-NightWing?* No wonder those dragons wanted a new city to live in — how could they ever return to their kingdoms, or choose one tribe while abandoning the other?

Snowfall had to admit to herself that she would have forbidden Crystal to see Gharial if she'd known about it when she first became queen. And he wouldn't have been able to cross the Great Ice Cliff alive. He still couldn't, so even if Snowfall gave them her blessing, they'd never be able to come to the Ice Palace.

She followed Thorn as they descended into the central clearing of Sanctuary, where Sundew and Tsunami were yelling at each other, surrounded by a wide-eyed audience.

"You could save us!" Sundew shouted. "It would be so easy for you!"

"I DID SAVE YOU!" Tsunami shouted back. "You're here, aren't you? And alive?"

"I mean everyone back there!" Sundew waved one wing at the western horizon. "All the mind-controlled dragons! You could save them with one spell!"

"That's — what?" Tsunami sputtered. "A what now?"

"A spell." Sundew clenched her fists. "The dragons on this continent have real *magic*," she announced to the LeafWings around her. "It's not only seeing the future and invisible armies. They can cast *any spell they want*. They could make a spell to free all the dragons in Pantala, but they won't! They've been *hiding* their magic from us!"

"All right, hang on," Tsunami said over the mutters from

the crowd. "That's a highly confused understanding of the situation."

"So un-confuse it!" Sundew barked.

"We don't all have magic!" Tsunami turned to Riptide, who had come up to stand supportively beside her. "Back me up! Hardly any of us have magic!"

"It's very rare," Riptide agreed. "Once in a generation, often less. Or at least, it's supposed to be."

"So right now you have, what?" Sundew demanded. "One magician? Two?"

Tsunami scrunched up her snout. "We call them animus dragons," she said. "And . . . four, we think, more or less."

FOUR? Snowfall tried to think. Did she know about this? There was Jerboa, and there was some animus dragon at Jade Mountain — she assumed a SeaWing — who'd cast the empathy spell. So who were the other two? What tribe did they work for? That was outrageous. Animus dragons all over the place! And none of them IceWings! No one was safe!

"So bring us one of them," Sundew said in a steely voice, "and have them cast *one spell* for us."

Tsunami's eyes slipped sideways into the crowd, but Snowfall didn't catch who she was looking at.

Whoa. Is there an animus dragon here right now?

"Here's the thing," Tsunami said slowly. "Animus magic has stopped working. Nobody knows why. That's why I didn't tell you all about it — because even though we want to help you, we can't do it with magic. We just can't."

"That sounds like another lie!" Sundew yelled.

Snowfall saw Queen Hazel in the crowd of LeafWings; at the same moment, Hazel caught her eye and gave a little start, as though she'd forgotten she was a figure of authority around here.

"Hey, hey," she said, stepping in between Sundew and Tsunami, her green wings spread out like giant leaf curtains. "It could be true, Sundew. If their magic isn't working, why would they tell us about it?"

"If their magic isn't working, why is *she* making armies invisible and having visions of Pantalan dragons?" Sundew asked, pointing at Snowfall.

Oh, great. Now the hundreds of puzzled eyes turned toward Snowfall.

"'I'm using old magic," she answered, holding up her talon with the ring on it. "Enchanted a long time ago. Those still work — it's only new spells that don't. Apparently. If we take the animus dragons' word for it."

Tsunami frowned at her and Snowfall scowled right back.

"The queens are starting to arrive," Riptide said, brushing Tsunami's wing with his own.

A wing of dragons was soaring down toward them, and farther off in the sky, Snowfall could see another group approaching. Everyone turned to look at them, whispering and murmuring — who would get here first? Would they come with any friends or family of the Sanctuary dragons?

Time to put on my super-queen face. My "the Ice Kingdom is

JUST FINE THANK YOU" face. *No advice needed, don't tell me what to do, I am an excellent queen who can handle — who can — what's — oh no —*

It was happening again. Darkness was crowding in around the corners of her eyes. Snowfall looked around wildly, spotted Winter, and sank her claws into his tail.

"Yowch!" he yelped, whipping around to look at her.

"Get me somewhere safe," she hissed. "Don't let them see!"

He didn't argue, didn't ask questions, didn't stand there with a dopey bewildered look on his face. He grabbed Qibli and the two of them spread their wings around Snowfall, hooking their arms under hers and carrying her away from the circle of dragons. With everyone looking up at the sky, Snowfall had to hope they wouldn't notice her being spirited away . . . but she only had a moment to worry about it before . . .

Tall grass brushes her wings and tickles her snout. She crouches lower, spreading her long wings. She's lucky they're a dark color, so it's easier to creep up on the Hives at night.

The dragon city towers over them, light glowing from the windows and archways on the higher levels. But she can't hear anything — voices, music, any of the sounds that usually carry across the savanna at night. It's too quiet.

And nothing moves in the webs overhead. They're empty and still, like she's never seen them before. All the SilkWings . . . where are they?

"Was this your Hive?" the small, dark orange dragon beside her whispers.

"Yes," she whispers back.

They should have come here first. All her Chrysalis friends . . . her parents . . . is she too late to save them?

She studies the map of Pantala in her head. They'd recruited SilkWings from Yellowjacket Hive, Wasp Hive, and Jewel Hive to bring to the Poison Jungle; those had gone across the sea with the escaping dragons. The SilkWings from Bloodworm Hive vanished into thin air after the Hive burned. No one knows where they are, but they can't be dead — no bodies and no survivors has to mean they all escaped somewhere, doesn't it?

She'd sent two dragons to Tsetse Hive, so it had only made sense for her and Cinnabar to fly the other way, stopping briefly at each Hive to warn whoever they could, then straight on to Mantis Hive. It was as far from the Poison Jungle as one could get — her wings were still sore from the frantic, full-speed flight. Which meant there was a chance of getting there before Queen Wasp's zombie minions.

And she'd been right. They'd found Mantis Hive empty of HiveWings. Bewildered SilkWings milled about its halls or rested on the webs, enjoying the unexpected days off while also wondering where everyone had gone.

Every HiveWing had left, even the smallest dragonets. Wasp had summoned every single one to the battlefield outside the Poison Jungle, determined to crush the LeafWings once and for all.

She clenches her talons. Those HiveWings hadn't had to lift a claw. The LeafWings, and the SilkWing allies she brought them, had lost before they even started to fight. They'd run away. And now Queen Wasp and the breath of evil were able to infect SilkWings, which meant the entire tribe might lose the last bit of freedom they'd had.

"Stop, Io," Cinnabar whispers, brushing one of her wings lightly. "Stop worrying. We got everyone out of Mantis Hive and safely into hiding. We'll save the SilkWings here, too."

"It's too quiet," she whispers back. "The HiveWings must be here. I bet they've got all the SilkWings trapped in there with them."

"Even if that's true," Cinnabar whispers, "they can't have put all the SilkWings in the Hive under the mind control yet. They don't have enough of the plant to do that. They'll have to grow more, and Sundew said that without Hawthorn or her, it'll take a while."

"Not as long as it should. Some of the LeafWings Wasp trapped have a little bit of leafspeak — they'll make it grow faster. And if the HiveWings keep all the SilkWings imprisoned until they have enough . . ."

"We'll get them out. That's why we're here."

Io sighs and looks up at the ghostly webs again. They're swaying slightly in a far-up breeze, silvery pale in the light of the three moons. Empty.

How are two dragons supposed to save all the SilkWings in Cicada Hive?

They'll help us, she reminds herself. *My friends will rise up when they realize it's time for the Chrysalis to break free.*

"The map is safe?" Cinnabar asks.

"Hidden," Io promises. "Where we agreed." Even if Queen Wasp captures them and steals their minds, she can't access their secrets. The map to the other continent is somewhere that only Io or Cinnabar can find with their minds free. Wasp won't even know it exists.

Cinnabar smiles, and her wings rustle in the darkness.

"Then let's go rescue our tribe."

CHAPTER 15

Snowfall floundered back into her own mind shouting, "It's a trap! Don't go in there!" She threw off the talons holding her down and tried to lunge into the air, but she was so disoriented that she crashed into somebody's wings and landed back in a soft pile of pine needles.

"Your Majesty," said Winter's voice, and somehow that was disorienting, too, her own cousin calling her that, when that voice and that name should only connect to Queen Glacier.

"Don't worry," Qibli said, touching one of her talons lightly. "You're back. You're Queen Snowfall again."

"They're going to catch her," Snowfall said breathlessly. "Cicada Hive is full of Wasp zombies lying in wait for Io and Cinnabar. I have to tell them. That's where Blue is. They can't go in there." She struggled up again and then stopped, standing with her wings outstretched along the ground, trying to breathe.

"I can't tell them," she said. "There's no way."

"Um," Qibli said, looking at Winter. "Maybe there is?"

"Don't you be needlessly optimistic at me," she snapped.

WHY? she screamed at the ring in her mind. *Why would you show me this when there's NOTHING I CAN DO?*

They were outside Winter's scavenger enclosure. The scavenger inside was squeaking loudly, like an overwrought squirrel. All around them, the bushes rustled in the wind, or maybe because of something else. Snowfall squinted at one of the trees and thought she saw something move that was bigger than a squirrel.

But then Lynx came darting through the woods and sprinted up to Snowfall's side.

"Are you all right?" she panted. "Who were you this time?"

"Someone very doomed," Snowfall bit out, frustrated. "Never mind. Are all the queens here?"

"Everyone but Queen Coral," Lynx said. "They've agreed to start without her, if you're ready. Are you ready?"

"I'm fine," Snowfall said, waving away Winter's talons as he tried to help her up. She didn't have to tell anyone that her heartbeat was still racing. Or that part of her was still inside the heat and smell of the savanna night.

Calm down. You are not currently creeping into a giant, terrifying dragon city full of mind-controlled monsters with bug powers.

But Io was — or would be — or already had? Snowfall shook herself. She had no idea how to figure out the time frame for her visions. That one might have happened days and days ago.

Io might be dead already. She flinched at the thought, then shot another glare at her ring. *You'd better not be sending me visions of totally dead dragons.*

The other queens were assembled in the mouth of a pebbly cave halfway up one of the mountain peaks. The wind whipped around the snowcaps above them, but the spot they'd chosen was an oasis of quiet. Each queen had brought one advisor as backup, and Snowfall debated all the way up the mountain about whether it was idiotic to bring Lynx, who was clearly still a dragonet, instead of one of her guards.

But Queen Thorn had summoned Qibli to join her, and he was about the same age as Lynx, surely. Queen Ruby's choice was a quiet older orange dragon who took notes the entire time in a kind of miniature scroll; Snowfall never caught his name. Queen Moorhen had a MudWing with her who looked so much like her that Snowfall nearly bowed at the wrong dragon — a sister, she guessed, remembering the way MudWings were about family.

And of course there was Queen Glory, with her floppy yawn-noodle of a sloth curled around her neck, as usual. She'd brought a fidgety NightWing with her, which Snowfall didn't like, but she thought it was an interesting choice. Why not a fellow RainWing? What did the RainWings think of Glory choosing a NightWing over them for this council?

Perhaps nothing at all. Did RainWings actually have opinions?

Queen Hazel was there, too, with Cricket and Luna.

Sundew had been left down in the village, most likely because Hazel didn't want her to do any more shouting in front of the queens.

Tsunami, Riptide, and Moon were the final three dragons in the council. If Snowfall hadn't been the last one to arrive, she might have complained and tried to get them kicked out, but it was too late by the time she got there. Well, fiiiiiiiine. Probably it made sense to get a report from one Pyrrhian dragon who'd actually been to Pantala.

Although there's also me. I could tell them WAY too much about what's happening on Pantala right now. She shivered a little, thinking of Io again.

The other queens exchanged polite greetings with Snowfall, the kind that would normally make her freak out about what they *really* meant and what they thought of her and whether they talked about her when she wasn't there.

Today she could barely even concentrate on saying the right things back to them. So what if Queen Ruby's smile looked suspiciously judgmental? Io and Cinnabar —

Wait.

Didn't Cinnabar say . . . something important . . . right at the end of the vision . . .

Her thoughts were interrupted by Tsunami standing up and calling the council to order, as though SHE was ANYBODY AT ALL. (All right, fine, she was a royal SeaWing princess, so technically she could be standing in for Queen Coral, BUT STILL it was VERY PRESUMPTUOUS.)

Tsunami told a long story about how Luna had been swept across the ocean in a storm, carried by her silk, and how that was their first sign there were dragons on a lost continent out beyond the sea. She explained that she and her brother had decided to swim across the ocean to find them — and to find out whether Luna's stories were true, that there were dragons over there who needed help.

Luna jumped in to talk about the political system in Pantala: how the HiveWings kept the SilkWings under their control, and how the HiveWings themselves were all controlled by Queen Wasp, who could take over any HiveWing's mind anytime she felt like it, from anywhere.

"Except mine," Cricket said quickly when Qibli turned to look at her. "And a few others — it's a whole thing."

Hazel added the story of the LeafWings, who had fought a war with Queen Wasp and almost been wiped out, except for a small remnant of the tribe that fled to hide in the Poison Jungle.

Snowfall drifted in and out for parts of the stories. She knew all this, from being Tau and Bryony and Blue and Io. She could still feel the weight of the history that rippled under their scales. She remembered knowing things they hadn't even thought consciously about; she could probably draw an accurate map of Pantala herself.

I am actually the most informed dragon here, she thought, glancing triumphantly around the circle. *The one and only upside to the visions.* Maybe that was why the ancient

IceWing queen had agreed to (or asked for) this gift in the first place. But knowing a lot about Pantala didn't seem like an even trade for Snowfall's sanity.

Finally, after a long explanation of the new war, Queen Wasp's attack on the jungle, and the discovery of the plant that gave her the mind-control power, the Pantalan dragons wound down into silence.

The queens exchanged glances. "So you need a new place to live?" Queen Moorhen asked. "I suppose you could stay here in Sanctuary, if it's all right with Queen Ruby and Queen Thorn. I'm afraid we don't have room in the Mud Kingdom."

Yeah, right, Snowfall thought. The Mud Kingdom wasn't exactly packed wall-to-wall with MudWings. They could easily fit a whole other city of dragons in those endless swamps if they wanted to.

"How many dragons are we talking about?" Ruby interjected. "Who will be in charge of them? You?" she asked Queen Hazel. "I mean, what if you keep having more dragonets and spreading out? Are we going to end up with a new kingdom in the middle of the continent — one that mostly takes over Sky Kingdom territory?" She shot Riptide a frown. "That's not what I had in mind when I agreed to this settlement."

"I know, Your Majesty," he said. "But we can't possibly send them back to Pantala." Beside him, Tsunami vigorously shook her head, and Moon looked horrified, as though someone had just suggested rounding up all the baby seals and setting them on fire.

"Is there anywhere else we can put them?" Ruby asked. She turned to Glory. "It sounds like they might be happiest in the rainforest."

"So Glory can be queen of *four* tribes?" Snowfall heard herself snap.

Glory made a face she couldn't interpret — was she laughing at Snowfall? Was she thinking that she could handle four tribes easily when Snowfall could barely manage one?

The part of her that had briefly been Blue the SilkWing thought, *or maybe she's thinking how impossible it would be to rule four tribes, and how much she's still struggling to bring together the two she has.*

SHUT UP, YOU MUSHBALL, Snowfall demanded.

"Wait, wait." Hazel stood up and spread her wings to catch their attention. "That's not — we're not thinking about where we could live yet. Most of us — all of us, I think — want to go back to Pantala."

Not Cobra Lily, Snowfall thought. She wondered if Hazel had actually asked anybody what they wanted. The LeafWings might be happier here, among trees that *weren't* constantly trying to eat them.

"Oh," Ruby said, taken aback. "Then . . . do that?"

"We all left dragons we care about over there," Hazel said. "They're all in awful danger."

That's true, Snowfall thought. *Extremely true.*

"We want to go back to rescue them," Hazel said, "but we can't go back alone. Our numbers are no match for Queen

Wasp, especially once she mind-controls everyone else in Pantala. We were hoping . . . maybe you could help us."

"Ohhhhh," Ruby breathed out softly.

"You mean with armies," Thorn said.

"You want us to send our soldiers all the way to the other side of the ocean," Moorhen said. "To fight in a war that — I'm so sorry, but — it has nothing to do with us."

"Nothing to do with us!" Qibli burst out. "Didn't you hear what's happening to those dragons?"

"Yes," Moorhen said, shooting a "get your dragon under control" look at Thorn. "But *our* dragons are safe here. That thing over there doesn't even know about us. If we go rile it up, it might come back to attack us and we could lose this whole continent, too. At least right now, this is a safe place — for us *and* for you."

"Plus, we just got out of a war," Ruby said. "And a follow-up almost-war."

Was that a dig at Snowfall? Was Ruby saying Snowfall was the kind of queen who would drag her tribe into war for no reason? OR was she saying that Snowfall couldn't even finish a war she *tried* to start?

"Darkstalker didn't do anything to your tribe," Qibli pointed out.

Oh. Was that the almost-war she meant — everyone against Darkstalker?

Well, if she was worried about that, she could have ALMOST been a lot more helpful trying to fight him!

"I have a lot of dragons who haven't recovered from the War of SandWing Succession," Ruby said. "Or, to be honest, from my mother's reign as the Super-Murdery Queen of the Mountains. I don't know if I can throw them back into another conflict." Both Moorhen and her sister started nodding.

"We have a similar problem," Glory said, looking thoughtful, as though she were running calculations in her head. "Half my dragons are not cut out for war — they wouldn't be any help to you even if I tried to send them. And the other half have been through a lot lately."

"Oh, have they?" Snowfall said icily. "Been through a lot? You mean such as raising an all-knowing magic evil dictator from the dead and then trying to help him murder a whole tribe and take over the continent? That does sound stressful. Poor things."

"What?" Hazel said, bewildered.

"*What?*" Cricket said at the same time, her eyes shining with curiosity.

"I think what we're all saying," Thorn interjected, "is that it would be tough to justify sending our soldiers into such a dangerous situation, when it sounds like they could have their minds taken over exactly like your dragons have. Isn't that right?"

"We don't know," Hazel said sadly. "I'd guess . . . probably."

"We can give you weapons, though," Glory said. "My

tribe makes these blowguns with darts that can put dragons to sleep. You'll be able to stop your friends from hurting you without having to hurt them."

"Oh, *wow*," Cricket said. "What's in the darts? Is it something that grows in your rainforest? Have you — um, sorry, I'll ask you later." She subsided as Hazel put one talon over hers.

"We would appreciate that so much," Hazel said to Glory.

"Make a note," Glory said to her NightWing. "We can triple production starting tonight if we send a messenger back."

"We have some dragonflame cacti," Ruby said, glancing awkwardly at Thorn. "You're welcome to that. But I don't think we can send any of our soldiers."

"Wait, wait," Qibli said. "Before you all decide, you have to hear Moon's prophecy."

Tsunami let out a small huff, and a few other dragons looked uneasy, but Thorn and Glory beckoned Moon forward.

"A new prophecy?" Glory asked.

Moon nodded. "It came with the vision that led me to Luna, on the western coast." She cleared her throat and recited it again. Snowfall listened a bit more carefully this time.

"Turn your eyes, your wings, your fire
To the land across the sea
Where dragons are poisoned and dragons are dying
And no one can ever be free.
A secret lurks inside their eggs.
A secret hides within their book.
A secret buried far below

May save those brave enough to look.
Open your hearts, your minds, your wings
To the dragons who flee from the Hive.
Face a great evil with talons united
Or none of the tribes will survive."

Moon glanced over at Tsunami when she finished. "Sorry," she added. "They just happen, I swear."

"You all heard that, right?" Qibli said. "Turn your eyes to the land across the sea? *Face a great evil with talons united?* As cryptic prophecies go, I think this one is PRETTY clear."

"*None of the tribes will survive*," Glory echoed. "Meaning all of us over here as well."

"But how is that possible?" Ruby said. "How would the danger even get to us? I thought someone said it was almost impossible to cross the ocean."

"It is," Hazel agreed. "We only made it because we found a map that was made a long time ago by Clearsight. I think that's what *a secret hides within their book* means. It showed a trail of islands where we could rest on our way across the ocean. Without it, we wouldn't have survived."

"There you go," Ruby said. "You had to use the map. The dragons over there, and whatever is controlling them, won't be able to follow you. So we're all safe here."

That was it. *That was it!* That was the thing Cinnabar had said!

"Actually, we're not," Snowfall interjected. She turned to Hazel, who looked as though she'd accidentally pushed them all into a Venus dragon-trap. "Because you left a copy of the map there, didn't you? With Io and Cinnabar."

"What?" Ruby cried.

"And Io and Cinnabar have been captured by HiveWings," Snowfall informed her. "So Queen Wasp getting her claws on that map? It's only a matter of time."

CHAPTER 16

Well. There was a LOT of shouting, and an UNREASONABLE AMOUNT of questions, far too many of them directed at Snowfall.

"You had a vision about Io and Cinnabar?" Cricket kept asking. "Did you see them get captured? Are you *sure* the HiveWings got them?"

"Unless my vision was of something that hasn't happened yet," Snowfall said. "That I don't know. But if it has happened, I definitely saw them going into Cicada Hive, which is definitely full of mind-controlled dragons, like Blue, lying in wait for them."

"We could try to warn them," Tsunami interjected. "We have a — thing — I'll go try."

She flew out of the cave and down the mountain, but that didn't help the noise levels because all the other queens were interrogating Hazel at once, and the poor LeafWing queen was trying to explain about the SilkWings they'd hoped to rescue.

"Let's go," Snowfall said to Lynx. "No one's going to make any great decisions today."

It was stressful enough knowing that map was floating around on the other continent; Snowfall did not want to add "explaining her visions (and by extension the cursed ring she'd blithely put on) to all the queens" to the list of things stressing her out today.

She slipped out of the cave quietly and Lynx followed her. They flew down the mountain and Snowfall found her wings turning toward Winter's corner of Sanctuary, where the scavenger enclosure was.

Must be nice to be a scavenger, Snowfall thought. *No problems in the world, no scary things coming from across the ocean to steal your brains.*

She couldn't believe Hazel had left a copy of the map with Io! What kind of nitwit — but then she thought of Tau and Jewel and Grayling and Blue's sad mothers, and then Io's fervent desperate hope to save them all swept through her so strongly, it felt like her own emotion. As ridiculous as that was.

Maybe Wasp won't find the map. But how will anyone else get it, if Io and Cinnabar are captured now, and they're the only ones who know where it's hidden?

What can we do? How can we save them?

Aaaaaaaaaaaaaaaaaaaaargh why do I care about this so much?

She tried halfheartedly to pull off her ring again, with no success.

They landed on the lake side of the enclosure, and Snowfall caught herself a fish while Lynx told Winter everything that had happened during the council.

"I think your visions are more helpful than you realize," Lynx said to Snowfall as she finished.

"Rubbish. Hazel would have told them about the map without me," Snowfall argued. "She's all honest and tortured like that."

"But you know what's happening over there," Lynx said. "You're the only one who can see what's happened to all those dragons since Hazel's group left."

"*I* think it would be *much more useful* if the ring actually *answered some of my actual questions*," Snowfall hissed at the opal.

"Have you tried lying down and closing your eyes and telling it to give you a vision?" Winter asked.

"NO," Snowfall barked. "I mean, sort of, when I went to sleep last night. But did it listen to me? NO, IT DID NOT."

"Maybe it's showing you the most important moments happening in the whole world," Lynx suggested. "That seems like something a queen might have asked for, right?"

"Perhaps you could try summoning a vision now," Winter said. "Maybe it would tell you what happened to Io and Cinnabar, or the map, or if they really got caught."

Snowfall sighed. "Fine. FINE. I hate this idea, but if I have to have a vision, I'd rather have it when it's convenient for me anyway." She looked around and spotted a tall flat boulder in the shade of the trees; in a moment she was on top of it, lying on the cool stone. From up there she could see the little scavenger scampering around its den.

It was pretty cute. Cuter than your average squirrel, not as cute as a polar bear cub.

"Stop staring at me!" she yelled at Lynx and Winter. "Mind your own business!"

They turned away quickly and started walking around the outside of the enclosure. Grumbling to herself, Snowfall rested her chin on her talons, took a deep breath, and closed her eyes.

What happened to Io and Cinnabar? she asked the ring. *Is the map safe? Does Queen Wasp know about it?*

She waited to fall into someone else's scales.

Nothing happened.

And then some more nothing happened.

Snowfall frowned and buried her head under one wing. She was definitely still herself. She had many very strong Snowfall emotions barging around inside her, such as for instance FURY. What was WRONG with this RING? Why couldn't it do what it was told?

Would it work properly for a better queen?

Is it trying to tell me it also thinks I'm terrible at this?

Snowfall waited for several more heartbeats of torture and insecurity and boredom, but she seemed to be lodged firmly inside her own anxious brain.

She sighed and opened her eyes.

Lynx and Winter were perched on top of the scavenger fence, staring at her again.

"Did it work?" Lynx called. "What did you see?"

"That was very boring and frustrating!" Snowfall shouted. "And it did NOT work! Probably because you were STARING AT ME! Go away!"

They exchanged a glance. "All right," Winter said. "We're going to find Tsunami and Qibli — will you be okay staying here?"

She glared at him. "Why wouldn't I be?"

"We could send your guards over," Lynx offered.

"Oh," Snowfall said, remembering she was supposed to be guarded at all times. "Yes, yes, sure, no rush."

"Can you keep an eye on Pumpkin for me?" Winter asked.

Snowfall flicked her tail across the smooth coolness of the boulder. "Do not tell me," she said, "that you *named* your scavenger. And moreover, that you chose the name *Pumpkin*."

"I think it's adorable," Lynx said, grinning at Winter, who looked gratifyingly embarrassed.

"I thought you wanted us NOT to eat your critter," Snowfall said. "So WHY would you name her after food?"

"It's supposed to be cute!" he said. "Because *she's* cute!"

"Come on, Winter, we'll be here forever if you start talking scavengers." Lynx batted his wing with hers and they lifted up into the air.

"She's been acting a little funny," Winter said to Snowfall. "She might be planning to break out of her enclosure again. If you wouldn't mind —"

"Yes, yes," Snowfall said, waving him away. "I'll watch her."

"Thank you, Your Majesty!" he called, and the two of them flew away, leaving Snowfall in blessed silence.

She watched the scavenger scamper around, piling leaves and sticks by the fence. She tried to think about all the visions she'd had so far. Why had the ring chosen those dragons to show her? What was the meaning of any of this?

Across the clearing, the bushes started rustling in a very odd way. In fact, they were more than rustling. They were thrashing about as though all the branches were wrestling furiously with one another, and then all of a sudden there was a very loud squeak, and at the same time, a dragon burst out of the leaves and careened into the open.

He fell over and sat there, blinking, for a moment, then hopped up to his feet and shook his wings. He lifted his head, saw Snowfall watching him, and grinned a huge, ridiculous, sweet-as-baby-hedgehogs grin.

"Good day!" he cried. "This day! So good! Right?"

She squinted at him. He was kind of weird-looking. Maybe he was one of the many hybrids here in Sanctuary, although he looked older than the little dragonets she'd seen — older than her, actually, if she had to guess. His scales were not quite SkyWing, not quite SandWing, but somewhere in between — a sort of pale orange. He had no tail barb, though, and his eyes were a washed-out blue. He didn't look at all dangerous, partly thanks to the crooked daisy chain wound around his horns.

"Can I help you?" Snowfall asked.

"I have come to here to bargain for this — uh, delicious scavenger!" the dragon declared. He waved one wing dramatically at the enclosure.

"Uh-huh," Snowfall said skeptically. "I don't think she's for sale."

"But I just ADORE scavenger — uh, chewing," he said. He made a weird, grimacey face. "Chewing scavengers. Meat! Yum. Want to eat them alllllllllll day, chomp chomp, yes."

"So go hunt down one of your own," Snowfall said. Somehow the more he talked, the less she believed he actually wanted to eat the scavenger.

"I *would*," he said, "but I . . ." He trailed off and shot a panicked look at the bushes. "Um. Don't . . . want to?"

Snowfall propped her chin on her front talons. This was the most entertainingly strange thing that had happened to her in days.

"You'd rather buy a scavenger that's not for sale than go catch your own."

"Could it be for sale?" he said hopefully. "I have blueberries!"

Snowfall laughed. "Winter is not going to sell you his pet, even for all the blueberries in the world."

"Oh!" he said. *"Ohh!"* He shot a look at the bushes like, "I told you so, bushes!" "She's a pet? Not for chewy delicious eating?"

Snowfall couldn't begin to guess why this dragon spoke so oddly now and then. "Yup, it's a pet," she said. "My cousin loves these critters. He's been trying to catch a good one for ages."

"And she's a good one?" he said, looking as pleased as if she'd complimented *him*.

"Well, she's energetic," Snowfall said, peeking over at her again. The scavenger was leaning innocently against the far wall, spinning a stick in her paws. "And Winter says she's a good mimic — she's made some very dragonlike noises at him. Which made him think she's terribly clever."

The stranger gave a little snort of laughter. "Hmmm," he said. "What if she . . . doesn't want to be his pet?"

Snowfall tilted her head at him. "Well, we can't exactly ask her! I'm sure she's perfectly happy. He feeds her, like, twice a day."

"What if *I* gave him a *different* pet? A better pet!" the odd dragon suggested with a triumphant flourish of his wings.

"I am quite sure he —"

"How about a SNAIL?!" the dragon cried, with a kind of rapturous delight Snowfall had only ever seen on dragonets tasting ice cream for the first time.

"A snail," Snowfall echoed.

"Snails are AMAZING!" he said adoringly. "Have you SEEN them?"

"I . . . have seen snails, yes," she said. Queen Coral had served sea snails during her visit to the Kingdom of the Sea, but Snowfall had a feeling this dragon's heart would explode if she told him that.

"Or a TURTLE!" he shouted. "I could give him a turtle! Awwww, don't you love turtles? With their little flippery flippers! And their sweet little shells! And their tiny heads HAVE YOU SEEN THEIR TINY HEADS? They look like they're smiling! Little tiny turtle smiles! Wouldn't he love a turtle?"

"He would not," Snowfall said positively. "I must say it sounds like *you* should get a turtle, though."

"Yes," he said dreamily. "That is exactly what *I have been saying.*" He shot another "did you hear that, bushes?" look at the shrubbery.

"How about you go get a turtle, then," Snowfall said, "and leave this scavenger to my obsessed cousin."

"Oh," he said, shaking his head as if he'd completely forgotten what he was there for. "Right, no, no, I would like this scavenger very much. *This* one, please."

The bushes behind him made some highly suspicious squeaking noises. Snowfall squinted at them. Did he already *have* a scavenger? Maybe he collected them. Maybe he was Winter's dream friend.

"If you're so interested in scavengers, wait and talk to Winter about them," she suggested. "He can tell you everything he's learned from studying them, if you have twenty days to listen to some outlandish theories."

"Can't I please have this scavenger?" he said with enormous, baby-seal eyes. "Please please please?"

"Being cute doesn't work on me! Nice try!" she barked. "I am the queen of the IceWings, and I have told you no!"

"Queen of the what? Really?" he said.

"Yes, really! How do you not know that?" She lashed her tail. "The settlement is full of queens right now! So you should practice being a little less adorable and a little more respectful, you — what the heck are you anyway? A hybrid of what?" A startling thought struck her. Could he possibly be an IceWing-SkyWing hybrid?

"Not a hybrid," he said. "Just a funny-looking SkyWing." He turned and hissed at the bushes. *"She thinks I'm adorable."*

"I DO NOT, three moons. Who are you talking to?"

"No one!" he blurted. "Sorry! Nothing! Never mind, I am not needing the scavenger after all, everything great, nice to meet you, bye forever!"

He turned and bolted into the woods; there was a bit more thrashing around in the greenery, and then Snowfall saw his tail darting away through the trees.

Weirdest dragon of all time! But she had to admit this feeling of amusement and slight confusion was preferable to the overwhelming anxiety she normally lived in. She wouldn't mind being distracted from the end of the world by him again.

Shaking her head, she glanced over to check the enclosure.

She should have noticed that it had gotten very quiet.

She should have been more suspicious of the scavenger standing so still for once.

She might have guessed that the scavenger had been standing right there to hide the new hole in the fence.

If she had, she might have caught the scavenger before it escaped — but it was too late.

Winter's pet was gone.

CHAPTER 17

"Oh, *walruses*," Snowfall hissed. This was the last thing she needed to deal with right now.

She flew down into the enclosure and marched around it, double-checking. Yes, Pumpkin was absolutely gone. The hole was just big enough for a scavenger, partly tunneled under the fence and partly hacked out of the wood.

Outside the fence, there was a scramble of marks in the dirt where the scavenger would have emerged, but it was hard to tell what kinds of marks they were.

Hang on.

Was that dragon distracting me so he could steal her?

But he hadn't moved from his spot while they talked, so he must have had an accomplice. Another dragon? Why would two dragons go to all the trouble of stealing one scavenger who was barely enough of a meal for one of them?

Snowfall frowned at the marks in the dirt. She didn't see anything that looked like a talon or tail had made it. And the scavenger must have been digging from her side, too — unlucky that she escaped right into a dragon's claws. If that's what happened.

This really made no sense.

Snowfall sighed deeply. She should *probably* go into the forest and try to catch that dragon, just in case he did have Pumpkin.

Grumbling to herself, she set off into the trees. *Should I wait for my guards?* No, she could handle an overly smiley dragon who went into raptures over turtles, no problem. Ooo, especially if she used her STEALTH ARMBANDS. She set them gleefully to make herself invisible and darted in the direction where she'd last seen his tail.

It didn't take long before she heard his voice burbling away up ahead. Snowfall slowed to a stealthier pace and crept toward him. He sounded utterly insane. Whatever he was saying was half words, half yips and chitters and meeping noises, as if his brain kept turning into a chipmunk mid-sentence.

She slipped through the trees to get ahead of him, which wasn't hard, as he was just ambling along chatting to thin air. There were clearly no other dragons with him, so perhaps his accomplice had gone in a different direction. Or perhaps she was wrong and this dragon hadn't stolen Pumpkin — but she smelled scavenger somewhere nearby, and his behavior had been *very suspicious* — so she didn't feel guilty about the heart attack she was about to give him.

"AHA!" she shouted, leaping into his path and flinging off the invisibility magic.

"YIIIIIIIIIIIIIIIIIIIIIIIIIIIIIIIIIIIIIIIIIIIIIPES!" he shrieked, in a very gratifyingly terrified way.

"Give it back!" she shouted. "You stole Winter's scavenger! Give it back now!"

"She wasn't *his*!" somebody yelled back at her. Not the dragon, though. He was standing there with his mouth closed and his eyes wide open. What the — ?

"You can't own a scavenger! We're not pets!"

There was a SCAVENGER. STANDING. ON THE DRAGON'S HEAD.

SHOUTING AT SNOWFALL *IN DRAGON*.

"Except you, you're *my* pet," the dragon said quickly, almost under his breath, and then made a face as if he was trying very hard not to laugh.

"Not helpful, Sky!" the scavenger barked at him, poking the top of his head with her foot.

"But — but —" Snowfall had never in her entire life been so at a loss for words.

A scavenger! Speaking Dragon! In a conversation! Like it was really talking to her!

"How is this happening?" She glanced down at her jewelry. Was this another animus curse? Was she hallucinating intelligent, talking scavengers now? "Where's Pumpkin?" she demanded.

The dragon started snorting with laughter so much that the scavenger on his head had to grab his horns so she wouldn't fall off.

"Her *name* is *Daffodil*," said the scavenger.

"Oh, ah," Snowfall said, very much in denial that this conversation was real. "Much more dignified."

A small face peeked out from behind the dragon's neck, surrounded by a halo of dark hair. She waved one of her little paws at Snowfall.

"Does she speak Dragon, too?" Snowfall asked.

"She's *supposed to*," said the scavenger on the dragon's head. "If she *paid attention* and *studied more*, she'd be able to *talk* to any dragons who try to kidnap her."

"Daffodil!" Daffodil/Pumpkin shouted in Dragon. "No eating!" The pitch of her voice was too high and the accents and growls were in all the wrong places, but now that Snowfall was listening for it, she could tell those were Dragon words. Winter's former pet shook her head huffily and squeaked something scavenger-ish in what looked like indignant outrage.

But scavengers *couldn't* be sentient; they couldn't be smart enough to learn Dragon and talk like dragons and argue with queens! They were just big squirrels! Prey! This had to be some kind of party trick. This weird SkyWing (if that's really what he was) must have trained his scavengers to make all the right funny noises. Surely that was it.

Or else Snowfall would have to believe that there was a

whole civilization of intelligent life living right under the dragons' talons all this time, stealing treasure and getting eaten. And having *feelings*? Surely not.

"This is" — Snowfall pressed her talons to her head — "I can't — this makes no —"

And then she realized the fuzziness and headache and creeping darkness weren't caused by the discovery that an everyday snack could have a conversation with her.

It was another vision, arriving now, whether she liked it or not.

"Oh no," she muttered, and then her eyes closed and she dropped . . .

down . . .

down . . .

down . . .

into . . . what?

She is very small.

She is tiny and soft and furry and nimble, leaping from rock to rock high above the cave floor, unafraid even though she has no wings.

Below her, the green dragon growls and spins, but it doesn't see her in the dark shadows of the cave ceiling.

Nice try, *she thinks jubilantly. This particular dragon has been trying to catch one of them for days, but with no luck, of course.* Ha ha, big old slow-moving lizard!

"Raven!" She holds on to a stalactite and turns toward the

voice. Of course it's Mole, peeking out of one of the secret upper passages.

"Hey, Mole," she says with a jaunty wave.

"Get in here before the dragon sees you!" he hisses.

Raven sighs, but Mole has enough stress without her adding to it. She leaps neatly to the ledge beside him and crawls through the hole in the wall.

On the other side, the passages are only big enough for humans. These winding tunnels are the safe parts of the cave, which is to say, the boring parts.

"Are you trying to get caught by a dragon?" he asks.

"Of course not," Raven says cheerfully. "I just think it's funny to watch them get all grumpy about it." They set off toward their cave village.

"You mustn't provoke them," Mole argues. "What if one of them catches you? Or gets really mad and smashes down some cave walls and finds all of us? There are too many dragons down here right now. We should stay hidden, not run around poking their noses and asking to be eaten."

Raven rolls her eyes. "Don't you want to know why they're suddenly here? Something is happening in the sky world. Something important."

"Important to dragons, maybe," he says. "Nothing to do with us."

"Unless it's related to the abyss," Raven points out.

"Shhh!" He looks around furtively. "You know the rules!"

"But it's acting weird, and everyone knows it," she says. "I don't think we can keep pretending it's not there."

"Well, if you *would* like to climb down into the deepest, darkest hole in the universe to figure out what those noises are, then go ahead," Mole says. "But leave me out of it — and stop teasing the dragons!" He runs on ahead of her, and she feels guilty for a moment that she's driven him past the edges of his patience once again.

Still. It is strange that so many dragons came crowding into the caves, acting weird, within days of the abyss changing for the first time in years.

Something is happening.

And Mole is wrong. Whatever it is, if it scared the dragons . . . then there's every chance it could be the end of the world for the humans.

— CHAPTER 18 —

"Is she all right?" a voice whispered near Snowfall's ear. "I've never seen a dragon faint before."

"I think Wren *yelled* her into fainting," the dragon's voice said disapprovingly.

"That's me, terrifier of dragons!" said someone else. "She was definitely scared of me, right?"

"No," Snowfall snapped, but she couldn't open her eyes yet. Everything was too strange; her limbs, her scales, her wings all felt wrong, and it was taking forever for her self to settle back into place.

"Wait — did she just understand me?" the third voice said.

They were speaking Human.

Human, a language of its own, not just a series of squeaks and grarghs and gurgles that the scavengers made.

I don't even want to know this word. Human.

"Should we be running awayrrplenerpchirp?" the first voice asked. Halfway through the sentence, the human language faded from Snowfall's brain and her inner dragon breathed comforting frost all through her.

I am Snowfall, she told herself frantically. *Queen of the IceWings. I am a DRAGON. This is really, truly me.*

She sat up, touching her head gingerly. The pale orange dragon was crouched beside her, with the Dragon-speaking human — scavenger — on his shoulder. Pumpkin was standing just behind one of his talons, as if she was prepared to either duck out of sight or run forward and attack, whichever was required.

"Sorry," the dragon said kindly, in Dragon, thank goodness. "We didn't mean to frighten you."

"You DID NOT frighten me," she growled. The scavenger on the dragon's shoulder put her hand on the sword at her belt. "I mean, I'm not scared. I get visions sometimes; that's all that was. It's a magic curse thing." She tugged on the intractable ring.

That seemed very intentional, you rotten accessory. Were you enchanted to prove me wrong every time I have a thought you don't like? Have you ever thrown any OTHER queens into the tiny edible body of something else? Why don't we all know about scavengers, if you have — and if you haven't, WHY ARE YOU TORTURING JUST ME?

"What did you see?" asked the strange scavenger.

"More of you," Snowfall answered, waving one of her wings at the creature. "But I think they were on the other continent." It was harder to hold on to the memories from this vision, because they made so little sense to her dragon brain. She could still *feel* the weird little hairs and flat face and upright balance of the human, but everything it knew, like the details of its life underground, was muddled and bewildering.

But — the dragons hiding in the caves. That sounded like Bryony and her group. And then something about an abyss?

"This is Wren," said the dragon, gently poking the scavenger on his shoulder with one claw. "You've already met Daffodil. And I'm Sky."

"No way," Snowfall said. He blinked innocently, and she added, "Sky the SkyWing? That's completely ridiculous."

"Oh," he said, his face relaxing. "Well, Wren named me, and she didn't know what SkyWings were called then-abouts." He shrugged, as if that made any sense, as if sure, scavengers named dragons all the time, totally normal.

"Winter is going to lose his *entire* mind," Snowfall suddenly realized. "A scavenger that can talk to dragons — I mean, I think his head might literally explode. Arrrrrrrrgh, I guess this means Moon was right." She contemplated not telling anybody about this; it would be insufferable to have to confirm that NightWing's "impressions" of scavenger emotions. But the thought of the look on Winter's face outweighed everything else.

"Wait," said Sky. "What?"

"We should go," Wren said, tugging on Sky's ear.

"No, no, no," Snowfall said. "No way! You CANNOT make me go back to Winter alone to say, 'oh, yes, Pumpkin escaped, but guess what, she has a scavenger friend who speaks Dragon, and a weirdo dragon who speaks scavenger, ah, well, but I let them go, didn't think you'd be interested.' SERIOUSLY."

Wren put her fists on her hips. "And *you* can't make us go back into that city full of dragons to say, 'hello, we escaped, no problem, but we thought it would be great fun to come back and get eaten instead.' SERIOUSLY."

Snowfall thought it was wildly funny that Wren seemed to speak Dragon better than Sky himself did, and that she could even master the exact right growly intonation of *SERIOUSLY*.

"No one's going to eat you," she said. "Obviously! We don't eat things that talk back to us! That would be very unsettling!"

"Guess what's more unsettling," Wren said. "Being eaten!"

"Wren, maybe it would be fun to meet them?" Sky said sweetly. "Maybe they're all nice dragons!"

"Well, not me," Snowfall said. "I'm definitely not nice. I'm probably the least nice dragon in Sanctuary right now, so if *I'm* not going to eat you, most likely nobody else will either."

"And don't you want to talk to more dragons?" Sky asked. "Building human-dragon communication? Isn't that our great quest or something?"

"No, that's *Ivy's* great quest!" Wren protested. "*My* great quest is to be left alone!"

Snowfall didn't know if it was the vision making her soft or this particular scavenger's personality, but she was starting to quite like Wren. *Maybe I should get myself a scavenger pet, too,* she thought.

The corners of her vision went blurry and she glanced down at the ring in alarm. *I mean, not a pet! Scavengers aren't pets! They're intelligent! I meant friend, a scavenger friend!*

To her enormous surprise, the blurriness vanished again, and she did not collapse or have a vision.

Hmmm. Can I actually talk this ring out of giving me visions?

If I convince it I've learned whatever lesson it's teaching me, I guess, she sighed. But still, that was a small, interesting glimmer of hope.

"Tell you what," Snowfall said to Wren. "You don't have to meet the entire city. Just come back and talk to Winter, so he'll believe me. Also, by the way, it's in your best interest to prove to him that scavengers are as smart as dragons, because then he'll stop chasing you and locking you up and giving you silly names."

"I *like* the name Pumpkin," Sky said. "Oooo, I want to know what he would call Wren." His eyes lit up. "Does he have any cute little hats?"

"Enough with the hats!" Wren hollered, whacking his neck, and then shaking out her hand with a grimace that suggested that had been a bad idea. "All right, fine. We will come back with you to meet *one* dragon."

"Excellent." Snowfall swept her wings behind her and led the way to Sanctuary.

Unfortunately, when they got there, Winter was pacing around the outside of the enclosure, lashing his tail, and there were three other dragons with him: Lynx, Cricket, and Qibli, who were all helpfully searching through the grass and bushes. No, wait, four: the small HiveWing was there as well, chasing a white butterfly.

It gave Snowfall a weird shiver to see the baby HiveWing try pouncing on the butterfly, even though she missed. She poked that discomfort for a moment, puzzled, and realized that must have come from Tau or Io, who would see it as a sign of a young HiveWing learning to capture and control SilkWings. *She's just playing with a bug, don't read into it!* Snowfall ordered herself, and by extension all the tangled-up others inside her.

"Snowfall!" Winter cried. "Pumpkin is missing!" He caught sight of Sky behind her. "Who — what —"

"That's not one dragon, that's *five* dragons," Wren hissed at Snowfall.

Snowfall shrugged. "They're all friendly turtles on the inside, though," she said, which earned her a gigantic grin from Sky. "I'm very sure none of these will hurt you, so calm down."

"He keeps saying *pumpkin*," Cricket said, pointing to

Winter, "but what he's describing sounds much more like a reading monkey than a pumpkin to me. I don't know whether I'm looking for an orange gourd or a small furry thing with cute paws."

"*I* can't believe he didn't show you Pumpkin earlier," Lynx said. "He would talk about scavengers *all day* if he could find someone to listen."

"Scavengers," Cricket said, testing out the word.

"Cousin," Snowfall called to Winter, "Pumpkin is fine. Get ready for your entire world to be flipped upside down, though."

Winter tilted his head and took a step toward Snowfall, but Cricket spotted the two scavengers on Sky's back first. She bounded over to them, her eyes as huge as the moons.

"Reading monkeys!" she cried. "He *did* mean reading monkeys! You have them here, too!"

"Is she talking about us?" Wren whispered to Snowfall. "And *what* the heck kind of dragon is that?"

"I mean, can yours read?" Cricket charged on. "Or are they more like regular monkeys? The one I saw was holding something that looked *just* like a book, can you imagine? Monkeys who can read must also be able to write, don't you think? Don't you wonder what they'd write about? Monkey stories! Can you think of anything more fascinating?"

"Yes, actually, if you'd shut up for a moment," Snowfall interrupted. "Try monkeys who can speak Dragon. Although they're not monkeys. We call them scavengers."

"And we call *ourselves* humans," Wren added.

Oh yes, here were the awestruck faces Snowfall was looking for. Cricket and Winter both seemed to be on the verge of floating right off the planet and hitting the moons.

Qibli recovered his voice first. "Did she — did she just —"

"My name is Wren," she said. She pointed to the dragon. "Sky. And that's Daffodil."

Daffodil squeaked something.

"Not Pumpkin," Wren added. "She would like me to say that a couple more times. Daffodil. Definitely not 'Pumpkin.'"

Winter put one talon to his face and rubbed it in a dazed way. "She kept making a noise that *sounded* like 'daffodil,'" he said. "But of course I knew it couldn't *be* 'daffodil,' because *that's impossible*."

Wren chirped something at Daffodil and Daffodil chirped indignantly back, waving her arms.

"Can all humans speak Dragon?" Cricket asked.

"Bandit couldn't," Winter answered. "Could he? Do you know Bandit?" he asked Wren.

She raised her eyebrows at him, and Qibli said, "I think we can safely assume that was not his real name."

"Wren speaks Dragon better than any other human in the world," Sky said proudly. "She's a natural. All that growling and roaring, you know, it matches her personality."

"Do you have books?" Cricket blurted. "I mean, the human I saw was back on the other continent and it looked like it was reading a book, so I just wondered if maybe you read books, too?"

"How is that your first question?" Winter asked.

"I do read books," Wren said. She tipped her head to study Cricket's delighted face and the octagonal spectacles that rested on her snout. "What kind of dragon are you?"

"Did you say 'other continent'?" Sky asked.

"I'm a HiveWing, from Pantala, on the far side of the ocean," Cricket said, waving vaguely westward.

"That's wild that you have scavengers over there, too," Qibli said. "I wonder if they speak the same language as these ones."

"They do," Snowfall said. She'd been replaying her vision in her mind. "They live in the cave systems underneath the savanna. And I think . . . I think they know something about the breath of evil."

— CHAPTER 19 —

Snowfall explained about her vision, about being inside a human on the other continent.

"She said something about an abyss. She said it was acting strangely, whatever that means." Snowfall looked around at the other dragons. "Perhaps it's connected to the mind control and the plant."

"We should find out!" Qibli said excitedly. "That's it! Your Majesty, you found the perfect solution!"

"Did I?" she said. "I mean, of course I did, but you explain it."

"We shouldn't send our armies to fight Queen Wasp," Qibli said. Cricket flinched, and he spread his front talons quickly. "Wait, listen. Armies are for wars where you want to kill as many of their dragons as possible before they kill you. But we don't want to kill their dragons. Most of them are friends and family who wouldn't be fighting if they weren't under Wasp's control. What we need is a way to free them, and not even all the armies in Pyrrhia would be able to do that."

"Sure, but if we send all the armies in Pyrrhia, they could at least kill Queen Wasp," Snowfall said. "Maybe that's all we have to do. I'm very into that plan."

"We don't think killing Queen Wasp will be enough," Cricket said with a little shiver. "There's something or someone else controlling *her*, and that's the thing we really have to fight."

"Still, our armies could help!" Snowfall said. "With those RainWing tranquilizer darts, we could knock out all the HiveWings and imprison them while we work on the freeing-them part and the killing-Queen-Wasp part."

Now Winter was giving her that look she kept getting, as though her horns had turned bright pink and were spouting lemonade.

"WHAAAAAAAAAAAAAAAAT?" Snowfall demanded. "Why is your face DOING THAT AT ME?"

"I'm sorry, Your Majesty," he said, ducking his head. "I just . . . never expected you to be one of the queens who argued *for* helping the Pantalan dragons."

"I am FAMILIAR with the concept of EMPATHY, cousin," Snowfall said frostily.

"Would you two please shut your glamorous IceWing snouts?" Qibli said. "I'm not finished! Listen to my awesome plan! Instead of armies, we have to send a *secret stealth team* of dragons to Pantala. Their mission: to find out the truth about the breath of evil and how to destroy it."

"That sounds . . . much easier said than done," Winter observed.

"I want to go with the secret stealth team!" Cricket said.

"ME!" the little HiveWing shouted from the top of the boulder. "MESTEALTH!" She leaped off the boulder, flapped her wings wildly for a moment, and then somersaulted into the grass. Daffodil crouched and held out one hand, and the tiny dragonet wobbled over to sniff it, warbling cheerfully.

"Find out the truth?" Lynx asked. "How, exactly?"

Qibli pointed at Snowfall. "By going into the abyss."

Everyone stared at him. He flapped his wings with dramatic exasperation. "Come *on*, everybody! Haven't you been listening to Moon's prophecy? *A secret buried far below may save those brave enough to look.* What's farther below than an abyss? Seriously, this one is *much* clearer than the last one!"

"Three moons," Winter said. "I sincerely hate to say this, but I think Qibli might be right."

"Also, bonus, a stealth team mission is something we can do without requiring armies and soldiers from all the queens," Qibli pointed out. "I think we could get everyone on board with this plan."

"And while the secret team is gone," Snowfall said, "we could get our armies ready just in case we *do* need them to fight at some point."

"Far below," Cricket echoed, staring off toward the setting sun. "It *does* make sense, if everything in that vision was true. But how are we going to find this abyss? Do we have to search all of Pantala?"

Qibli scratched his head awkwardly. "Well," he said, "it would be helpful if we had someone who could talk to the scavengers for us." He glanced sideways at Sky and Wren.

"Absolutely not," Wren said. "I don't know what you're talking about, but I'm very sure I don't like the sound of it."

"What?" Sky tore his gaze away from a chipmunk that was adorably nibbling something near his talons. "Sorry? What?"

"We're offering to take you to the other continent," Cricket said. "To meet humans from all the way across the sea! Can you imagine? Just think — what are they like? How different are their lives from yours, and how much is the same? Isn't that just amazing to think about?"

"I'm all right where I am, thank you," Wren said. "I don't need another continent full of people to worry about; this one is quite sufficient."

"But you could save so many dragons," Qibli said. "If you help us find the Pantalan humans, and they can take us to the abyss, and we can stop the breath of evil — I mean, you'd be saving the entire world, basically."

Wren pointed at him. "That does sound fun. Except for the part where I probably get eaten and Sky probably gets evil breath, whatever that is."

Sky snort-chuckled. "Leaf's the one with evil breath! At least first thing in the morning!"

"Hush, you," Wren said, nudging him.

"We won't let you get eaten," Winter said in his most noble voice. "Every dragon on the quest would protect you with his or her life! I would gladly sacrifice myself to keep you safe!"

"Too much," Qibli said, patting Winter's talon gently. "Very heroic and dashing, but you can take it down a notch."

"*I* can take care of myself. Sky's the one I'm worried about," Wren explained. "He is not a 'super-stealth' or a 'fighting evil' kind of dragon. He is a 'but do the bad guys know about pandas because then I bet they wouldn't be evil anymore' kind of dragon."

"Well, but," Sky protested, "I mean . . . pandas! Have you SEEN pandas?"

"Is there any chance you're actually a RainWing?" Winter asked.

"You can't take Sky into a war zone," Wren said, wrapping her arms around his neck as far as they would go.

"I'd be all right," Sky said, nudging her head with his snout. "Everyone else could do the shouty stabby parts, and I could just talk to the humans. And maybe the other continent has something even *cuter* than pandas."

"We have lots of different kinds of monkeys," Cricket said hopefully.

Snowfall could tell that Wren was not buying any of this, and that she was the one who made the decisions for these two. *Think like a scaven — human*, she thought. *Remember what it felt like to be Raven. What did they want? What did they worry about? What do I know that could change Wren's mind?*

"Human," she said. "I mean, Wren. Listen. What if the agreement went two ways? You and Sky help us save dragons, and we help you save humans."

Wren glanced over at Daffodil, who was tossing the baby HiveWing up in the air and then catching her again as the dragonet giggled. "Keep talking."

"All the queens of the dragon tribes are here in Sanctuary right now," Snowfall said. "In exchange for your help, we could issue an edict that dragons are no longer allowed to hunt or eat humans in any of our kingdoms."

"Ooooooooooooooooooo," Sky said, nudging Wren again. "Ivy would *loooooooooove* that!"

"Every human would love that," Wren said. "But would it work? Do dragons listen to their queens? How would it be enforced? And what if the next queen reverses the edict?"

"*My* tribe listens to their queen," Snowfall said haughtily. "And there isn't going to *be* a 'next queen' for a VERY long time."

"It's worth a try, isn't it?" Qibli said to Wren. "It would probably save a lot of humans, even if some dragons disobeyed the orders."

"I *love* this plan," Sky said happily. "Let's *do* this plan!"

"It is a great idea," Qibli said to Snowfall.

"See?" Lynx said, thwacking Qibli's wing with her own. "I told you. Best queen ever."

Snowfall fluffed out her wings and gave Winter a "who's the best cousin for the throne NOW?" face, which was a little unwarranted since he'd never shown any sign of preferring Crystal. But he was the nearest IceWing she could make a smug face at.

Truthfully she thought the other queens would probably issue an edict like that with or without Wren's agreement to come to Pantala. Once they realized that scavengers could think and read and talk like dragons, she assumed they wouldn't be at all interested in eating them anymore.

"No more pet scavengers either," Wren said, wagging her finger at Winter again. She might have noticed the wistful glances he kept casting at Daffodil. "That should be in there, too."

"Unless they *want* to be dragon pets," Sky said. "Or the hats are *very cute*."

"Do humans love hats?" Winter asked hopefully. "I could get P — Daffodil a hat!"

"No, we do NOT love hats." Wren glared at Sky. "And Daffodil would be the worst pet, really. She might be willing to stay and practice her Dragon with you for a while, though, if you'd actually *listen* and not lock her up."

"And if you let her keep playing with Bumblebee," Cricket observed. The HiveWing dragonet was now curled around

Daffodil's shoulders, winding the human's hair between her claws.

"I promise," Winter said meekly. "No more pets. I'll tell everyone else." He gave Qibli a suddenly horrified look. "Smolder has a pet human! He's had her for *years*! We must fly at once to convince him to free her!"

"Oh, no, she's fine," Wren said. "We've met, and she's happy, don't worry about her."

"Hmph," Winter said, subsiding.

"Let's go talk to the other queens," Snowfall said. "You two can stay here and think about our offer, and we hope you'll still be here to discuss it when we return." She beckoned imperiously to Qibli and swept across the clearing with Lynx trotting along beside her.

Will this work? Snowfall flicked her tail. *Sending a small group of dragons over to Pantala, armed with a talonful of tranquilizer darts, a line from a prophecy, and a scavenger?*

She thought of the chillingly malevolent feel of Wasp's brain, and the evil tendrils she'd felt wound all the way through it.

Is there anything that can save Tau and Bryony and Blue and Io and everyone else?

Or is the prophecy right . . . and none of the tribes will survive?

PART THREE

WALLS OF ICE

CHAPTER 20

The night before their return to the Ice Kingdom, Snowfall had no dreams at all. She slept peacefully until quite some time past dawn, and woke up slowly to rustling leaves, bars of sunlight, and several worried IceWing faces ducking away as she opened her eyes.

Except for two. Lynx and Crystal stayed where they were, watching her. Lynx looked disgustingly cheerful, as usual, and Crystal wore a mask of boredom over something Snowfall now realized was nervousness. Her tail kept twitching, and she glanced at the trees occasionally as if she was thinking about flying away.

"Good morning," Snowfall said, stretching. "Crystal, I have made a decision. If you would like to return to the Ice Kingdom anytime, for any reason, I give you my word I will not have you killed. Wait — unless you come with an army to try and steal my throne. Then I will probably have to kill you. So I guess I mean, if you would like to return to the

Ice Kingdom anytime for any not-deposing-Snowfall reason, you are welcome, and you'll be safe."

"Oh," Crystal said. "I — thank you. If it helps, I have no intention of ever bringing an army to steal the throne. I really don't want it."

"Weirdo," Snowfall said, but nicely. "Also, you have my permission to marry Gharial."

"I wasn't aware I needed that," Crystal said wryly, "but thank you for that as well."

Snowfall waved one talon. "Permission, blessing, whatever you want to call it. Your queen will not be mad. You will not be banished."

Crystal tipped her snout down for a moment, then looked back up with suspiciously shiny eyes. "I appreciate that," she said.

"It is very silly," Snowfall said, "that you are more emotional about me approving your MudWing than you were about me promising not to kill you."

"I know," Crystal said with a little laugh, wiping her eyes. "I just came to say good-bye. I heard you're flying home today."

"Yes," Snowfall said. "We had an excellent council of queens yesterday and I was an extremely excellent queen part of it, wasn't I, Lynx?"

"Absolutely marvelous," Lynx said.

"We need a better name than 'secret stealth team,' though," Snowfall said. "Anyway, the queens agreed that we'll all stop eating scavengers, and we chose the group that's going to go to Pantala to search for the abyss and the Pantalan humans. Which means they'll have to carry another map back over to that continent, but it can't be helped. Personally, I think they should eat it when they get there."

"I can't believe it about scavengers," Crystal said, looking a little green. "When I think . . . I just can't think about it."

"I have a feeling a lot of dragons are going to be pretty horrified," Lynx said.

"And some others are going to violently deny that it's true, so that they don't have to feel bad about themselves," Snowfall pointed out. "But that is a problem for another day. Today my problem is that going home means I'll have to rearrange all the names on the stupid wall again."

"Oh, wow, the wall," Crystal said with a laugh. "I totally forgot about that."

"How can you forget about the wall?" Snowfall said, shocked. "You're still near the top of the First Circle! I kept you there!"

Crystal shrugged. "I guess when you're away from it for long enough, you realize how pointless it is."

Lynx made a face at Snowfall, like "this is what I was saying! Remember that time you totally yelled at me? I was totally right and look, she thinks so, too!"

"Well, fine," Snowfall said. "Say good-bye to your MudWing for us. I must go be inanely polite to the other queens for half the day before we can leave."

"You sound a lot more like yourself today," Lynx observed.

Was that true? Maybe a night with no visions had brought her back to herself completely. Maybe the visions were over? Snowfall tugged hopefully on the ring.

Nope. Still stuck. She'd have to tell the guards to stay close enough to catch her in case she suddenly fell out of the sky on the flight home.

The queens had decided that *face a great evil with talons united* meant they should send one dragon from each tribe on the mission. Personally, Snowfall thought a team of ten dragons wasn't the *most* stealthy idea, but she wasn't about to wade into the question of which tribes should be left out.

Some of the choices were easy — they only had one HiveWing, for instance, and Sky had to be the SkyWing, and Tsunami didn't bother to ask anyone's permission to be the SeaWing, although Queen Coral seemed fine with it once she arrived.

Luna and Sundew convinced Hazel to let them be the SilkWing and LeafWing representatives. Queen Thorn looked worried when Qibli said he wanted to go, but she agreed that he was the best choice. Snowfall could see how much she didn't want to lose him.

Queen Moorhen offered a brawny MudWing nearly twice the size of most of the other dragons, a volunteer named Bullfrog. Queen Glory had to choose two dragons; she settled on a serious-looking RainWing with the very silly name of Pineapple, and Moon for the NightWing.

Snowfall had the hardest choice, in her opinion, because she had two IceWings who *really* wanted to go. On the one talon, she wanted Lynx to come back to the Ice Kingdom with her, to join her new council and keep Snowfall sane. On the other talon, she trusted Lynx more than any other IceWing, and Snowfall knew for certain that Lynx was smart and clever enough to be very valuable on the mission.

On the third talon, Winter was occasionally quite smart, too, and she wouldn't miss him nearly as much. But on the fourth talon, would sending him really count, if he was technically banished and not part of the tribe? Would Snowfall be risking the whole mission, just because she wanted to keep her friend close to her?

She didn't say any of that to them, but she did grouchily admit to herself that *friend* was the right word for Lynx after all.

In the end, she chose Lynx. Winter would be useful in Sanctuary, overseeing the scavenger outreach project and keeping Daffodil safe. Snowfall did not like to think about how Wren would react if she came back from Pantala and someone had accidentally stepped on Daffodil.

So the stealth team was gathered, and there was a ceremony for them that involved a lot of awkward talon-holding and speeches from the queens. *Boring boring*, Snowfall thought, and tried not to look at Lynx too often in case something stupid and wet happened to her eyeballs.

She'll be back. She has to come back.

She watched Sky instead, who was SO EXCITED about all his new dragon friends and his valiant purpose and heroic destiny and absolutely EVERYTHING. Then she realized how much she was going to worry about his sweet, grinning face going into danger, and she had to fix her gaze on Bullfrog instead. There was no risk that she'd get sappy and sentimental about *him*.

When the polite farewells finally began, Snowfall took a deep breath. There was something she had to do, even though it made her anxiety spike right up to the moons.

She crossed the clearing to Sundew, who was sitting with her tail twined around Willow's, holding one of her talons. Willow looked as though she'd been crying all morning.

Sundew tilted her head to meet Snowfall's eyes. "Yes?"

"We don't have weapons like the RainWing darts to offer you," Snowfall said, nodding to the pile that Pineapple was sorting into pouches. "But I wanted to give you something else, since I'm guessing you're going to be the leader of this team, or you should be, no matter what Tsunami thinks. And you're right that our magic should have been able to help you, and if any piece of magic can help defeat that thing over there, I think you should have it."

She unclipped the gift of stealth from her wrists and Sundew sat up, shining like the northern lights. "Magic?" the LeafWing echoed.

"This is how I made my army invisible," Snowfall said, passing the wristbands to her. It felt a bit like snapping off her horns and passing them over, after so many days of having the reassuring magic weight of them on her arms. "We call them the gift of stealth, and since stealth is literally in the name, and that's your whole mission, I mean . . . it just makes sense."

Sundew put them on reverently, the pale silver metal strange against her dark green and gold scales. "How do they work?"

Snowfall explained everything from the notes in the treasury, and Sundew practiced turning herself, then Willow, then both of them invisible. When they reappeared, Willow wrapped her wings around Snowfall.

"Thank you," she whispered in Snowfall's ear. "I feel a little less worried now."

What am I doing? Snowfall thought. *Giving away one of the only animus treasures my tribe has? Maybe one of the last ones that will ever be made in this world?*

Giving up IceWing magic . . . to a strange dragon from a faraway land.

Snowfall straightened her shoulders as Willow went back to Sundew's side.

I'm choosing to trust them. This is the right thing to do. They need it to defeat the breath of evil, and we all need them to succeed.

"I'll bring them back," Sundew promised. "When we've won and everyone is safe, I'll return them to you. Thank you, Queen Snowfall."

"Good luck," Snowfall said. She took a step back, glancing at the gift of stealth one last time. And then she turned and went up to the lake to find Winter.

"Hello," she said, startling him into dropping the fish he'd just caught. "I hereby decree that you are not banished anymore. Unless you would like to be. Also, you can go back to that school, if you want to. I still don't care." She hesitated. "But . . . I guess there's a VERY TINY part of me that . . . wantsyoutobehappy," she finished in a rush.

Winter dipped his front talons in the cold lake and smiled down at the water, looking a little surprised and embarrassed and pleased at the same time. "Thank you, Your Majesty," he said.

"Gaah," she said. "It's too weird. Just call me Queen Snowfall."

He laughed, and then his face turned serious again. "Snowfall, you're my queen and the IceWings will always be my tribe, whether I'm banished or not. But Jade Mountain and Sanctuary . . . they've made me feel like I'm part of a bigger tribe. Like I'm worth something more than a place on a wall."

"Hmmm. I *suppose* you are," Snowfall said. "It's *possible* everyone is, but you didn't hear that from me. Good luck with that little Daffodil human. Stay in touch, Winter."

Snowfall made her way through all the polite good-byes to the other queens and eventually found her guards waiting for her, ready to fly. Standing with them was Lynx, who also looked ready to fly.

"Aren't you leaving on a mission tomorrow?" Snowfall demanded, frowning at her.

"Day after tomorrow, actually," Lynx said. "I'm going to fly home with you first and then meet the others on Jerboa's beach."

Snowfall did not let herself make the silly Sky face she felt her inner dragon making. "Oh," she said. "Very well, I suppose that's fine with me. Because you need something from the palace? Dragons to say good-bye to?"

Lynx nudged her side and smiled. "Just want to hang out with you for a couple more days."

Snowfall scrunched her snout at her so that she wouldn't either start beaming or burst into tears. "Well. Fine. All right. I SUPPOSE THAT'S FINE WITH ME, TOO."

It was late in the day when Snowfall and Lynx and the other ten IceWings reached the Great Ice Cliff. Snowfall saw it first, ahead of them in the distance, huge and glowing red-gold in the sunset.

For thousands of years, it's kept all other tribes out of the Ice Kingdom. We always thought it kept us safe. I thought it was so important, I wanted to extend it all around us, so my tribe could huddle safely in our igloos and ice palaces and no one would ever be able to get through our walls of ice.

But if we'd all stayed hidden in the Ice Kingdom,

Darkstalker's plague would have killed us. We needed dragons from other tribes, working together, to recognize his magic and find a way to save us. We needed hybrids like Typhoon, who could cross the wall and were spared the plague, to bring us those earrings.

We only survived because of our connections to the other kingdoms.

Her wingbeats slowed. *And if the breath of evil comes here . . . if it lands in the Ice Kingdom first . . . we may need those connections again.*

Besides, I want to know what happens on Pantala. I want dragons to be able to come tell me!

I want Sundew and Sky to be able to fly right into my kingdom and find me, if they need to.

She veered suddenly into a wind current that dropped toward the cliff. Startled, the others wheeled around to follow her.

Snowfall landed on top of the cliff; she could see the sheer face of it dropping away on either side of her talons. Lynx hovered beside her, beating the air with her wings.

"What's happening?" Lynx asked.

Snowfall adjusted her small, elegant crown. "Did I ever tell you what this does?" she asked, pointing to it. "It's the tiara of strength. All right, all right, stop laughing. It makes me very, very, very strong, so laughing at me is an even less good idea than it usually is! Anyway, my point is that I've hardly gotten to play with it at all, since this turned out not to be the punching-dragons-in-the-snout expedition I thought it was going to be."

"I, for one, am quite glad we didn't have to punch any dragons in the snout," Lynx observed.

"Want to see how strong I am?" Snowfall asked. She slammed her fist into the ice below her.

Cracks shot out from the spot where her talons met the ice, and the surface below her shook. She punched it again, as hard as she could, and then had to lift into the air as the cliff began to shake harder, and chunks of ice broke off and started avalanching down toward the snow below.

Snowfall hit the cliff again and again, triggering more cascades of ice and snow, until she had punched a pretty impressive hole in it, if she did say so herself.

Ooof. Now her fists hurt, and her muscles ached, and she was VERY tired.

But the look on the other IceWings' faces was worth it.

"That's amazing," Lynx said, flying down to swoop through the gap in the cliff, as if to make sure it was real. "Does that break the spell? Can other tribes fly through here safely now?"

"I'm not sure," Snowfall said. "We'll come back soon with many more dragons and tear down the rest of it." She shook out her claws with a wince. "Maybe I will let someone else wear the magic strength tiara, and I will do the ordering-everybody-around part instead."

"Wow." Lynx gathered a talonful of snow and packed it

around Snowfall's claws. "What happened to 'everyone is evil and can't be trusted'?"

Snowfall looked at her severely. "I have been six different dragons and a human this week, and only one of them was evil. I am basically an expert on other dragons now. And with my knowledge of everything, I can now say for a fact that *several* dragons are *not evil after all*."

"*Several* dragons!" Lynx said in mock surprise. "Are you sure?"

Snowfall flicked her with her tail. "I might even say *most* dragons. Still dubious about you, though. Pretty sure that face you make when you think you've won puts you right into the evil category."

"Fair," said Lynx, grinning. "As long as I still win." She glanced up at the darkening sky, where stars were starting to glitter. "It's getting a bit late to fly the rest of the way to the Ice Palace. Maybe we could make camp in the snow. What do you think? One more night away from the palace?"

"Yes. Let's do that," Snowfall said. She turned to the guards. "If that's all right with all of you."

They did a lot of startled blinking before one of them said, "Of course, Your Majesty, whatever you wish is fine with us."

It was pretty thrilling to be back in the Ice Kingdom, to be making their beds in piles of snow again. Snowfall rolled around in hers for a while, cleaning all the dust off her scales, until she felt shiny and cold again.

Then she curled up and stared at the opal ring. It had

been silent all day. Were the visions really gone? If so, why was it still stuck on her finger? Was it just lying in wait to spring a whole bunch of terrible dragons on her at once?

"Hey, magic ring," she whispered. "I put up with all your visions. I told those Pantalan dragons what you showed me. I made peace with scavengers! Is that what you wanted?"

Twinkle, twinkle, smug twinkle.

"I'm all right with no more visions," Snowfall whispered. "No more visions would be totally fine. But if you *do* have to give me another one tonight, could it please be the one I asked for? Can you tell me what happened to animus magic, and why it's not working? If there's a way to fix it, we could use it to help the Pantalan dragons. Or if not . . . then it would be good to know that, too, so we can stop worrying about it, at least. What do you think?"

Twinkle twinkle twinkle, mysterious opal thoughts.

"All right," Snowfall said, feeling her eyelids droop. "Whatever you can do." She yawned "Thanks," and let herself slip into sleep.

— CHAPTER 21 —

It is raining. As always. She hates the Mud Kingdom; hates everything about it, from the gloppy swamp between her talons to the incessant gurgling sound of water coming from somewhere. It's never warm enough and she never feels dry, even when she retreats to her cave. She is constantly worried that Queen Crane might find her and she'll have to flee to yet another kingdom.

But she couldn't stay in the Stronghold anymore. She's not sure she'll ever be able to set her talons in the desert again — at least, not until Queen Scorpion is dead. Which won't be for a long time, thanks to those healing and longevity spells Jerboa was forced to make for her.

I said no when it mattered, though, *she reminds herself.* I saved the SkyWings.

And probably even more dragons than that. Queen Scorpion wouldn't have stopped. She would always want more: more land, more power, more of Jerboa's magic.

It's almost as if she was the one losing her soul, not me.

Jerboa flexes her talons, trying to test herself. Do I feel like murdering anyone today? Not particularly. How about some senseless violence, is that on the agenda? Don't think so. How do we feel about tiny dragonets? Still think they're cute? No impulse to kill any of those, right?

She sighs and rests her head on her claws. She's always wanted a dragonet of her own, but Queen Scorpion kept her away from other dragons. And now that she's a fugitive, that dream is even further away than ever.

Unless I use my magic.

She sits up, startled to full alert by the idea.

I could do that. I think I could. I could enchant a rock to turn into a dragon egg — would that work? Maybe it needs to already contain some kind of life . . . I've never brought something to life before. That might be on the list of things animus magic can't do.

But I *could* steal someone else's egg and change the dragon inside into a SandWing like me.

Hang on. That might have been an evil thought.

She rubs her temples, reviewing the choices.

Right, yes: Stealing someone else's egg would be bad.

What if I found a different kind of egg — a snake egg or ostrich egg — and changed it into a dragon egg?

And whatever's alive inside, I make it a dragonet? My own dragonet, who would love only me, forever?

She is so delighted with this plan that she almost runs out into the rain to find an egg right away. But she stops herself on the threshold of the cave.

Wait. Be cautious. It would not be safe for a dragonet to be part of my life right now. If Scorpion found us, she could use it against me.

Bide your time, Jerboa. Scorpion's not the only one enchanted with longevity. I could live forever if I wanted to.

If I'm patient, she'll be gone, and then I can create my dragonet and we could return to the Kingdom of Sand and live in peace.

Yes. Really good plan. Not evil, right?

Right. Not evil.

Hugging herself with her wings, she rolls against the cave wall and falls asleep dreaming of her beautiful dragonet.

She is standing in the desert again at last. Sixty years of hiding was quite long enough. And quite long enough for anyone to be queen, especially the power-mad kind.

Queens die in their sleep of unexpected heart attacks all the time. It might have happened at any moment even without any magic help.

And really, I mean — sixty years. More than long enough.

Her daughter is perfect, and now she is perfect here, in this perfect place, surrounded by sand and wind and wide wide open sky.

"Welcome home," she says.

Jerboa the third doesn't answer. She is in a bit of a snit because she just found out about Jerboa the second, which was an accident. Jerboa herself, the first Jerboa, hadn't planned to ever talk about the daughter who went wrong. Because it didn't matter. *She was gone, and now Jerboa and the next Jerboa were together and they could just be happy, couldn't they?*

"I want a different name," says the smaller Jerboa. "One of my own."

"Why? Jerboa is a lovely name."

"Because I WANT to be my OWN DRAGON," she huffs. "Not just one of your hundreds of copies of you."

"I haven't made hundreds of copies of me," Jerboa argues. *Although, come to think of it, she could, couldn't she? She could test them out and see which ones are pleasant company and which ones end up as sullen grouches. She's sure she was never this bad-tempered, so it's not like the current version is THAT close a copy of her. Maybe a closer copy would be nicer to have around.*

Was that an evil thought? *her mental voice whispers, as if from very far away.*

"You could have made hundreds, and I would never know," little Jerboa points out. "I could be number 847 or something."

Eight hundred and forty-seven dragonets sounds exhausting. Even if she only tried them one at a time, Jerboa wouldn't want to go through that again and again, teaching each one how to hunt, listening to their endless questions.

But I could try a few, until I get a quiet, pleasant one.

"Jerboa doesn't even have a good nickname," *her daughter mutters.* "Jerb? Jerbie? Boa . . . I guess you could call me Boa."

Jerboa shrugs. Ungrateful, that's what this one is. "If I call you Boa," she says, "will you stop sulking and appreciate this lovely desert?"

"Fine," Boa snaps, which doesn't SOUND like not sulking to Jerboa, but she lets it go for the moment.

I don't have to put up with this forever. If she becomes unbearable, I can always start over.

Wait, wait, *whispers the voice*. And then what? You'd kill this one? Didn't we decide once, long ago, that killing dragonets was always evil?

Even my own? *she argues back*. Ones I made myself?

Yes . . . I think so . . .

Hmmm. It is *hard to imagine disposing of this one neatly — and she can't just let her go wandering off. No one can find out that the long-missing SandWing animus is still alive. Jerboa does not want the hassle.*

What if I simply . . . fix her a little, then? Just a little spell to make her more agreeable. Obedient would be a good start. Helpful would be nice, too.

She sinks her claws into the warm sand, picturing how perfect small Jerboa could be.

But . . . evil? *whispers the little voice again*. Maybe?

Shush, you, *she whispers back*. I made this dragon. I can perfect her if I want to. Nobody gets hurt.

No, no, I don't have to worry. That's not evil at all.

She is flying over the ocean, wondering if they should try shark again. The last time it was a bit oily, but this time Boa could prepare it differently.

That was such a good idea, making Boa an excellent cook.

A shame she had to add an extra spell to also make her enjoy *cooking; she'd thought just being good at it would be enough, but no. Boa tends to be lazy. If she could do nothing at all, that would be her preferred life.*

Jerboa thinks she wasn't always like this. When she was little, Boa had so much energy. Perhaps one of the spells went a little awry. Perhaps making her more placid, less argumentative, more likely to say yes to everything . . . perhaps that resulted in a bit of laziness, too.

She'll try again. Calibrating the right personality can be quite difficult, it turns out, even with magic.

She isn't in the mood for shark, after all. She'll make Boa go get them a camel; it'll be good exercise for her.

As she swoops back down to the beach, she spots something odd.

Boa is crouched in the surf building a sand castle . . . but the castle is building itself.

Jerboa flips through several stages of panic before she realizes what's really happening. Boa is using one of the objects Jerboa enchanted — the stone that builds them a new home each time they move.

But for a moment, she thought Boa had her own magic, and that was terrifying.

"What are you doing?" she asks as she lands in a squelch of wet sand.

"Sand castle," Boa replies serenely. Her tail swishes lightly as the waves wash over her talons.

"This is not a toy," Jerboa hisses. She snatches the stone out of Boa's claws. Boa blinks and bows her head.

"Sorry."

"You never touch Mother's magic things."

Boa tips her head and looks slowly up at her. "Can I have magic, too? I think I'd like some magic things of my own."

"No, no, no." Jerboa shakes her head. "Magic isn't safe. It's very very dangerous. Only very special dragons should have it, and that's why it's so rare. Only one animus dragon at a time, that's the rule."

This is a lie, but Boa will never know that. For a while, Jerboa knows, there were five animus dragons coexisting in Pyrrhia — one in the Ice Kingdom, two in the Kingdom of the Sea, one in the Night Kingdom, and herself. She doesn't know exactly what happened to each of them, but they're all gone now. Everyone but her. Sometimes she casts a spell, just to check, but everything is quiet. Peaceful. Much less worrying that way.

Maybe she's a little bit right — maybe that much animus magic in the world at once was like too many dragons drinking from an oasis at the same time. Maybe they sucked all the magic out of the world. Or maybe the magic is taking a break, waiting for a future generation of dragons before letting another animus hatch.

"There are rules?" Boa says. "About the magic?"

Three moons, she talks SO SLOWLY. It's like all her words have to wade through the MudWing swamps to make it out of her mouth.

"Absolutely," Jerboa says. "One animus dragon at a time — if there are too many, can you imagine how dangerous that would be? They could get in a fight, start throwing spells around, and destroy the whole world by accident!"

"But," Boa says even more slowly, "one animus dragon could also destroy the whole world, just by herself."

"You don't have to worry about that," Jerboa says. "I'm the only animus dragon right now, and I'm not going to destroy anything."

Boa looks out at the sea, thinking something at the speed of fossils forming. "Couldn't I have just . . . a little bit of magic?" she says finally.

"Magic is also dangerous for your soul, remember?" Jerboa says. "I want to protect your soul, sweetheart. Let me do all the magic and take all the risk on myself, and you stay safe."

"All right," Boa says with a sigh, and Jerboa can sense that one of her spells is kicking in — the one that stops Boa from arguing with her. That was a great one.

Still, this Boa definitely needs a few tweaks. And something to make her stop growing. Jerboa enchanted herself to stop at a normal dragon size. If they both live for thousands of years, as Jerboa is planning, it would be very inconvenient if they wound up absurdly gigantic. She'll make Boa stop just a bit smaller than her, so they'll always look like mother and daughter.

Maybe she could add a little fear into the mix as well. If Boa is more scared of animus magic, she won't keep asking for it. And then she'll keep her grubby talons off Jerboa's stash of magic items. Yes, this is a good idea.

Did she once have second thoughts about her magic spells? Wasn't there once a voice in her head that asked . . . something?

She shrugs it off. It probably wasn't important.

She is curled beside the campfire at night, with stars twinkling overhead and Boa nestled against her side. Boa is small again, and Jerboa has tripled the dragonet's usual love for her, so she's extra cute and affectionate. It was getting boring having another full-grown dragon around who never did anything new or surprising. Shrinking her down and starting her over as a two-year-old dragonet has made things much more fun for the last couple of years.

They've both been alive a very, very long time. Over eight hundred years? Can that be right? Jerboa tries to think. Boa has started over as a dragonet several times in those centuries. And Jerboa has lightly kept track of any other animus dragons over the years.

She spotted two in the Night Kingdom — the granddaughter of a dragon named Whiteout, and then that dragon's great-grandson. None in the Ice Kingdom in all that time. One in the Kingdom of the Sea, in the royal family, but she didn't live very long after having her own eggs. Jerboa doesn't know why; she hasn't gone digging for more information. As long as they don't find out about her or do anything earth-shattering, she can ignore them.

"Mother, I think you should make me an animus dragon," Boa chirps out of nowhere.

THIS again? Jerboa thought she'd stomped down all of Boa's curiosity about magic. But it keeps coming up, year after year, despite all the memory wipes and implanted nightmares and personality adjustments. What is wrong with this dragonet? Why can't Jerboa fix it?

She sighs. "If you did have magic," she asks, "or, let's say, if you could cast just one spell, what would it be?"

Boa thinks and thinks and thinks. Rewinding her age made her a faster thinker again, but she's gotten slower with each new spell since then.

"I know!" she says sweetly. "It would be a teleportation spell. One that would bring me home to you anytime I wanted, no matter where I was."

"Aww," Jerboa says, snuggling her closer. "But you don't need that. We're never apart."

Is that a shadow flickering across Boa's face?

"I know," she says. "It would be just in case. Just in case something very bad happened, and we got separated."

Jerboa is pleased. "I can make that for you," she says. She plucks a seashell from the sand, a pale fan shape edged with dark pink.

"Can't I —" Boa starts, but Jerboa gently taps her snout with her tail, and she falls silent.

It only takes a moment, and the spell is cast. This seashell will bring Boa to her mother instantly, at just a flicker of a thought from either one of them.

It's quite neat, actually. Six hundred and twenty years ago, and four hundred years ago, and two hundred and fifty years ago, and a few other times — Jerboa can't remember exactly — Boa tried to run away.

She doesn't remember any of that misbehavior now, of course. Each time Boa runs, she thinks it's the first time. And it has been a real pain in the tail to drag her back, so it's perfect that now Jerboa will be able to do it with a snap of her claws.

Jerboa pokes a hole in the shell, threads a coconut-fiber rope through it, and loops it over Boa's neck.

"There," she says. "See, you don't need magic. Just ask me for whatever you need, and if I think it's a good idea, I'll make it for you."

Boa nods faintly. She doesn't seem as delighted with the gift as Jerboa would like. For a moment, Jerboa considers making her more grateful — but really, it's too late now. Boa has ruined what could have been a very nice moment.

Jerboa sighs. A thousand years. Maybe it's time for something new.

"What if I made you a brother?" she asks Boa. "Wouldn't that be fun?"

Something flickers in Boa's eyes again. Jealousy? Poor dear, it would be hard to share her mother after all this time. "Would his name be Jerboa, too?" she asks.

Jerboa laughs. "No, of course not. What do you want him to be like? Funny? Clever?"

Boa traces a shape in the sand with her claw. "You can do that?" she asks. "Make him turn out any way you want?"

"Of course," Jerboa says. "We can even make him love to do all the boring stuff we hate, like gathering firewood or cracking the lobster shells."

Boa stares at her talons with a strange expression. "I love gathering firewood," she says in an odd voice.

Oh, that's right. Jerboa added that to the spell a little while ago, when she got tired of either doing it herself or listening to Boa whine about it.

"Something else, then," she says. "Whatever we don't want to do. We can also make him age very slowly so he stays a cute little dragonet for as long as we want. Oh, and we'll make him a really good sleeper, so he'll nap easily and fall asleep whenever he starts fussing. Not like you, Miss Up All Night."

Boa tips her head up to the stars. "But . . . I sleep really well," she says. "I sleep all night and sometimes during the day. I'm a 'really good sleeper.'"

"Of course you are now," Jerboa says impatiently. "So what do you think? Wouldn't you like a new toy to play with?"

Her daughter doesn't answer for a boringly long time. Just as Jerboa is about to snap at her, she suddenly turns and burrows under Jerboa's wing.

"No," she says. "No, thank you, please. I don't want

a brother. I like it just us. I want to be your only dragonet. Please?"

Jerboa is surprised. Well, this is her own fault, phrasing it like a question instead of presenting the idea in a way that Boa couldn't argue with.

Anyway, it's fine. Boa is enough entertainment on her own, especially during the periods when Jerboa makes her a talented musician or storyteller. Another dragonet would probably be a lot of trouble.

Boa is trembling, shivers running through both their scales.

"All right, all right," Jerboa says. "Just us. No more dragonets. Don't worry." Look at her, sounding all nurturing and kind. She's such a great mom.

"Promise?" Boa asks.

"I promise," Jerboa says easily. It's always easy to make promises to Boa, since she can erase them from Boa's mind just as easily. If Jerboa decides she does want another dragonet one day, she'll have one, and Boa won't complain or even remember this conversation.

For now, she'll have to think of something else to make their lives interesting. They haven't abducted an enchanted servant in a while. Maybe a RainWing this time. That would be pretty, and they don't eat very much. Yes, that would be a nice change of pace around here.

She is very tired. They have been flying all day to get to their summer hut, and they weren't able to stop at an oasis on the way because there were so many SandWings milling about below. Every century it seems like there are more and more dragons everywhere. Jerboa prefers to avoid them, after a few awkward incidents where Boa tried to get someone to "rescue" her, of all the nonsense.

Her wings ache and her head is fuzzy, and that is the only reason Boa is able to catch her unawares.

Jerboa doesn't realize what has happened at first. She is frozen one step inside the doorway of the cabin. Literally frozen; no part of her can move, and ice is starting to travel rapidly up from her claws.

She whips her head from side to side and finally spots Boa in the far corner, pointing something at her.

The porcupine quills. Boa had gathered them all so carefully in the mountain forest, then bound them together with a length of thin vines. She'd shown them to Jerboa, proud and sweet, and asked for a new spell.

"When I point this at my prey," she'd said, "I want them to freeze in place, so I can catch them more easily."

Jerboa had chuckled at her lazy, lazy daughter, but she'd given her the spell. Why not? Boa hadn't asked for a spell in so many years, and she'd been so good and quiet and biddable lately. Easier hunting was a harmless request.

Or so she'd thought.

"What are you doing?" Jerboa says with a hiss. She catches herself, and in the long pause before Boa speaks, she tries pouring honey through her voice instead. "Boa, dear, you've accidentally used your hunting weapon on me. Let me go."

"It's not an accident," Boa says, trembling. "You're stuck now."

"It seems that way," Jerboa says. She's trying to remember the words of the spell. Does Boa have to say something specific to release the prey? The cold is crawling higher on her legs. She tries to breathe fire on the blocks of ice around her talons, but this is magic ice, and her fire does nothing.

"So now you have to listen to me," Boa says. "I want you to tell me the truth for once. How many spells have you cast on me?"

Jerboa barks a laugh. "I couldn't possibly remember all of them. I've been trying to fix you for literally centuries."

Boa's eyes go a little unfocused for a moment. "Centuries?" she whispers.

Jerboa tries to remember when the last memory wipe was, but she's too cold to think straight. "Yes," she hisses instead. "Nearly eleven centuries."

"Three moons." Boa presses her free talon to her eyes. "Why don't I remember that?"

Jerboa would shrug if she could move her shoulders.

"Because you keep erasing my memory," Boa answers herself. "That's why I get so confused. That's why you keep talking about things I don't remember at all."

"Let's be fair," says Jerboa. "You also have an uncommonly stupid brain."

"How would we know?" Boa flares. "Is any of it really me

anymore?" She brandishes the quills at Jerboa. "I only love you because of magic," she says. "Right? You've been enchanting me to love you."

"No, that's all real," Jerboa lies, silkier now. "If you love me so much, let me go." She looks down at the ice that now encases her legs and tail. Her scales are so cold. Her wings are raised slightly, immobile, but the ice will reach them any moment.

"It's not fair to make me love you when you don't love me at all." Boa angrily wipes her tears away.

"I love you when you're not like THIS," Jerboa points out. "You're exceptionally unlovable right now."

"Well," Boa says. "I guess we can fix that, can't we? Just a little tweak here, a correction there — all you need is this, right?" She holds up an unrolled scroll.

Uh-oh. Her Boa spells.

She should have been more careful, kept them all in her head the way she used to. But it was getting so hard to keep track of them, and some of them were complicated . . . it was just easier to make an enchanted scroll where she could write down whatever she wanted to change about Boa, and it would happen.

But Boa wasn't supposed to see it. She wasn't supposed to get her claws on it.

"Where did you find that?" Jerboa snaps.

"MORE OBEDIENT," Boa reads from the scroll. "EVEN MORE OBEDIENT. CHEW WITH HER MOUTH CLOSED. STOP ASKING

ABOUT TALKING TO OTHER DRAGONS. FORGET THAT OTHER DRAGONS EXIST. REMEMBER THAT OTHER DRAGONS EXIST AND STOP ASKING INANE QUESTIONS. ALWAYS LET MOTHER HAVE THE BIGGER FISH." *She narrows her eyes. "This certainly explains a lot."*

Jerboa has never been so cold.

"Guess what?" Boa says. "It turns out, anybody can add notes to this scroll. Watch." She picks up Jerboa's quill and writes on the scroll. "GRE-EN TAIL BAR-B," *she says slowly as she writes.*

Her tail barb turns a beautiful shade of emerald green.

"See? Exciting, isn't it?" Boa writes on the scroll again. "NORMAL COLOR TAIL BARB." *And her tail goes back to normal.*

Jerboa can't feel her wings. The ice is up around her neck now; she can't even move her head to look at the rest of her.

"But you know what I really want?" Boa says. "More than a green tail, Mother? You might remember this, because I've asked for it before. More than once, I think. Maybe quite a lot, in all those memories you erased.

"I'd like to be an animus dragon."

No! Never!

Jerboa tries to cast a spell with her mind. She tries to rip the scroll out of Boa's claws, but it only flutters feebly.

"Oh, sorry to disappoint you — for what, the eight millionth time?" Boa says as the quill snaps in half. "You actually can't stop me from writing it down. Because I already did."

She looks down at the quill with a smile, and it smooths back into one piece.

She's not going to save me, *Jerboa realizes for the first time.* Not ever. This isn't a negotiation. It's a final performance. *Boa has freed herself from her mother's spells. She doesn't need Jerboa anymore.*

These are my last moments, after all this time.

She finds she's not as sad as she would have expected. She has lived a really, really long time. And most of it was quite delightful, when it wasn't irritating.

"Good-bye, Mother," Boa says, and she actually looks much sadder than Jerboa feels. She's crying, but Jerboa doesn't know if those are real tears, or ones caused by the spell that makes Boa love her.

I only have a moment.

One last spell.

Not to save myself. Just to make sure that Boa isn't as triumphant as she thinks. Something to ensure she never, never forgets me.

She casts the spell on Boa herself, making her daughter her last animus-touched object.

And then she is gone.

~ CHAPTER 22 ~

She is free.

She can't believe it.

Boa steps toward the block of ice that has her mother trapped inside. It is fascinating to see her like this, through the bubbles and glaze of the ice walls. It's hard to see her expression, although Boa will always remember the contorted fury on her face.

I did it. I tricked her. I freed myself. Finally, after all this time. *Longer than she could possibly have guessed.*

I'm the only Jerboa now.

She hesitates, then writes in the scroll: RETURN ALL BOA'S MEMORIES. GENTLY, *she adds in a hasty scrawl.*

It's still too much.

It's so much.

All the times they fought, and Jerboa just flicked the memories away like bugs so Boa would be pleasant again.

All the promises she made and broke with a snap of her claws.

The conversation about making a brother came back, and Boa clutched her stomach — did it ever happen? Was there another damaged dragonet in their past, or had she convinced her mother and spared someone else her fate?

No brothers appeared; no sisters either. Boa was alone with her mother throughout all the centuries of memories.

But there were servants here and there — dragons that Jerboa kidnapped and enchanted. Boa had loved some of them. She would have run away with them if she could have.

Her memories gave her no clues about what happened to them when Jerboa was done . . . did she wipe their memories and throw them back out into the world? Or something worse? All Boa could see were days where she was happy, building sand castles with a RainWing or swimming with a SeaWing, and then the next day they'd be gone, along with all her memories of them.

I have had friends. I just . . . never knew it.

Maybe she can cast a spell to find them. Maybe some of them are still alive. Maybe she can restore their memories, and they'll be so happy to see her.

What if I search for them and find out something terrible, though?

She's not sure she's ready to face every truth about her mother right now. And there are so many other, less traumatizing things she can do with all her wonderful magic. She can make everyone on the whole continent be friends with her! She can make herself queen of the Kingdom of Sand, if she wants to.

She has all the power her mother had, but she's not going to use it to torture one dragonet for hundreds of years. She's going to use it to be happy. To have a completely different life.

But first things first: She needs to get this frozen monster out of her doorway.

Boa touches the shell around her neck. It gives her instant teleportation to wherever her mother is — the first spell Jerboa ever made at her request. That could still be useful, if she puts her mother in the right place.

She rests one talon lightly against the chilly ice wall and looks through the dark whorls to where she thinks she can see her mother's eyes.

"I enchant this block of ice to bury itself under this hut and stay frozen there forever."

The ice and her mother vanish and the hut shakes slightly, as though something is settling in the sand below it.

But Boa doesn't even get a moment to be thrilled. Pain lances through her, sharp and blinding, and she shrieks at the unexpected agony.

When the first wave of pain passes, she opens her eyes, gasping, and sees that one of her claws is gone. It's been sliced off as if someone took a hatchet to it, and there is blood EVERYWHERE, although the claw itself has vanished into thin air.

"What?" she whispers. "What?"

Did she cast the spell wrong? Maybe she was accidentally

touching the ice block with that talon, and it took a piece of her with it?

Or . . .

No. No, no, no.

Somehow she knows, in a space beyond knowing. She can't see the shape of it yet; she still has to figure out how and what exactly this is, but she is certain of one thing.

Her mother did this to her.

She is sitting by the freshwater pond, washing the blood off her newest stump. Six claws gone. When she has lost all of them, what will go next? Her ears? Her horns? Her tail barb?

Her wings? She shudders.

She has to be so, so careful with her spells. There's no way to know which one will cause enough damage to kill her.

She lost her second claw trying to heal the first one, and it only half worked. The wound closed, covered over with a shiny new layer of scales, but her claw did not grow back.

She used a normal bandage on the second injury and thought for a long time.

Her third claw: sacrificed for information. She enchanted a scroll to truthfully answer any question she asked of it. Through the pain and the spinning stars around her head, she made it tell her what her mother had done.

One final curse. She should have expected it, should have enchanted something to protect herself. But she'd had to move fast when she found the Boa-changing scroll in the piles of bags her mother had forced her to carry across the desert. Her mother was so rarely careless, or perhaps Boa was rarely smart and alert enough to catch her when she was.

And now Jerboa has left her this: a last spell that was a masterpiece of awfulness. Every time Boa tries to use animus magic, she will lose a piece of herself, bit by bit, until she dies of her wounds. The spell specifies that the pieces could not grow back, even with magic, and it is reinforced with words of binding that mean there is no way to reverse it or fight it.

Boa tried anyway, which is how she lost claws four and five. It didn't seem fair that she could be injured by spells that didn't even work.

Her mother learned a lot over the years, about what animus dragons could do to each other, and how to word spells so other dragons couldn't break them. Boa remembers all the horror stories now — everything her mother told her to try to scare her away from animus magic. But she'd never taught her anything. Boa knows nothing about protecting herself as an animus.

And I'm not a normal animus. I'm cursed.

All right. So. She can live without magic. She is still free of her mother. This is her chance to have the normal life she always wanted — free in the world, meeting other dragons. Maybe it wouldn't be the glamorous enchanted whirlwind she'd imagined, but it would be a thousand times happier than her life up to now. She would be herself. She would choose her own path. She would be free.

At that point she had looked at her maimed talons and realized it would be hard to walk into any dragon village and make friends looking like this. She'd have a lot of explaining to do.

So, then, good-bye to her sixth claw as a new spell was added to the shell necklace, casting a glamor so that she looks normal and intact to any dragons who see her. No one will ever see what her mother did to her, or know how much pain she is in.

Boa still has several objects her mother enchanted, and she knows what about half of them do. Her information scroll can tell her the rest. She might even be able to sell a few of them to a queen somewhere, if she dares to risk it.

And if she's ever in danger, one thought will bring her right back here, to this hut by the ocean, to the floorboards that cover her mother's grave. Where she can dance and dance and no one will ever tell her to stop or cast a spell to make her fall over or enchant away her love of music for a hundred years.

"I hope you didn't die thinking you'd won, Mother," she says out loud. "Because unlike you, I can control myself. I don't need to use my magic. I'm going to be happy, despite everything you've done to me."

She spreads her wings and lifts into the sky.

She is taking a break from other dragons. She does this occasionally — goes back to her hut for fifty years or longer, until everyone she's met this time around has forgotten about her and she can come back as someone new.

It might have been longer than fifty years this time, though. Has it been closer to a hundred? It's so peaceful on her beach, all alone with the waves. In the cities, around other dragons, she is constantly tempted to use her magic, even knowing the pain it will cause her. But here she never thinks of spells she wishes she could use. She can just be.

She has one friend, a dragon who knows the truth about her. They met by accident before Glacier became queen, but Glacier is not like other queens. She believes in solving her own problems, and she knows how dangerous animus magic can be. She also knows the cost Jerboa has to pay every time she uses her magic. Jerboa took off her glamor once, so Glacier could see her as she really is. She was surprised when Glacier cried. No one has ever felt sorry for her before, or told her that it's not fair, everything she went through.

In all the years they've known each other, even through the recent war, Glacier has never asked Jerboa for a single spell.

Once, Jerboa asked her about that, and Glacier said, "You should save your magic. Someday, the world might really need it, and you'll be the only dragon who can save everyone."

Jerboa had laughed. "Me? Like a hero?"

"Why not?" Glacier had answered. "Don't you think you're here for a purpose?"

Two thousand years was a long time to wait for a "purpose," Jerboa thinks. Maybe she'll have to invent one, eventually.

She is strolling down the empty beach toward the water,

thinking about what kind of fish she'll catch for dinner, when the universe suddenly crumples inward, and an unfamiliar voice says, clear as a bell:

"Bring them here. Every animus dragon in all the seven tribes. Bring them here to my throne room right now."

And before she can think or breathe or run, she finds herself standing in a sunlit black marble throne room.

In front of her is the largest dragon she's ever seen, a NightWing-IceWing hybrid, menace radiating off him. He has his back to her, and as she appears, three more dragons appear in front of him — two SeaWings and another NightWing, all looking completely terrified.

Jerboa doesn't hesitate. Centuries of reacting to fear have trained her well; she is barely in the room for a moment before she seizes her necklace and whisks herself home again.

She is in her hut, her heart pounding. Her claws sinking into the weathered wooden floor, which she has replaced several times over the years, but always in the same spot. Where her mother is buried.

Thank you, Mother. For once, one of your spells has saved me.

The magic has brought her home, but is she actually safe? Who was that?

And all those other dragons — are there really five animus dragons in Pyrrhia right now? Didn't Mother say the limit was one? How is this possible?

She scrambles over to her trunk and tosses everything in

it aside to get to her answers scroll. "Tell me who that was," she says.

The writing goes on for a while. The scroll is usually very concise, but it seems to have a lot to say about this Darkstalker. His past, his history — he was alive back when my mother was, she thinks — the spell that tucked him away, the mistake that freed him, the NightWings who follow him.

"What does he want with animus dragons?" she asks.

TO CONTROL THEM, the scroll answers. TO USE THEIR MAGIC INSTEAD OF HIS OWN, TO PRESERVE HIS SOUL. AND TO BE SURE THAT THEY CAN NEVER BE ANY THREAT TO HIM.

Jerboa shudders, feeling sick. What if he'd been facing her? What if he'd gotten his claws on her and forced her to use her magic? What if he found it amusing to watch her slowly sliced into pieces until she died?

I have to protect myself against him. I have to cast something to make myself invulnerable to his spells. Or something to make me more powerful than him.

She reaches for one of her copper bracelets, then hesitates, struck by a chilling thought.

"Why did he summon all the animus dragons right now?"

BECAUSE HIS MAGIC TOLD HIM SOMEONE WAS CASTING ANIMUS SPELLS, AND HE WAS AFRAID THEY MIGHT BE AGAINST HIM.

She asks quietly, "He can tell when someone uses animus magic?"

YES.

"Can he sense me right now?"

NO. HIS SPELL ONLY SEARCHES FOR NEW ENCHANTMENTS.

"How can I protect myself against him?"

THAT ANSWER IS NOT AVAILABLE YET.

She knew it would say that. It can't see the future or tell her what's going to happen; it is sort of useless when she needs to hide or make plans or, for instance, when there's a big ominous magic user haunting the land. Once she tried asking it: "how long will I live?" and it answered: UNTIL YOU DIE, which was neither comforting nor helpful.

Maybe this is it. Her purpose. Maybe she's the only dragon in Pyrrhia who can stop him. If she can come up with just the right spell . . .

"Is this my purpose?" she asks the scroll, knowing what it will say.

THAT ANSWER IS NOT AVAILABLE YET.

I could kill him, couldn't I? With one stroke of magic? Or put him back to sleep under the mountain, the way he was before?

Except . . . if he's as old and dangerous and powerful as her scroll says . . .

"Has Darkstalker protected himself from other dragons' animus magic?" she asks.

YES.

She stands up and starts pacing around the hut. The world is in danger and there's nothing she can do. In a way, it's a relief, *because she would rather hide here. But it feels wrong. It feels as though there should be something, if she can only think of it . . .*

She is outside, recovering her fishing nets before the storm destroys them, when she sees a flare of golden fabric up in the rain clouds.

She watches for a moment, and then sees that it's attached to an unconscious dragon. The wind is blowing her in to shore, some ways south of Jerboa's hut.

Jerboa holds the nets in her talons, thinking for a moment, and then she hurries back inside.

Darkstalker was defeated not long ago. No thanks to her; she did nothing at all. She had the perfect spell, but she was too afraid to use it — that it wouldn't work, that it would backfire somehow and she'd be caught and lose all her freedom again.

But she can't stop thinking about it. Five animus dragons, all alive at the same time. It was so wrong. The universe was out of joint. Even with Darkstalker gone, how could the rest be trusted? What if they turned on one another and took the world down with them?

What if one of them found out about her and forced her to use her magic?

What if any of them were like her mother?

Or, almost equally scary, there's the new IceWing queen. Jerboa wishes she had met Snowfall in time to save Glacier. But she didn't, and now she's linked to this tempestuous, paranoid, terrified young queen who wants to use Jerboa's magic all the time. *She has ideas upon ideas for animus spells that will benefit her kingdom — or at least, keep them walled off and away from all other dragons forever.*

Jerboa doesn't know how many times she can safely say no. What if Queen Snowfall brings her army next time? What if she locks Jerboa up and tortures her into doing magic? She could be on a path to becoming another Queen Scorpion — Jerboa remembers all those stories from her mother very clearly.

She pulls out her scroll. "Who is the dragon that just blew in on the storm?" she asks.

HER NAME IS LUNA. SHE COMES FROM PANTALA, THE LAND ACROSS THE SEA.

Jerboa's ears twitch. A dragon from across the sea? "Why is she here?"

BY ACCIDENT.

"Is she dangerous?"

ONLY TO THOSE WHO THREATEN THE DRAGONS SHE LOVES.

Jerboa likes the sound of that. "Is she my purpose?"

THAT ANSWER IS NOT AVAILABLE YET.

"Does she need help?"

YES.

"Does anyone else know she's here?"

A NIGHTWING HAS HAD A VISION ABOUT HER, AND WILL BE HERE TO FIND HER SOON.

Jerboa is a little nervous of NightWings at the moment. But if she finds Luna first, if she introduces them — she could be part of something important. Bringing the continents together.

Is that a good idea, though?

"Does Pantala have animus magic?" she asks.

NO.

What if the animus dragons here decide to take over Pantala? They could do anything to them, with all that magic here and none over there.

It's time to use her spell.

Time to fix everything.

Dragons can't be trusted with animus magic. Jerboa knows that better than anyone.

She lifts a small glass candleholder down from a shelf. It's curved and glittering, and she loves it, but sacrificing it will make the spell more powerful.

"I hereby enchant this candleholder," she whispers. "When I shatter it, I shatter the power of all current animus dragons. From now on, no new spells cast by any animus dragon alive today will ever work again. Also, from this point forward, I will grow old and die, like any normal dragon. I make this spell irreversible by any animus, including myself."

She cups her talons around the candleholder, then hurls it to the floor.

It explodes into a million shimmering pieces, and Jerboa screams with pain.

Her tail barb is gone. She guesses the price for such a big spell was necessarily higher than all the others she's cast, but it's hard to think through the agony.

Jerboa drags herself outside, trying to stem the flow of blood and get to the pond.

I did it. I think. I hope it worked. *She is in too much pain to test it by trying another spell right now.* With luck, that was my last animus spell ever.

Tomorrow I will find Luna, bring her back here, and keep her safe until the NightWing comes for her.

Then they can figure out how to unite the continents safely, without any magic at all.

And I won't have to be afraid of someone controlling me. I don't have to be scared of what animus magic can do anymore. And no one will ever ask me for anything ever again.

— CHAPTER 23 —

Snowfall was awake before anyone else the next morning, which surprised her, because she felt as though she'd been asleep for centuries. For two thousand years, to be more specific.

That was the first time her visions had done that — dragged her from one into another, on and on through someone's lifetime and then into a different dragon's, hopping through time. But she understood why. She needed to see all of that to understand Jerboa, her Jerboa, and what she'd done.

She made a small pile of snow and started sculpting it into a shape while she waited for Lynx and her guards to wake up. The sun was only a thin line of gold off to the east, and the morning air was gloriously cold. Everything was so quiet, so much quieter than the noisy rustling forest or the incessant background chatter of Sanctuary.

Jerboa broke animus magic. Mostly because of me. It's all gone because she was afraid of what I'd make her do.

Snowfall knew there was more to it than that. She'd felt

everything Jerboa had felt, and she recognized it. She knew so clearly what it was like to be that scared. She'd had her own nightmares about the idea that someone else could take control of you and you'd be powerless — the way Queen Wasp treated the Pantalan dragons, or the way Darkstalker had used his magic against the IceWings (and against his own NightWings, in fact).

And she understood why Jerboa hadn't told anybody. Snowfall herself would have been furious if she'd found out even a few days ago, before the dragons arrived from Pantala. *Before I put on the ring.*

Now, though, she realized she wasn't angry at all. She couldn't imagine being angry at Jerboa anymore, now that she'd experienced a tiny bit of Jerboa's life.

And she wondered if Jerboa was right to do what she did. How could you be sure who could be trusted with animus magic? The first Jerboa had seemed like a good, normal dragon in the first vision, but the magic or the power had obviously changed her over time.

Maybe it's not so terrible if we have to figure out how to save the world without magic.

She hoped they could do it, the dragons who were on their way to Pantala. She'd do what she could over here, preparing her army in case they were needed.

And maybe soon she'd visit Jerboa, just to check on her. It seemed like she needed a friend.

That had never even occurred to Snowfall — that Glacier

and Jerboa had just been friends, rather than queen and animus dragon who served her. That maybe Jerboa missed Glacier as much as Snowfall did.

"Hey," Lynx said, wandering over to her and yawning at the same time. "What are you making?" She waved her tail at the little snow creature.

"Can't you tell?" Snowfall asked.

Lynx peered at it.

"I'm afraid I'll have to have you executed if you guess wrong," Snowfall added conversationally.

"Add it to my treason list," Lynx replied. "Is it a snail?"

"It is!" Snowfall beamed at it. "In honor of that abso*lute*ly ridiculous SkyWing."

"It is suuuuuuuuuuuuper cute that you keep thinking about him," Lynx teased, and Snowfall threw a clump of snow at her. "All your guards are awake, by the way, and looking very embarrassed that someone wasn't awake and on watch when you woke up."

Snowfall shrugged. "I was tired, too. I mean, let's give them some stern looks, but I don't feel like decapitating anyone this morning."

Lynx laughed.

On their way back to the palace, Snowfall kept thinking about the two Jerboas — and the fact that the ring had actually answered her question! That was exciting. Even if it had been slightly horrible to experience the first Jerboa's gradual loss of her soul. Snowfall hoped she wouldn't ever become like her, too far removed from other dragons to remember that they had feelings, too.

I need to keep dragons like Lynx close by, to ask me things like: "Wait, is that maybe evil?" in case I forget to.

They swooped down through the gates, and Snowfall waved at the guards as she flew by. They both looked startled, and a little nervous, but those were expressions she was pretty used to seeing on her own IceWings by now. She'd work on that.

Low voices were coming from the throne room, so Snowfall headed there first. That was sort of suspicious, actually. Why would anyone be in the throne room while she was away?

Don't be paranoid, she reminded herself. *Not everyone is out to get me. I am not Queen Wasp.*

She swept through the window and landed right in the center of the grand room. Conversation slammed to a halt all around her.

On one side of the throne stood General Ivory, flanked by a few soldiers, looking fierce and bristly. On the other side were Tundra and Permafrost, calm and gleaming and toothy.

And on the throne itself, wearing Snowfall's hideous crown, was her little sister, Mink.

Snowfall raised her eyebrows at the gathered dragons. "Hello, Mink," she said. "That's way too big for you."

Mink reached up and clutched the crown to her head, her giant eyes blinking quickly.

"We thought you weren't coming back," Tundra said in her slippery whale-blubber voice.

"I said she was!" Ivory growled. "You wouldn't listen!"

"We thought it was highly unlikely that you'd leave a lowly soldier in charge rather than one of us," Permafrost smarmed, flicking his tail between himself and Tundra. "So we assumed something terrible must have happened to you."

"You were wrong," Snowfall said pleasantly, "and now something terrible is going to happen to you. Thank you for trying, Ivory. Mink, budge over, that's my seat."

"No!" Mink yelled, bursting into tears. "I have to be queen! I have to stop the awful hateful terrible bad NightWings!"

Snowfall squinted at her, then exchanged a puzzled glance with Lynx. "The what?" she asked.

"The NightWings!" Mink sobbed. "I hate them so m-much! They're going to hurt us!"

Well. So this made no sense at all. Mink had never mentioned NightWings before, that Snowfall could remember. And Mink loved *everybody*. It didn't even seem possible for Mink to hate someone, let alone an entire tribe.

Was it something I said? Snowfall tried to remember, but she thought she would have noticed if she'd said, "the NightWings are the worst, Mink," and Mink had said, "yeah! let's hate them!"

"Did you do this?" she asked Tundra and Permafrost. "Did you make her afraid of the NightWings?"

Tundra lifted her wings. "We haven't said anything about them. I don't know where this came from."

Snowfall was inclined not to believe her, but Tundra

looked as confused as Snowfall felt, and it was rare to see her aunt have an actual emotion on her face.

"When did she start talking about them?"

"The moment we made her queen," Tundra said. "I mean . . . temporary queen, of course. Just in case you weren't returning."

Uh-huh. A queen you could control a little better than me, I suppose, Snowfall thought. So where did Mink get this new fear of NightWings? If Tundra hadn't said anything . . . but somehow when she became queen . . .

Snowfall strode across the room and knocked the crown off Mink's head. Mink yelped and tried to grab for it, but Snowfall held her at arm's length with the crown in her other talon.

"Aunt Tundra," she said, "what do you know about this crown? When was it made?"

"It's been in the royal family for hundreds of years!" Tundra said, sounding quite scandalized. "It's one of the most treasured IceWing heirlooms!"

"Yes, yes," Snowfall said, "but who made it?"

Tundra looked at Permafrost, who scratched his neck and mumbled, "I'm not sure. I believe maybe it's from the time of Queen Diamond?"

"Queen Diamond," Snowfall said. "As in, the one whose son ran off with a NightWing."

"Was KIDNAPPED by a NightWing!" Tundra objected.

"The queen who happened to be an animus herself," Snowfall said. "Correct?"

"Oh!" Lynx cried. Tundra shot her a quelling look, but Lynx ignored her, taking a step toward Snowfall. "You think the crown could be enchanted to make every queen who wears it hate NightWings as much as Diamond did? But nobody knew it for all this time. That's awful!"

Permafrost flapped his jaw for a moment, as if a sealskin rug had come back to life and started questioning his moral authority. "It's true Queen Diamond was an animus," he said, "but — but she wouldn't just — that is, she couldn't use her power beyond her one gift to the tribe! She *wouldn't*, I'm sure of it!"

"Well, I'm not," Snowfall said. "And I don't like this thing anyway. So let's be safe *and* fashionable and destroy it."

"Destroy it?" Tundra gasped faintly.

"Oooooo, we can do that?" Mink asked. "Because I really really don't like it either. Snowfall, it's so heavy! It hurt my head, did it hurt yours?"

"Yes, it hurt my head a lot," Snowfall told her. "Ivory, would you take charge of destroying this for me?"

"At once, Your Majesty," Ivory said with a respectful bow. She lifted the crown out of Snowfall's talons and flew out of the room with two of her soldiers.

Snowfall climbed up on the throne next to Mink. It was big enough for a very old queen, so there was enough room for her to scoot in beside her sister. She put one of her wings around Mink, who snuggled into her side, closed her eyes, and sighed with relief.

"I don't have to be queen?" Mink whispered.

"You are not allowed to be queen right now," Snowfall said kindly. "I'm going to be queen for a long time."

"Good," Mink said. "I'm sorry so many d-dragons keep telling you what to do, though. That was my least favorite part."

"It'll be better if it's the right dragons," Snowfall said. "I just have to ignore the ones I don't trust." She shot a significant look at Tundra and Permafrost.

"The crown was magic?" Mink asked. "Does that mean I don't have to hate the NightWings?"

"That's right. It was just a spell." Snowfall bopped Mink's head with her snout. "It'll wear off. I feel much better about NightWings after being away from the crown for a few days. Plus, I bet if you meet any, you'll love them immediately just like you love everybody else."

"Oh, I'd like that," Mink said. "I love you the *most*, though."

Snowfall laughed. "I met a SkyWing you would adore," she said. "I didn't realize until right now that he reminded me of you."

"Your Majesty," Tundra said frostily, "as the wall has been neglected for a number of days, despite my best efforts, perhaps you would appreciate a few updates about the behavior of the palace IceWings in your absence."

"Ah, yes," Snowfall said. "Thank you for reminding me. Mink, want to see something cool?"

"I do I do!" Mink sang as Snowfall led her through the

halls and out into the courtyard. Tundra trailed after them, protesting that the queen needed more information before she started rearranging names. Permafrost had made himself scarce, perhaps realizing that the farther out of Snowfall's sight he was, the fewer spots he'd drop on the list.

There were several IceWings out in the courtyard, gathered near the wall or on benches, chatting to one another. A hush spread through them as Snowfall swept by, and she saw a few starting to edge toward the nearest doors.

"Mink," Snowfall said, stopping beside the gift of order. "Do you know what this is?"

"Of course I do," Mink said with wide eyes. "Everybody knows what the wall is! Look, there's m-me." She pointed to her name on the dragonet side. "I'm here, which means those dragons up there are better than me. But I'm still better than this dragon and this dragon and this dragon and this dragon and allllll these dragons," she said, tapping one name after another below hers.

Snowfall winced. It was somehow so much worse to hear something like that from someone as little and sweet as Mink.

"That's what I thought, too," she said to her sister. "But it turns out, that makes no sense."

"It makes no sense?" Mink echoed, blinking up at her.

"You might do better on a math test than this dragon," Snowfall said, pointing to a name below Mink's, "but what if he carves a better ice sculpture than you? Then who should be higher on the list?"

"What?" Mink cried, outraged. "B-better than mine?! Where? I want to see!"

"I just mean *if* he did," Snowfall said.

"Hmph," Mink said. "Not possible. But I love you anyway, Polar Bear!" she shouted at one of the little faces peeking out of a window overhead.

"What I mean," Snowfall said, "is that if you spend all your time worrying about where you are on the list and who's higher than you and who's below you, you can't focus on what *you* do well, or how everybody can do *something* important or kind or clever, no matter where they are on the list. And maybe you start to think the dragons below you aren't as important or special as you are, which is silly."

"Hmmmm," Mink said thoughtfully. She tipped her head up again and yelled, "Polar Bear, I think you're very special and important!"

"Thank you?" he called back.

Snowfall wasn't sure this lesson was going quite as well as she'd pictured it in her head. Maybe she should break stuff first, explain it all later.

She called up the tiara's strength and slammed her fist into the wall of names. Cracks shot out in all directions like bolts of lightning, ripping through every name on the list.

Tundra shrieked in horror and tried to grab her arm. But Snowfall shook her off easily and did it again, and then again, smashing the wall until it was obliterated and she was surrounded by a rubble of broken chunks of ice.

"Whew," she said into the cloud of glittering ice dust around her. "That's better."

"But — but —" Tundra cried. Snowfall realized that Lynx was standing between them, wings spread, to stop Tundra from charging at Snowfall again. Tundra seemed unable to move at the moment, though. She was staring at the space where the wall had been as though she thought it might magically rebuild itself if she stared hard enough.

Can it do that? Snowfall gave the broken bits of ice a hard stare of her own. They stayed where they were; no sign of any magical rebuilding. *Don't even try it, ancient ice wall.*

As the echoes died away, Lynx started clapping. Mink immediately joined in, beaming, although Snowfall suspected she just loved clapping and didn't entirely understand the enormity of what Snowfall had done.

I just smashed centuries of tradition into literal pieces, she thought, feeling a little dizzy.

But then another IceWing started to clap, and another, across the courtyard. Snowfall saw a few more at their windows applauding, although she also saw some older dragons duck out of sight when she looked, as though they didn't want to be caught with disapproving expressions on.

It's all right. Eventually they'll see that it's better this way.

"The gift of order," Tundra said faintly, and then she collapsed into the snow.

Snowfall beckoned two of her guards over and told them

to carry Tundra gently to her room and stay until she recovered, in case she needed anything.

"This is so exciting!" Mink said to Snowfall, scrambling over and sitting on her foot. "What else can we break? Can I smash something next?"

"Maybe tomorrow," Snowfall said, resting one wing around her sister. "I'll let you wear my tiara and everything. Tonight I think I need to have some ice cream and go to sleep." Snowflakes were drifting from the gray sky, covering everything in quiet sparkles.

"I love it when I'm right," Lynx said.

Snowfall bristled at her. "Who said you were? Maybe I smashed it for my own reasons! I have many opinions that have nothing to do with you!"

Lynx gave her a sideways grin.

"What?" Snowfall said. "Did you mean something else? Right about what?"

Lynx flicked her tail gently at Snowfall's wings. "About you being the best queen ever, Madame Spiky Face."

"Oh." Snowfall resettled her spikes and nodded regally. "Yes. Well. That is the plan."

CHAPTER 24

She opens her eyes.

She is standing in the Forbidden Treasury. She can't see a light globe anywhere, but the niches glow pale blue and the walls glimmer as though icy fireflies are swimming through them.

She is herself. She is Queen Snowfall. She feels that she is, but she holds her talons out and turns them over, just to be sure. The opal ring is still there, on her claw. She took off everything else before bed, though — the tiara and all her weapons. This is her palace, she is the queen, and she decided she wasn't going to be afraid all the time anymore.

But . . . she is having a vision, isn't she? How can she be having a vision of herself?

"Because this is the last one," says a voice behind her.

Snowfall turns. An IceWing is standing there, next to the empty niche labeled GIFT OF VISION. *Even in the weird light, Snowfall can see that she has unusual scales, like there's a hint of another color beyond the white in each one.*

Like an opal.

The dragon smiles. "That's me. Opal. Nice to meet you, Queen Snowfall."

Snowfall gives her a wry look. "I have a feeling I've been yelling at you for the last several days."

Opal shrugs her wings elegantly. "No more than any of the queens who used the ring before you."

"Have there been a lot?" Snowfall asks. "Does every queen put it on at some point?"

"Not every one," Opal answers. "It's enchanted to appear to those who need it most."

Snowfall regards the ring for a moment. "So I needed it because . . . we had to find out what was happening in Pantala? And make a connection with the scavengers, so they'd help us defeat Queen Wasp?"

Opal laughs. "I'm glad you used it so well," she says. "But no. It's for dragons who become queen before they are ready, to help them take steps toward becoming even stronger queens."

Snowfall raises an eyebrow at her. "That's a polite way of putting it," she says. "But you mean it's for queens who are a total mess, to teach them to see the world through other dragons' eyes, so they won't be so selfish. Isn't that it?"

"We don't say that part out loud!" Opal admonishes her, but she's clearly hiding a smile. "And you weren't a total mess."

"Are you really here?" Snowfall asks. "In the Forbidden Treasury? Just wondering how to find you so I can throw you in my dungeon forever."

Opal laughs again. "No, I died a long time ago — I created

my one animus gift, and then had a long happy normal life as an IceWing. I just left a bit of my spirit in the ring to keep track of the visions and have this last conversation when the ring has finished its work."

"I can't believe your original queen agreed to this," Snowfall says, holding up her talon with the ring on it.

"She fully did not," Opal says. "Why do you think I made the enchantment the way it is? She became queen before she was ready, too, and she was so scared and furious all the time. She asked me for an animus gift that would let her spy on all her enemies — both outside the kingdom and inside her own tribe. I made her this instead."

"Wow." Snowfall touches the opal lightly with one claw. "I can't believe she didn't execute you the moment she realized she couldn't take it off. That's probably what I would have done," she adds ruefully.

"No, you wouldn't have," Opal says with certainty. "You would have thrown me in the dungeon, like she did. And then after a few weeks, if the ring worked the way I enchanted it to, you'd have forgiven me, like she did."

"A few weeks?" Snowfall lifts her chin proudly and sweeps her tail across the floor. "I learned all my vision lessons in just a few days."

"Maybe you were closer to ready than even you realized," Opal says.

Snowfall looks down at the ice below her feet and hesitates

for a moment. "What if — what if I'm not sure I am ready?" she asks. "Maybe I need a few more visions."

"No," Opal says. "The ring is magic; it knows exactly how much you need. There's just one more you have to see." Suddenly she is standing right in front of Snowfall, and she rests her talons on Snowfall's temples.

And then

Snowfall is

not Snowfall anymore

but her mother instead.

Queen Glacier is flying in from a meeting with Blaze, thinking about what a cheerful brain-dead goose that SandWing is. Below her in the courtyard, she sees dragonets playing, and she lands on one of the upper ledges to watch them.

Three of them are her daughters: Crystal, Snowfall, and tiny Mink, who tries to keep up with the other two but keeps getting stuck in snowbanks. They're playing some kind of made-up game; Glacier can't figure out the rules from up here, but it involves a lot of running and defending particular corners of the courtyard, and snowballs are flying everywhere.

Mink tumbles into another pile of snow and Snowfall grabs her, lifting her to sit on Snowfall's back. "Come on, we can't let them win!" she shouts. She hurtles across the courtyard at ferocious speed, even with Mink clinging to her shoulders, and tackles one of the other IceWings before he can throw a snowball into her corner. She rolls over him, slides him back toward his team, bowling two of them over when he crashes into them, and leaps up with her wings spread wide to block another snowball from another direction.

Back in the middle of the courtyard, Crystal is standing still and yawning. "Is it time for lunch yet?" she calls.

"No!" Snowfall shouts back, fending off another snowball and flinging one of her own into her opponent's face. "After this you're going to quiz me on my kingdom geography, remember?"

Crystal sighs elegantly and wanders over to the nearest bench. "If you say so."

The sun warms Glacier's wings as she watches them. Her three perfect dragonets. Crystal's serenity, Mink's affectionate loveliness, and Snowfall's indomitable ferocity. She loves them so much.

She's already decided she won't fight them for the throne. Whichever one decides to challenge her first, she'll step aside and let them have it.

She hopes it's Snowfall. She loves them all, but Snowfall will fight for this kingdom like nobody else will. She has some growing up to do first, and Glacier hopes to pay more attention to her after the war is over . . . but even now, watching her, Glacier can see what a great queen Snowfall could be.

Being queen is not easy. Glacier is often exhausted, frustrated, confused, uncertain; she worries for her tribe all the time, and she has inexplicable nightmares about NightWings. She has to work hard to seem confident in front of the tribe.

The crown would be too much for Crystal or Mink; it would crush them. Glacier knows perfectly well that the same is true of Blaze and the SandWing throne, but she plans to be a strong ally to help her hold it, if Blaze can get herself together and win the war.

But Snowfall is strong enough to rule a kingdom and do it well. Glacier is sure of it. Snowfall earns her place at the top of the dragonet side of the wall, day after day, and she struggles and cares and tries and fights, and that's who the IceWings need.

We're going to be all right, Glacier thinks, feeling her shoulders relax for the first time in a while. Watching Snowfall fills her with hope. No matter what happens, I'll be able to leave the tribe in the right talons.

The courtyard fades away.

Snowfall wipes the tears from her snout.

"Thank you," she says to Opal.

"I just made the magic," Opal says with another shrug. "You had to walk the visions." She holds out one talon. "And now you're done."

"Shouldn't I keep it a bit longer?" Snowfall asks. "So I can see what happens to the dragons who are going to Pantala?"

"It doesn't work that way," Opal says. "The gift of vision serves its purpose, and then it disappears again, until the next dragon comes along who needs it."

Snowfall slides the ring off. She can't believe how easily it

moves, after all those days of wrestling with it. Now it feels
too big again, wobbling around her claw. She gives it to Opal,
who puts it back in the empty niche. Dark ice slides across the
hole, and the words GIFT OF VISION *vanish, until the ring is*
completely hidden.

"Good luck," Opal says with a smile.

Snowfall woke up late in the morning. She'd finally had a
real night's sleep in the royal bed, despite the tiny snuggle
monster who'd climbed in beside her during the night. Mink
was still asleep, one wing flopped over Snowfall's snout.

The ring was gone, which didn't surprise her. *Stupid
magic*, she thought, but didn't really feel. She would miss the
visions, she realized. A little bit. She preferred being herself,
always Snowfall, but it felt oddly empty to think she'd never
get to walk in someone else's talons again.

*Mother believed in me after all. She didn't just choose me
because she couldn't have Crystal. She thought I was the right
choice.*

Snowfall moved Mink's wing off her face and rolled out
of bed. Outside the window, the sun was up and IceWings
were darting through the sky, each one catching the light
like a flying star. Beyond them, Snowfall could see the ocean,
all that moving, glittering water between here and the lost
continent of Pantala. Lynx was out there somewhere, flying

to meet the rest of the dragons whose talons held the fate of the world.

I hope they survive. They BETTER survive or I'm going to be SO FURIOUS at them.

I hope they stop Queen Wasp and the breath of evil. I hope I see Sky and Wren again . . . and Sundew and Cricket and all the rest of them.

I hope we're doing enough to save the world.

~ EPILOGUE ~

Raven crept through the tunnel, listening for any sign she was being followed, but she couldn't hear anyone behind her. The darkness pressed in like panther fur, brushing the hairs on her arms. But she knew the path to the abyss well enough to navigate without sight — and as she got closer, she could see the dim green glow that came from its depths.

She could also see the skeletal figure that huddled by the edge of the glow. He crouched so close to the terrifying drop, it made Raven dizzy. He didn't turn toward her. His eyes were always fixed on the chasm.

"Vole," she whispered. "I brought you food." She set her little bundle down as close to him as she dared, then stepped back out of reach.

It had been a long time since Vole threw someone into the abyss, but that was most likely because no one else dared to approach him anymore. Only Raven, who came even though it was forbidden, and his brother, Mole, who was allowed to keep him alive but never allowed to speak of him.

"Can you hear it?" Vole said in his shivery rasp of a voice. He still didn't look at her. He never did.

"I think so," Raven said, sitting on one of the rock formations. "I mean, I hear something, but I don't know what it's saying. Do you?"

The whispers reached the upper caves, winding like long clinging spiderwebs around the people of the village. She knew they could hear it, too, from the way they flinched or hunched their shoulders or hurried away from one another. But no one would talk about it except Vole.

"It's growing," he said softly. "It's reaching. Soon it will be now. But it needs . . ." He trailed off.

"Needs what?" Raven asked.

Suddenly Vole whipped his head around and met her eyes for the first time in years. Raven jumped and nearly fled back into the dark. His eyes were nothing like they'd been when he was just her friend's funny older brother. Now they were haunted and overlaid with a green shimmer, and they seemed to look right through her.

"It needs a dragon," he hissed.

"A dragon?" Raven curled her fingers around the rough edges of the stone below her. "Any dragon?"

She wanted to run away screaming. But if something was changing in the abyss, Vole would be the only one who could tell her, and she had to know.

"You must find the dragon," Vole said, and now his voice was like the crawling cave centipedes, thousands of them, with millions of scuttling legs crossing her skin. "Bring it the dragon. Save the village."

"Wait," Raven said as he turned back toward the abyss. "What does that mean? Save the village? From what?"

"Find the dragon," Vole said, leaning toward the glow. "Bring it here."

He let out a long, slithering breath that twined around the whispers from below.

"Or everyone you know will die."

DISCOVER THE #1 *NEW YORK TIMES* BESTSELLING SERIES!